THE NIGHTMARE WITHIN

Glen R. Krisch

DEDICATION

For Aidan, who assured the way before he was even born.

CHAPTER ONE

The memory of heat and burning, of smoke and searing pain, shaped every moment of Maury Bennett's life. When he was eight years old, fire gutted his family's apartment building, killing seven people before the firefighters, some from two towns over, could contain it. Maury was lucky enough to regain consciousness in the hospital, thirty percent of his body charred black and nerveless, his skin as crisp as fried chicken. He had been the first of his family to smell the smoke and to see the flames as the living room curtains caught fire, the first to feel the raging heat bursting down the hallway, throttling his body like a malevolent spirit. Flames quickly engulfed everything, forcing his younger brother, Maury, and their parents to run, heads covered with soaked bath towels, through a gauntlet of swirling flames to reach the front door. The shared hallway outside their apartment was little better, the old faux-wood paneling a mass of tumbling embers and seething smoke.

Upon reaching the sidewalk outside the apartment building, the fresh air was intoxicating. But Maury was on fire, his Incredible Hulk pajamas combusting, his throat hoarse from smoke and screaming. Shocked neighbors stood on the trampled courtyard grass, their glassy eyes reflecting the shimmering fire consuming their homes. Maury's father pulled him into an unyielding embrace. He rolled on top of him, smothering the fire.

Maury had lost all sense of reality. Only momentary fragments rooted him to the conscious world. His father, still struggling to choke out the flames feeding on Maury's flesh, whispered repeatedly into his ear: "I never should have left you alone, never should have left you, never should have left..."

Rosemarie Clement reclined her ample body on Maury Bennett's leather office couch. She was staring into a panel of drop-tile ceiling, not focusing on anything in particular. She was trying to probe her soul, searching for a meaning to it all, trying to figure out why she had to be such a perfectionist. Why did she have to iron her bed linens? Sure, a small segment of the population ironed their bed linens, but she felt worthless if she didn't strip the bed naked before it had a chance to cool after her husband got up for work. Why did she incessantly wash, iron, buff, shine, scrub, boil, sanitize? Does asking that question lead to answers that she didn't want to face, that she couldn't face even if she wanted to?

Maury wondered how a woman could let herself become so insignificant.

The couch hadn't been a part of his practice during the early years. But he learned the hard way, that even when he wanted to, he couldn't accomplish the simple act of looking at his patients as they spoke. His palms would become clammy, and he would wait for the subtle hint of pity in their eyes. They would twitch after glancing at his melted-wax scars and then look away, ashamed. Their self-consciousness offended him more than if they gaped without giving it a second thought.

"I'm on the edge of this cliff..." she was speaking about a dream she had the night before. As if it were interesting enough to bring up in a meeting with her psychiatrist.

Maury closed his eyes and thought of his younger brother, and the night of the fire. Little Dale, with his dark brown hair covering his eyes, cowering in their mother's lap as she tried to soothe him. Maury remembered hearing the shrieking sirens and seeing flashing lights washing across the slate gray apartment building in chaotic waves. His father was resting his cheek on Maury's forehead. He cried as he held Maury, rocking him against his chest. The flames were gone; the searing pain attacking his skin was nearly gone, too.

Maury heard his skin crackle under the pressure of his father's touch. When he looked down he saw the scorched flesh of his arm crack and split, saw blood seep and bubble from his wounds. The worst part was that he felt nothing.

Though Maury was in shock when they loaded him into the ambulance, he clearly remembered and had since become haunted by the image of Rocky, their mangy pound cat. Before the ambulance doors closed, Maury saw Dale pointing at the building. Maury looked up in time to see Rocky jump from their third floor balcony. The cat was a ball of flames streaking across the grass until the fire stole the last ounce of his life. As the ambulance doors closed, Maury drifted from consciousness.

Countless surgeries, skin grafts, and physical therapy patched together Maury's body until he looked as normal as someone recovering from his condition could look. That's what the doctors said, at least. They always told him how lucky he was, how some people from his building didn't make it out alive. Until he was ten years-old, he spent more time in hospitals than not. At first, his left arm was little more than a dead limb. Whorls of pink and brown scars ran up his shoulder and melted across his ear. He went through the torture of his formative years wearing ball caps to hide the spots where his hair wouldn't grow back. He wore long sleeves to hide the easy target of his disfigurement from the other kids. By the time he received a new prosthetic ear, he had learned how to conceal the worst of his remaining frailty.

Through all of his struggles, he learned a valuable lesson. Doctors possessed true power. They could salvage the unsalvageable; they could extend life and raise the level of comfort for those in their final days. Doctors looked at Maury with an unflinching eye. They saw his ravaged body as a canvas--their medium of choice to practice the highest of intellectual arts. Maury watched these people wield their power and learned from an early age what his calling would be. But he soon discovered, that even with his impressive academic record, he had to give up his dream of becoming a surgeon. His left hand carried with it an invariable impairment. He would never be able to practice surgery. Instead of salvaging the flesh, Maury turned his attentions to salvaging the mind.

"Can you understand how I have trouble sleeping at night?" Rosemarie asked from her reclined position.

Maury blinked away the memories of his childhood. "Hmm... yes, I think I do." He opened a desk drawer and took out his script pad. "Your time is almost up, and from listening to what you've said, I think I have something that might help you with your sleep issue." He scribbled something slightly legible on the pad and handed it to her.

"You really think I need to go on a prescription?"

"I think it would help you find the root of this problem," he said. "You need to look at this issue from a new perspective. This script will help you unclutter your mind and lead you in the right direction."

She looked at the paper doubtfully. "Are we through for the day? I thought I still had more time left?"

"If you use the rest of the time to get the prescription filled, that will be part of your therapy," he said, getting up from his chair. Rosemarie followed, a confused look on her face. Maury handed her the slip and walked with her to the door.

"So... same time next week? Good. It was nice seeing you again, Mrs..." Before he could fumble with her name, he rushed her out the door, the prescription fluttering between her fingers as the door shut behind her.

Maury leaned against the edge of his desk and exhaled slowly. He didn't know how he was going to keep up this hectic pace. His practice was a safe bet; he would never be out of a job, but ever since meeting Nolan Gage, his whole outlook on life had changed. Dr. Edwardson, a family physician, had introduced him to Gage at a fundraiser for the Loyola Children's Hospital. Dr. Edwardson knew that Maury specialized in the treatment of patients suffering from traumatic dreams, and that Gage desired to fund a research project in a similar field. When they met, Gage had spoken about groundbreaking research with dreams, and particularly, the transmutation of dreams. Nolan Gage didn't know what he was getting himself into.

Three months ago, Maury accepted an offer to join Gage's research team. Maury soon realized that he could never again live his simple life. Treating the Rosemarie Clements of the world would leave him hollow and unfulfilled. He only kept his practice going as a safety net until he learned the end result of the dream research. As time went by, the prospects looked more and more promising that he would close shop and work exclusively for Nolan Gage.

Reaching for his coffee mug, he absently spilled it across a stack of notes. Using the tissue that he always kept handy for his patients, Maury wiped up the mess. He picked up a potted plant and pushed aside a few family photos to make sure he didn't miss a spot. As he dried the corner of one of the picture frames, he realized the family portrait taken under an azure summer sky at Cape Cod was probably their last family picture before the apartment fire. His parents stood shoulder to shoulder with their arms wrapped around one another. Maury and Dale sat at their feet, while everyone wore big smiles and squinted against the water's glare. The picture brought painful emotions to the surface as he fought off tears.

He finished drying the frame, tossed out the tissues, and went over to his couch. As he sat down, his emotions were back in check, but his mounting fatigue felt like a physical weight on every inch of his skin. He pulled his legs up on the couch, held the Cape Cod picture against his chest, and closed his eyes.

Eight months after the fire, Maury came home from the hospital for good. The first night, after an unbearably awkward dinner, he excused himself and turned in early. His parents were treating him differently, as if he were a fragile object instead of their son. Dale also wouldn't stop staring at him as they ate. They lived in a new house and none of the stuff in his new bedroom felt like his. Maury felt more comfortable in bed with the light turned off.

At some point, he must have fallen asleep. The room was completely dark when Dale woke him, shaking his leg.

"Maury, Rocky won't leave me alone." Dale was sitting on the edge of Maury's bed and sounded terribly upset.

"What do you mean?"

"When I go to sleep he's always there. He's on fire just like that night."

Maury couldn't see his brother's eyes in the darkness, but he could hear in his voice that he believed every word he said. "It's only a dream. Dreams can't hurt you, Dale. Go back to bed."

"But he's after me, he's gonna..." Dale said, stopping mid-sentence. Maury's eyes adjusted to the dark bedroom. Dale's face was all shadow and gloom.

"What's Rocky going to do?"

"Nothin'. He just scares me."

"That's not what you were going to say. Spill your guts. What's Rocky going to do?"

"He's gonna... burn me," Dale said, turning away.

He knew he couldn't calm his brother with words. He patted his bed, and Dale climbed up next to him. "You can sleep here tonight. Rocky won't hurt you. I'll make sure of it."

Dale looked skeptically at Maury, but he seemed more at ease. He climbed under the covers and gave off a worried grunt. Maury turned on his bedside lamp and started reading the newest Incredible Hulk comic. He was really into it, enthralled by the concept of an outsider housing monstrous powers deep inside his soul. By the time he had finished reading it for the third time, Dale was snoozing fitfully next to him.

Maury snapped off the light and pulled the covers up over his shoulders. His eyes burned from reading so much, and he felt like he could fall asleep in about two seconds. He was in the gray area between sleeping and waking when Dale began to stir. He could feel his brother's tension next to him, but Maury was frozen in some kind of in-between state.

It wasn't until Dale screamed that Maury sat up, fully awake.

"Hey... you okay?"

Dale didn't seem to hear his brother and continued thrashing about the bed. His eyes were closed while his legs tangled with the sheets.

Maury shook his brother, trying to wake him. When his fingers touched Dale's shoulder, the fiery image of Rocky burned behind Maury's eyelids. Every time he blinked, the cat was there. He could feel Rocky's pain. His calico fur blazed with six inch flames and his green eyes were watery and skittish. Maury had to pull away, had to get away from Dale and the image of the burning cat. When he removed his hand from his brother's shoulder, he felt a magnetic pull under his dead, nerveless skin. And in the gap between his trembling hand and his still sleeping brother, a bundle of flames emerged. The more Maury pulled away, the more the form took shape. It was as if he were pulling a calf from its mother's womb. Rocky, his fur burning, his skin sizzling, appeared right there on Maury's pillow. By touching Dale, he had flipped some type of switch. He had somehow pulled his brother's dream into the waking world. Maury felt the cat's burning body.

He dragged Dale away from the cat, while a humming noise filled their bedroom. It could've been the cat purring, or possibly his flesh burning, he couldn't tell. Maury still had bandages over much of his torso and had trouble moving his left arm. He hooked his right arm under Dale's armpits and pulled until stars shot across his vision. His brother inched along the floor with him, the effort aggravating his wounds.

Rocky slinked along the bed as he always had, not seeming to notice the flames. He meowed as if he wanted them to pet him, and then jumped from the bed. Every step he took left a small flaming paw print on the floor. The paw prints burned brightly for a few seconds before extinguishing to a black sooty mark on the floor. The scorch marks faded to a silt-brown, before disappearing altogether.

"Dale, wake up. Come on...I can't carry you!" Dale didn't stir, the cat only a few steps away. "Come on, Dale, wake up!" Maury yelled into his brother's ear. Maury slapped his face, startling him awake. As soon as Dale saw how close Rocky was to touching them, he started to scream.

The bedroom door flew open and their parents stormed into the room. Rocky darted for the open door and meowed angrily, bolting down the hallway.

"What's going on in here? Are you two okay?" their father called out. Dale leaped into their mother's arms and wrapped his legs around her waist, hugging her, new tears soaking into the shoulder of her nightgown.

"Rocky... the cat. He came, and then..." Maury tried to explain, but how could he explain what had just happened?

He felt a mixture of fear and awe, and as the seconds ticked away, this mixture was joined by curiosity. Since the paw prints had disappeared by the time they looked for the cat, they all began to doubt if Rocky had been there in the first place.

Their father was going to call the fire department, but there wasn't a fire to report, or any damage to indicate there was a fire at all. Their father, an overwhelmingly practical man who was afraid to sound just the opposite, called no one.

The next morning, their mother discovered a half-healed burn hole in a screen of a living room window. It was oval shaped, and just big enough for a cat to slip through. The family never brought up the subject of Rocky again. Their dad replaced the screen with a new one, and Dale didn't have any more dreams about their dead cat.

Maury found the Cape Cod picture on the floor next to his office couch. When he picked it up, emotions once again threatened to surface. This time the emotions were different; he felt joy and a growing pride at seeing the Maury in the picture. He had left that Maury behind in that world of innocence--the world of happy summertime vacations, trips to the ice cream stand on hot nights, and building snowmen with Dale during the endless gray winters. But it was okay.

For many years, he had regretted the night of the fire. He had been marred forever and seven of his neighbors had died. And it was all because of a silly cartoon. Maury had seen Jerry set Tom's tail on fire and had laughed hysterically when the cat ran around until he finally dipped his hind end in a sink full of soaking dishes. At the time, Maury knew that trying a similar stunt with Rocky would never end with the same result. No one would laugh, and no one would be left unscathed. But he did it anyway, childhood whimsy getting the better of him.

He remembered the spark as he struck the wooden match against the box. The flame sped along the trail of lighter fluid faster than he could have ever imagined. When Rocky felt the fire bite into his tail, he was off like a pinball, running into furniture, bumping into walls, setting anything he touched ablaze.

After all those years of guilt, and wishing he could only have a chance to do things differently, Maury finally accepted what he had done. In fact, he was swiftly coming to the conclusion that he appreciated what he had done. If he hadn't done such a stupid thing as a child, he would have never become the man he was; a man who could pull dreams--the essence of fear, guilt, rage, or lust--directly from people's minds. After years of turmoil, he could finally harness and wield a power that no one could ever imagine.

He stared at the photo, a momentary glimpse into the life of those photographed. The transmuted dream-beings were somewhat like that. Once birthed from the mind of a dreamer, the transmuted dream was a still-photo of the dream taken at the moment of transmutation. But unlike the Cape Cod photo, transmuted dreams changed. They evolved, adapting to and absorbing surrounding details. Depending on the strength of the dream, this evolution could be limitless.

He supposed he owed a debt to his poor dead cat. If someone forced the issue, he would also have to thank Nolan Gage for his money and patience. Now all he needed was a star. A main attraction. Nolan Gage's money was leading to the eventual unveiling of the transmuted dreams in a museum called Lucidity. All Maury needed was a dream so devastating to the museum goers' psyche that they would leave the museum of dreams changed forever, clutching their chests in both horror and joy, certain to return to Lucidity again and again.

CHAPTER TWO

Just inside the doors of the Warren Cove bus station, Kevin already lagged behind his parents. He couldn't help it. His excitement about the trip to Chicago made him have to take a leak that could put out a forest fire. The station wasn't crowded since it was so early in the morning. Even so, a woman clipped Kevin on the shoulder as she rushed to catch a bus on time.

"Sorry," the woman said, barely giving him a glance.

"No problem, Mrs. Hepner." Warren Cove was a small town, nothing more than a rest stop in a long journey through the endless farm fields of central Illinois. Kevin had started a newspaper route when school let out two weeks ago, and he already knew every customer on his route by name and face. Mrs. Hepner lived four blocks away. Kevin delivered to her the thin Cove Herald every other weekday and on weekends.

"Oh... Hi." Mrs. Hepner gave him a vague look of recognition, her freshly applied makeup making her look like a clown.

"Kevin Dvorak. I deliver your paper."

"Yes. Sorry, Kevin. I'm running late." Mrs. Hepner looked at her watch, looked even more exasperated, and gave him a slight wave. "You're doing a fine job with the paper. Better than that Callahan boy ever did. I'll see you later."

Whenever he saw one of his customers, he made an effort to acknowledge them, hopefully resulting in better tips. His parents trudged on ahead, distracted, without looking back to see if he was keeping up. He could probably ditch them and duck into a restroom, but they would throw a fit even though he felt old enough. They let him ride his bike at 5:30 in the morning for his route, but wouldn't let him go to a public restroom on his own. Go figure.

He was getting desperate. His palms were sweaty and it pained him to walk. Stopping in mid-stride, he called out to his dad, but he didn't seem to hear. The overhead lights were so white, like the lights he imagined shining down in an operating room. The tile floor echoed his mom's heel clicks, seeming to amplify them. His dad tried to take hold of her hand, as he often did when they walked together, but she shrugged off the attempt. She increased her distance from him and their hands swept by at their sides, alone and empty.

He felt like screaming, anything to get their attention. But he didn't want to anger his dad. He was angry a lot lately. Something about his job, and people at his job. Whatever it was made his mom angry, too. She focused her anger more at his dad, while at the same time, his dad would grumble under his breath about things Kevin didn't really know about. Things like entrapment. Things like harassment.

Kevin had an idea about harassment. People talked about it all the time on T.V., boring him to the point he'd change the channel in search of cartoons. He was fuzzy about entrapment. It sounded like something straight from one of the army movies his dad liked.

Walking faster through the station, Kevin focused on keeping his bladder full, trying not to think of anything wet or anything cold. Or anything wet *and* cold.

"Dad!" This time tension strengthened his voice, cutting through the empty bus station. His dad turned around, and after a couple of steps so did his mom.

"For God's sake, what is it, Kevin?" His dad looked tired, like he hadn't slept in a thousand years.

"I have to go…" Kevin started to say, but then just nodded his head and bugged out his eyes, the obvious universal sign for MY BLADDER IS ABOUT TO EXPLODE!

"Can't this wait? The bus is about to board. You can use the bus toilet after you find your seat."

It would be a mad thrill to take a leak while on a moving bus, but Kevin couldn't wait."I-Have-To-Go…" Kevin explained.

"Carin, I better take him."

She already had her arms folded and tense in front of her. "Fine. I'll be right here. Hurry up. The bus is leaving in ten minutes," she said and then leaned forward. She whispered to his dad, trying to keep her voice from Kevin's ears, but he heard anyway. "Don't take so long that you can't say a decent goodbye to your son."

Kevin had no idea what his mom was talking about. Goodbye? What was that all about? He thought they were all going to his grandma's house. He was excited because he envisioned the trip bringing happiness back to their family. Sure, he had been aware of the tension between his parents, but it wasn't the end of the world. Or so he hoped. Just awkward silences during meals, or his dad working late and missing dinnertime altogether. They didn't fight all of the time. They never had any shouting matches, and thank God, never threw any punches. And now this... goodbye?

His dad placed a hand on his shoulder to guide him toward the restroom, but Kevin was still looking back at his mom.

Goodbye?

He tried reading her face, but just as his dad looked really tired lately, her face seemed as expressive as a clean chalkboard. She watched him watching her, but her look was cold, the pained glassiness of her eyes the only sign of any emotion.

Kevin's dad led him to the restroom, and his mom disappeared from view. Finally, he was going to take a leak.

Kevin, feeling considerably lighter in the bladder, was washing his hands when a man entered the restroom. He wore his black denim shirt tucked into his faded tan carpenter pants. His sleeves rolled to the elbow, Kevin couldn't help noticing that his thick gray arm hair matched the color of the unruly hair on his head. He stepped up to a urinal next to a balding guy with a gut so big he had to stand back about a foot to avoid bumping into the white porcelain.

The new guy stared intently at his urinal neighbor as if trying to memorize his features for future reference. A number of silent seconds ticked away, and when the fat guy became uncomfortable with the invasion of privacy, he gave the man a scowl. The old man frowned, his unshaven face sagging as he looked away. He seemed to be stuttering under his breath, small bursts of air escaping between his clenched teeth.

Kevin was getting a bad feeling. His dad was in a stall smoking a cigarette, and he wished he would hurry up so they could get out of here. He turned on the hand dryer, but his eyes didn't leave the two men.

The old guy turned, once again studying the other man's face. His hair stuck out in weird spikes, as if he hadn't brushed it in a week. His eyes were yellow and seemed somehow both fatigued and frantic. When his urinal neighbor faced him, he didn't look away.

"Do you have a problem?"

The old man paused, as if considering the question, a puzzled look deepening the wrinkles across his forehead. "I'm afraid I don't."

"Keep your eyes to yourself."

The fat man hunched over, grunted, and closed his fly. He tucked in a loose tail of his shirt, glowering over his shoulder as he walked over to the sinks. As he washed his hands, he nodded to Kevin. "Stay clear of that guy. I think he's a perv."

Kevin wondered if his dad was ever coming out. First that weirdo came in, and now this other stranger was talking to him. He was uncomfortable and just wanted to get on the bus, even if his dad wasn't coming with. He could sort out his family problems later.

The guy wiped his hands on a paper towel, and then turned to exit. The old man was already blocking his path, his back against the swinging exit door. He casually zipped his own fly.

"I'm only going to say this once, get the fuck away from me." The strength of the big guy's voice deflated with uncertainty as he faced this odd crossroad.

"Hey now. I'm *talking*. You're *listening*."

"Why you little shit--" The big guy snapped, charging with his shoulder lowered like a battering ram. The old man sidestepped the charge and shoved him shoulder-first into the cinderblock wall. Kevin, seeing the pained contortion of the man's face, backed away from the sinks.

The old guy grabbed the stranger's neck with both hands, his fingers twisting into his considerable jowls. The wounded man cradled his shoulder and fell to his knees, but didn't slip away from the old man's grip. The old guy's yellow eyes were bloodshot and a rope of drool descended from his lower lip. Suddenly stirred by rage, he was panting, forcing the fat guy to stand up. He then pressed the man's meaty face against the mirror, the steam of his frantic breath clouding his reflection.

The hand dryer stopped. The man's breathing, a wet near-sob, sounded incredibly loud without the whir of the dryer.

"What'd I do!" the fat man cried, the old guy's palm pressing his face into a morbid sneer.

"It's your turn, jackass. Just your turn is all. Ain't no shame in taking your turn."

Kevin inched away, his back against a stall. The toilet flushed behind him and his dad opened the door.

"What the hell's going on?" His fists tightened at his sides, the muscles alive under his skin. Kevin cowered on the floor next to him.

The old man didn't even flinch at the interruption and didn't seem to notice anyone else in the restroom. The fat man was still smashed against the mirror and he couldn't move at all. Kevin had no idea how such a feeble-looking man could manhandle someone so large so easily.

With sympathy in his eyes the old man looked at his victim, as if he might even decide to let him go. But then swiftly, violently, he slammed the man's skull against the foggy metallic mirror. The stranger's unconscious eyes rolled back to full whites as he fell to the floor. Before anyone could react, the old man started stabbing him with what looked like a steak knife.

His dad rushed forward to grab his arm on the back swing. Kevin knew his dad was strong, just about the strongest person he knew, but the old man somehow lifted him off the floor with his stabbing motion. His dad lost his grip and tumbled across the stranger's body.

"Dad!" Kevin cried, tears clinging to his cheeks.

"Looks like it's your turn now," the old man hissed as he feverishly attacked his dad, the knife a big blurring motion of metal and blood. His dad tried to deflect the stabs with his forearms which were soon littered with wounds. He looked defeated, afraid. His eyes met Kevin's, even as the crazed man continued his assault. His lips moved wordlessly, his life drifting away.

But something steeled in his dad's eyes, and the fear disappeared. He struggled to one knee and then stood fully. Ignoring the knife, he grabbed the old man's face between either hand, leaving his abdomen unprotected. The old man took advantage by pressing the knife in deeply, just below the ribs. As the stranger lifted the knife handle, his dad slammed his gray head into the wall, hard.

Kevin wanted to look away, but couldn't. Not even as both his dad and the old man fell with dual thuds to the floor.

"No, Daddy. No..." Kevin whimpered, losing coherence. He slumped down the side of the stall until he sat with his legs sprawled out before him. He blinked and saw the nightmare in front of him: his dad's ravaged body, his wheezing last breath, his empty eyes left staring at Kevin.

Kevin's eyes glazed and his mind cowed away, finding shelter in a safer place. When he opened his eyes again, how long later, he had no idea, he began to scream for his mom. He screamed with a fear bordering on madness. He screamed until his words became a simple wailing pain.

CHAPTER THREE

As she pulled the Ford Explorer into her mother's driveway in Chicago, Carin's heart felt empty. Kevin sat in the passenger seat, wearing the same blank expression as the previous two weeks. She was hoping that completing the move to her mother's house would help draw him out of his grief. It would take some time, but she was hoping to see some inkling of her sweet little boy still inside him somewhere.

The front yard was so lush and green that it looked like a bed of emeralds. Newly planted baby pine trees lined the drive on either side. The leaves of the two large oaks in the front yard hung limply and had curled in the heat. The yard was mostly shadow and cool air, a luxury during the heat of summer.

She eased the Explorer to a stop, and shut off the engine, leaving them in silence. It was as if with the turn of the ignition key she expected Kevin to snap out of it, for him to show the same joy he always did when they would go to her mother's house. A minute or more slipped by and neither one of them stirred. The mounting pain behind her eyelids wanted release. It would be so easy to let it overwhelm her, to let it drown her in its violent and brackish waves. Her temples pounded and if she didn't get things under control, she was going to start crying again. She didn't want to be in that condition around her mother.

She took a deep breath, fighting the hitching in her chest with every inhaled ounce of air. Her hands still gripped the steering wheel, her knuckles white and trembling.

Come on Carin, you can do this. You have to do this.

She slowly let out the pent up air from her lungs. She had to do this. "Hey, bud, let's go inside. Your grandma's waiting for us."

Kevin didn't say anything or even look at her. Tucking his baseball glove under his arm, he opened the passenger door. He was nearly to the front door before she remembered to move. She grabbed her purse and hurried to catch up to him.

That wasn't so hard, was it? Carin thought. But getting out of the car wasn't the worst of their problems. Moving on with the rest of their lives would be their true challenge.

Kevin stood staring at the door, his eyes rimmed with brown bags. Carin was digging in her purse for her key when the door opened.

"Oh, my babies, you made it." Carin's mother reached out to touch them. She had been blind since childhood, but she got around so well that Carin sometimes forgot.

"Hi, Mom. Thanks. Thanks for everything."

They didn't say anything else. Her mother leaned in for a deep hug with Carin, and then shared a dead-fish embrace with Kevin. He slinked away to the living room and turned on the T.V. He flipped the channels until he landed on cartoons, and then he watched like a zombie, barely blinking.

When the door closed behind them, darkness shrouded the interior of the house, even with the sun still high in the sky. All the curtains were closed and not a single lamp was alight. A rush of air that bordered on an arctic freeze greeted Carin and she realized her mother had the air conditioning cranked up high. Her mother was raised poor, and not until Carin was into her early thirties, did her parents pull out of it. Some of the frugal practices never went away, and Carin doubted her mother was aware of most of her quirks. She almost never used the air conditioning, even during the blistering heat of summer. Her mother had consciously cooled the house for their benefit.

The smell of the house was comforting and familiar. The well-oiled molding and oak shelving her father had built into their home, a little each year until it looked so much more than the cookie cutter G.I. housing it had once been. A repotted plant, moist and freshly turned soil, fragrant leaves and snaking tendrils, probably in the kitchen window where it would get the best light. The rose-scented powder her mother dusted the carpet with before vacuuming. For the first time in months, even long before James's murder, Carin felt a measurable amount of ease. Walking into the home of her youth and knowing she would find solace here once again seemed to wash away the coppery tinge of anxiety from her mouth. In its wake, she was aware of how emotionally raw she felt. It was a palpable feeling, yet distant, almost as if they were someone else's emotions mentioned to Carin in hushed tones.

"Would you like some chamomile tea?" her mother asked, hopefully.

"That sounds wonderful." And it did. Carin suddenly felt tired. She could imagine taking a nap after a soothing cup of tea.

Carin followed her mother into the kitchen and sat down at the dinette. She thought about helping, but knew that her mother wanted to make it herself, mothering her as if she had never moved away. "I should probably get the suitcases from the car while you make the tea."

"Don't be silly. You're home now and your car is in the driveway. It isn't going anywhere and neither are you," she said, nodding for emphasis. "We can unload it after we catch our breath." She put the teapot on to boil, and then took a tin of tea from the cabinet.

"Jeremiah is dead," Carin said. She didn't want to bring up her husband's killer, at least not this soon after coming home. He didn't deserve to be spoken about, not in such a welcoming environment. But she had to get the weight off her chest.

Her mother turned from the stove and stood quietly.

"He had a heart attack, or at least that's what the police told me."

"When?"

"Two nights ago. He was asleep. They told me he went painlessly."

"I don't exactly know what to say."

"Neither do I. But I do know I feel cheated. I was praying that the prosecuting attorney would be able to steer away from the insanity plea. I knew that probably would've never happened, and he'd end up at some cushy mental hospital. I wanted him to suffer in prison, I wanted him to see those bars and feel the loneliness and see them every minute of every day and I wanted him to suffer for seeing them."

"At least he's gone." The teapot began to whistle. Her mother turned off the stove and poured the steaming water over the teabags to steep. Her movements were flawless, her light, flickering fingers comprehending details from the slightest surfaces of her world, a sense of touch keener than most people's sense of sight.

"I know I should be grateful," Carin said. She took the enameled cup offered by her mother. "At least he won't hurt anyone else."

They both sat at the dinette, sipping the steaming tea.

With the burden of Jeremiah's death off her chest, Carin wanted to change the subject. She couldn't remember the last pleasant conversation she'd had. First it was the police, and then a brief talk with the F.B.I., then the funeral home, the insurance company, the realtor, and the moving company. It never seemed to end. "You look good, Mom."

"Thank you, dear. You seem to be getting on all right, all things considered. But, Kevin, he doesn't seem to be doing the same." Her voice softened upon mentioning Kevin.

No matter what Carin tried, her conversations always turned to unsavory subjects. "I know it's only been two weeks, but I'm worried about him, Mom. I can understand his behavior around me and when we're in public. No one his age would feel like being social under the circumstances. What bothers me is how he's having those dreams I was telling you about. They seem to be getting worse."

"That pains me to hear."

"It's one nightmare in particular, a dream monster he calls Mr. Freakshow. He says Mr. Freakshow is going to take over the world, stare everyone in the eye one by one and see their weaknesses. Every night he dreams that this Mr. Freakshow is coming for him, is coming to kill him."

"Dear God, that poor boy." Her mother reached out, covering Carin's hand with her own.

"I'm going to take him to see a doctor," Carin said and there was another pause in their conversation. She didn't want her mother to respond. She wanted the whole idea of some horrible dream monster tormenting her son to go away. All she wanted was for them to move on, but they couldn't do that as long as Kevin had these nightmares.

Kevin normally liked watching Ben 10, but he hadn't paid attention since it started. Instead, he listened to every word spoken in the kitchen, keeping his eyes glued to the T.V. While he listened in on the conversation, his own conflicting thoughts threatened to overpower his outside world. He knew from overhearing his parents' arguments that his dad had been acting inappropriately at work, acting in ways that wouldn't seem right for a married man. Or for someone's dad. Kevin was so mad at him. Anger broiled in his gut and he didn't want to love him anymore. But then his mind returned to the final moments of his dad's life. How he tried to save that stranger from being butchered, and how he'd given his life to protect Kevin. People he didn't want to love anymore shouldn't act so selflessly, without regard for their own life.

"If it comes down to it, you can take him to see Dr. Edwardson," his grandma said.

Kevin didn't want to see a doctor. What was the point when he didn't remember much from his dreams? Sure, he remembered who Mr. Freakshow was. But the monster always seemed to change. If Kevin closed his eyes he couldn't see the nightmare man. Upon waking, Mr.

Freakshow became faceless, void of detail. Only the fear remained, haunting his every thought.

He didn't want to hear anymore. He shut off the T.V. and went to the bedroom that had been Kevin's whenever they visited. He closed the door and leaned against it, taking in the room. The bed was too hard and he never slept well on it. Now he would have to sleep on it every night. A red and blue lamp with toy soldiers on the shade stood on top of the dresser. A Chicago Bears poster hung on one wall, a life-sized Michael Jordan poster on another. While he liked Jordan, he didn't even watch football. This was his bedroom, but it sure didn't feel like his.

Everyone asked how he was doing, how he was sleeping, or not sleeping. He was just glad that it was still summer break and he didn't have to face the kids at school. They would've looked at him funny and forever know him as the guy whose dad was killed in a bus station bathroom by the Steak Knife Killer. At least he was starting fresh at a new school and no one would know. He would miss his friends, but he didn't want to face them, either. Even with school out for the summer, his classmates had sent condolence cards made out of construction paper and white school glue. He didn't read any of them. At the insistence of his teachers, he had made similar cards for people when a grandparent had died, or when a car had run over someone's dog. When he had made those cards, he'd felt like he was being kind and that the people would appreciate his thoughtfulness. Now he realized none of that mattered, and that his teachers had used the students' tragedies as a way to fill their art hour requirements.

He lay down on the stiff bed and twined his fingers behind his head. He didn't want to hear his mom and grandma talk anymore. He didn't want to think about his dad anymore. Or school or distant friends, or their move to his grandma's or anything else. All he wanted was for his mind to stop whirling at a million miles a minute.

When he took a deep breath and closed his eyes, it did. He was swiftly off to sleep, the sun beginning its arc to the horizon.

The night swallowed the sun, leaving his room draped in long, skeletal shadows. Enough moonlight shined from the window for Kevin to see through the ethereal gloaming. He sat up from the stiff mattress, groggy as usual. His back ached and his right hand had fallen asleep, making it feel like a battalion of fire ants marched across his skin.

Shaking his throbbing hand back to life, he swung his legs over the edge of the bed.

That's when he saw the bulky shape in the window.

He stood, feeling the cool hardwood under his feet as he approached the window. The bulky shape shifted, becoming less a mass of shadow and mystery. The moon illuminated details in shades of somber blue and bruised indigo. A broad, muscled back, with tree trunk arms outspread in the shape of a crucifix. Raised gray scars lined his back like grubs burrowed under tree bark. Greasy swaths of black hair fell forward over mountainous shoulders. Each inhaled breath defined his spine--sledge-hammered stones piled one on top of another; his shoulders heaved, his head bowed in thought.

Kevin was close enough to the window to feel the cold glass pulling at his body heat. He touched the glass with his finger and felt a shiver quake through the digit, up his arm and beyond, until his whole body trembled.

With arms still outspread, the monster turned to face Kevin. Endless black irises surrounded pupils that swirled with liquid fire. Intricate henna tattoos covered his massive chest--the artwork's reddish hue contrasting the deadman-blue of his skin. Blood-caked wooden splinters pierced his nipples, and iron shackles bound his wrists, trailing clinking chains to the ground.

Mr. Freakshow smiled at Kevin. An openly lascivious smile.

"Hello, boy." The monster's breath steamed the glass. Mr. Freakshow's voice was deep and discordant, the sound of the earth's plates grinding on one another.

Kevin couldn't move away from the window.

"I see you've moved to your dear old grandma's house. So far away, and yet I found you." Mr. Freakshow ran an index finger over the glass separating them. He traced a circle in one of the central panes, his claw-like fingernail scratching a trail into the glass.

Kevin's voice caught in his throat, but he fought through the turgid thickness of his fear. "What do you want?"

Mr. Freakshow tapped the circle and the cut glass fell to the bedroom floor. Reaching through the hole in the window, he flipped open the locking mechanism. Corrupted air seeped into the bedroom as the window opened. Open sewers on a hot day, rotting fish floating in a dead lake.

"Leave me alone." Kevin staggered away until the backs of his legs bumped into the bed. He lost his balance, falling to a sitting position on the mattress.

"Oh, Kevin, I'm not going to hurt you. Not yet. It's way too early for that. I've come to teach you a thing or two, to enlighten you. All I ask is for you to pay attention." Mr. Freakshow stepped aside and waved his shackled arm like a game show diva showing off a shining brand new car. The window widened, the whole bedroom wall seemed to fall away.

What Kevin saw made his heart ache and forced a sluggish surge of adrenaline to drop into his bloodstream. The canopy of oak branches and the emerald green yard were gone. It was no longer night. Blinding sunlight broke through a lead-lined stained glass window. The multi-colored puzzle pieces of the window focused, revealing Christ on the cross, the two Marys at his feet--their time of mourning. Dust motes spiraled in the broken beams of light, twirling down away from the window, down to the smell of burning incense, down to the sight of his dad's funeral.

A stooped and ancient priest spoke in Latin, his palms raised heavenward in benediction over his dad's coffin. Sunlight gleamed on the coffin's polished lid. The six pallbearers, all strangers except for his Uncle David, stood in the aisle behind the coffin, their heads lowered, their hands clasped respectfully in front of them.

"Such a sorry sight, isn't it?"

Kevin felt a tear spill from his eye. He blinked and it blazed a trail down his cheek.

"The sadness of this spectacle is not the fact that a perfectly healthy man, still young in years, was cut down so mercilessly, so viciously. The sadness, at least in my eyes and I assume probably in yours, stems from the fact that Amber Winstrom, the petite blonde standing three rows behind your own mother is actually the last woman that your daddy ever... how shall I put it, knew."

Kevin's vantage point was high up in the rafters, even higher than the choir balcony at the back of the nave, but he still saw of whom Mr. Freakshow was speaking. His mom was standing at the end of the first pew, her arm over Kevin's shoulder. His grandma stood next to him, holding his hand. He could see his own head bobbing, unable to control his tears. He was far from alone. Everyone appeared to have a tissue or kerchief in hand, or with tears on their faces, untouched. And yes, Kevin could plainly see, Amber Winstrom had her face buried in a lace hanky.

"That's not true. My dad wasn't like that," Kevin was able to blurt out.

"Oh, I'm afraid it is. Your mom only learned of his indiscretion after your dad was fired for sexual harassment. You see, once she was in good with your dad, Amber tried to weasel her way up to the management ranks in his office. Of course, she was unqualified, and while your daddy enjoyed his tryst with Amber, he knew she was not management material. Pardon the pun, but your daddy was screwed. Either he would push for her promotion, with his intentions as obvious to everyone in the office as if they had actually witnessed your dad's spurious rutting, or he would not mention a word of her ambitions for management and have her spill all the lewd details to anyone who would listen."

"You lie. He'd never..." Kevin wanted to argue, but deep inside he knew Mr. Freakshow's words were true.

"At least your daddy had the dignity to not promote someone unworthy."

Kevin was crying now. Seeing the funeral for a second time, knowing his dad was in that shining box, and knowing that the woman with whom he had been having an affair stood only a few feet away from his own mother, made him feel like he would be sick.

"Why... why are you doing this? Why don't you just leave me alone?"

"I can't do that, Kevin, my boy. I can't leave you alone, because I'm a part of you." Mr. Freakshow rattled his shackled wrists. "See these? I'm bound to you and you to me." The monster walked down the center aisle of the church. The funeral goers didn't seem to be aware of his presence. He shoved the pallbearers out of his way, punching one in the back of the head, while elbowing another over several pews. "I want to show you one more thing. I'll need your help, of course, since we have this whole brotherhood thing going on, this bond of ours." Mr. Freakshow rested his palm against the top of the coffin. The priest droned on nearby about dust and earth and the sins of man. Mr. Freakshow backhanded him until the gray balled-up priest tumbled down the aisle, hitting a lectern with a clamorous crash.

"Leave me alone."

A knocking came from within the coffin. Mr. Freakshow seemed surprised. "You hear that? Do you know what that is? I think I know what that is. Let's find out. I need for you to come here." Mr. Freakshow waved at Kevin, his wrist shackles jangling, gesturing for him to join him next to the coffin.

"No!" Kevin screamed as he floated past the choir balcony, descending toward the coffin.

The knocking became louder. "You hear that, Kevin? That's your daddy banging against the coffin lid. Let's pry this lid open so we can

25

find out which woman he chooses. Is it going to be contestant number one, Amber Winstrom, the ambitious whore-secretary who would go down on anyone to get a leg up? Or is it contestant number two, his dear wife, your mother, the woman who bored him to the point of such a succulent temptation!" Mr. Freakshow yanked on the corner of the lid with both hands, one grotesquely clawed foot propped up on one of the handles for leverage. "Come on, give me a hand!"

From a far off place, a warm voice tore through the nightmare. It tickled his ear and stirred his heart. He turned away from the sight of Mr. Freakshow violently shaking the coffin, and began to rise from his slumber. The church pulled away, becoming smaller, darker. The bedroom wall fell back into place, and then the window began to shrink, stopping at its original size. The darkness outside lightened, and the oak canopy soon cast shadows across his bedroom floor.

"I'll see you again, Kevin. Real soon," Mr. Freakshow's voice hissed, fading away to nothing.

"Kevin, dinner. Come on and get washed up," his grandma's voice cut through the last tenuous strands of sleep.

Kevin's eyes opened, this time for real. He touched his wet cheeks and the puffy skin around his eyes. He didn't want his mom to know he had been dreaming. He felt like he had slept the night away, but was probably out for only an hour. He cracked open the bedroom door and saw the coast was clear down the hall to the bathroom. He hurried out and reached the bathroom before his mom could see him.

He splashed cold water over his face until the puffiness around his eyes subsided. By the time his mom knocked on the door to call him again to dinner, he looked as close to normal as possible. When he sat down to a dinner of batter-dipped chicken, fried rice and honey-glazed carrots, he had little memory of his dream. Just glimpses, flashes of thought, fragments of emotion. As he ate, he thought about how he didn't want to see a doctor, and how he would do anything to prevent his family from knowing how scared he was to fall asleep.

CHAPTER FOUR

Nolan Gage stood in the Serenity Wing of his museum of dreams, transfixed by the mural he had commissioned. Behind him was a wall of state-of-the-art impact-resistant glass. Beyond the glass, austere and empty rooms awaited the arrival of the dreams.

The nearly finished mural was much closer to his original concept than he could have hoped. A silvery rush of water crashed over a boulder-strewn cliff, leaving the wooded vale below shrouded in a cool mist. The pale lemon sun hung low at the start of a new day. Reeds knifed skyward from the hidden reservoir's spongy shoreline at the bottom of the falls. Thick, downy grass carpeted the ground. Two people dwarfed by the enormity and natural beauty of the vale cast their fishing lines into the shimmering water.

He was one of those minute people lost in the gray morning mist. The other was his daughter, Nicole. His little Nika. He was teaching her how to cast the line with a sharp flick of her wrist, letting gravity take the bait-laden hook through an arc to splash the water. Every time Nika would cast during the day that inspired the mural, she would want to reel in the hook right away. She didn't want to wait for the fish to find her bait. But she had learned. She had learned, and she had been adorable and innocent. And whole. A whole person, not the withered form he now visited on a daily basis.

His mind seemed to drift through the unmoving air of the museum, crossing through to the otherworldly air of the painting. As he absorbed the depth and detail of the shore, the texture of his painted fisherman's vest, the thatch of the picnic basket they had taken along on that lost morning, a hint of movement played at the far reaches of his peripheral vision. The movement tore his attention from the fond remembrance captured in the painting. He quickly looked up to see a pair of painted birds flying higher than the falls, above the mist, cutting the air with their sharp, weightless wings. He couldn't remember seeing the birds before. They couldn't be new. Sophie wasn't at the museum and there was no way they had painted themselves.

He had only looked in that direction because he sensed movement. It was an instantaneous reaction, subconscious and altogether instinctive. But the birds were only smudges of different shades of paint. Highly realized and beautifully idealized, but smudges nonetheless. He chalked it up to the mural's breadth of detail. He had simply missed seeing them before.

"I didn't know you were here, Nolan."

The sudden voice startled him. When he turned, he felt disoriented.

"Sophie. Hi. I didn't know you were here, either. I thought I had the place to myself."

"I was just getting my coat from the office," Sophie Marigold said, zipping her yellow slicker. A loose bun held her silver hair. She wore bright red lipstick and a long denim skirt that swept the floor as she walked. Streaks of red and cream colored paint stained her clothes. Her right cheek carried a fresh daub of yellow paint like misplaced makeup. She was the only person who worked for Nolan Gage who called him by his first name, and the only person who could get away with it.

They had met in college. Gage had majored in finance while Sophie had studied art. He'd needed to take an art class to graduate, and when the semester was half over and Gage was on the verge of getting a B and ruining his perfect GPA, Sophie took pity on him and helped him get his A. They were soon inseparable.

"Done for the night?" he asked.

"I'm so close to finishing, I want to gut it out to the end, but I'm exhausted."

"And I suppose you would like to get home to Andrew."

While in college they had nearly fallen in love, but their lives were too different, their worldviews would never travel the same path. Not long after their break up, a fellow art student named Andrew Morton captured Sophie's heart. They married less than a year later. Nolan Gage graduated and made his first million before his thirtieth birthday.

"Yes... Andrew." An underlying sadness weakened her voice.

"He's probably busy at home. Painting."

"Even if I wasn't so tired, I should go. He misses me."

"That's understandable," Gage said softly. They were quiet then, standing at the base of the mural, seeming only a step away from entering the grassy vale. "This piece is better than I deserve."

"You are too hard on yourself. You've given me something no one else could have. Andrew and I haven't been this happy in so long."

"Good. That's good. Then I guess it worked out for everyone. You have your happiness, and I have the perfect image of a perfect day to look on whenever I want."

"Can you walk me to the door? I'm afraid I don't have a key to lock up behind me. I should have realized when the last of the workers were leaving, but I was a bit distracted by the painting."

"Of course." Gage watched Sophie as they left the Serenity Wing and entered the expansive foyer. He had often wondered what it would have been like if they would have tried harder to keep their relationship together. He imagined they could have been happy, but then he would never have had Nika. For the briefest moment, he felt like his life would have been better off. He felt a twinge of guilt when he remembered why he had come to the museum so late in the first place.

They reached the wooden double doors. Sophie flipped the deadbolt and pulled open the heavy door. "I hope Maury can help you."

"It's what I live for."

Sophie surprised Gage by touching his face with the back of her thin, gentle fingers. She caressed his cheek. She smelled of turpentine and flowery perfume.

He saw tears forming in her eyes. "You've always been a sweet man."

"I'm glad you're in my life again." Gage felt both discomfort and warmth from her touch. Gage took hold of her hand as it lingered at his cheek. He squeezed it before letting go.

"Are you leaving soon?" Sophie asked.

"I came to see my daughter."

She nodded with understanding and gave him a weak smile as she left the museum.

"Drive safely," Gage said. He stepped outside to make sure she made it out safely.

As Sophie walked to her car, Gage noticed the normal sprightly bounce to her step had disappeared and she clutched her purse tightly. She looked so vulnerable. Tired. Maybe it was just age. He didn't get around as well as he once had, either.

After her car's headlights disappeared, and the loud clatter of its muffler faded, he looked at the outside walls of the weathered limestone building. The sunken twelve-panel windows of the old Carnegie Library looked like entrances to abandoned caves. Navy-blue drapes held in the meager interior light. Still thinking of Sophie Marigold, he entered the building, hoping he was making the right decision in opening this museum.

Novelties and concessions would soon fill the island at the middle of the open foyer. T-shirts, cheap plush animals, rainbows of cotton candy. Posters and autographs. A pair of curving stairwells framed the far end of the foyer like a giant's embracing arms. The second floor housed the adult-natured dreams. One branching hallway led to the Nightmare Wing, the other to the Erotica Wing. Originally, Gage didn't want any part of displaying such fodder, but Maury Bennett argued vehemently that their display would more accurately represent the human psyche. Gage eventually conceded after Maury assured him ID checks would be required of anyone wanting to enter the second floor.

The first floor was family-oriented. The Serenity Wing would soon house lush dreamscapes inhabited by liquid flowing pastiches of human-animal hybrids, flocks of laughing, flying children, and any number of indescribable dream-folk. The dream-folk changed both their own shape and the symbolism embedded within their environs with equal ease. Bunches of floating balloons tied to razor sharp ribbon, became bunched ripe grapes, became pillowcases stuffed with goose down and one hundred dollar bills. A dream child, transmuted from the mind of an alcohol abusing truck driver, became an eye-patch wearing pirate, became a green and crimson-clothed elf using his saliva to join pieces of a balsa wood airplane became…

The possibilities were limitless.

Gage marveled at the complexity of the dreams, the ironic simplicity of their lives. A year ago, if someone would have told him he would soon walk through a building full of embodied dream people, he would have insisted upon their consignment to a padded cell. The fact that he now owned and financed such a business? Perhaps he too should be committed.

He walked to the elevator set in the back wall of the foyer. He hit the down button and waited for the doors to open. His mind drifted to the day Sophie Marigold reentered his life. Periodically, Maury would update Gage on the dreams he had encountered and the possibilities of including them in the museum. Many of the museum's dreams had come from his work with patients at his private practice. Others had turned up after Maury posted want ads on bulletin boards in the courtyards and hallways at the University of Chicago. The ads solicited lab technicians interested in groundbreaking dream therapy. No experience necessary. While at the university attending an art seminar, Sophie came across one of these ads. A long-time sufferer of recurring dreams, Sophie was immediately interested in hearing what Maury Bennett had to say.

A week after her initial phone call to Maury, she was at the former Carnegie library, gutted of its bookshelves and magazine racks and antiquated card catalogs, walking side by side with her former love, Nolan Gage. They hadn't spoken since their ten year reunion in 1973. Nolan had been amazed by how little she had changed.

The elevator doors inched open, and Gage entered, descending into the bowels of the building.

After exchanging awkward pleasantries, he had shown her his doorway to the sleeping mind. He had explained how the dreams would be divided into separate "wings" of the museum. It wasn't long after Gage had started their impromptu tour of Lucidity that Sophie had stopped walking and had given him a quizzical look.

"I didn't know people were so interested in dreams. Or at least enough to have an entire museum dedicated to them. Aren't you going to do anything about Freud or Jung?"

"Lucidity is a museum dedicated to dreams, but not how you're thinking. It has very little to do with psychology and the interpretation of dreams. Lucidity is a modern museum with a goal of attracting a young, forward-thinking demo."

"What do you mean?"

"Actually, I guess you can consider Lucidity to be more of a zoo than a museum."

Sophie had thought about it for a moment, but was still just as confused.

"All those displays with the four-inch thick glass, the empty chambers roped off from the public--those displays are going to house dreams."

Sophie had no idea what he was talking about.

"I know, it sounds crazy, and I don't really know how it works. I'm just in charge of bankrolling all of this. Maury Bennett is the guy who brings us the dreams."

"Slow down a second. He *brings* you the dreams?"

"Like I said, it's more like a zoo. It's not the entire dream we house, just people or creatures from within the dream, for the most part."

"Really?"

"I've seen it myself. It's amazing, kind of dumbfounding, really."

An hour later, they had parted company, their decades apart forgotten, and a new bond formed. She had agreed to paint his mural, and in exchange, Maury Bennett would help her with her recurring dreams.

The elevator doors opened to the museum's basement. For decades, the library had been the county's local history archive. The cavernous Carnegie Library basement had been a depository for the largest historical collection for Chicago's history. From shortly before World War I until the early 1960's, collegians and professors alike ventured to the basement, a place that seemed downright cold even on the hottest summer days, to thumb through volume after volume of forgotten news and discarded artifacts.

With the opening of the museum only two weeks away, most of the dreams occupied enclosures in the basement, in the former archives, tucked away in secure environments, unbeknownst to the people walking above them. As the workers finished with their remaining work, Maury would move the dreams to their appropriate locations in the wings of the museum's upper levels. By the day of Lucidity's grand opening, the basement would be empty with the exception of one room. The room held a single, well-worn recliner, an occupied hospital bed, and the brightly colored accoutrements of a child's bedroom.

He would visit his daughter regardless of the success or failure of the museum, until hopefully she would awaken. The doctors had told him there was little point in holding on to hope; there was little chance of her regaining consciousness. As this almost certain situation became clearer, he noticed himself putting more faith into Maury Bennett and his mysterious abilities. If Nika should never awaken, Gage awaited the day when Maury Bennett would transmute a dream-Nika from her comatose mind. As long as her mind continued to function on that most basic and primal level, Gage had something to hold onto.

He could find Nika's room in the dimly lit hallway with his eyes closed. He turned left, walked a short distance, and then made another left. At the end of the hallway was a small antechamber with a number of brown-painted metal doors recessed in the rough stone walls. Behind three of the doors were small rooms with glassed-in enclosures. All kinds of nasty creatures lurked within. In the fourth room, his daughter slept her endless sleep. Safely away from the world above, left in a perpetual dream state. His hand was on the knob to her room when he heard what sounded like thunder emanating from the ground itself. The air seemed to become heavier and much cooler. The hair stood up on his arms, and he had to suppress a shiver.

He tried the nearest doorknob, but it was locked. The museum should have been empty, especially with Sophie gone for the night, so any kind of disturbance might mean trouble. He tried another door and found it unlocked. When he opened the door, he found Maury Bennett seated at a battered desk scavenged from the leftover library furniture. He had reams of paper spread before him, a cup of coffee in his hand.

"Hello, Mr. Gage."

"What are you doing here?"

Maury gave him a wry smile. "Working."

"I thought the museum was empty."

"I just brought in a dream." Maury pointed to the wall of glass in front of him.

Behind the glass lurked a woman, or what Gage thought was a woman.

"This is Juliet. She'll be displayed in our Nightmare wing," Maury said, letting Gage step into the room completely to get a better view. "She seems nice enough most of the time, but when she gets in certain moods, it just wouldn't be right for kids to be around."

Within the enclosure, a young woman was sitting on a green park bench, her summer dress hanging limply on her shoulders. Succulent red berries dotted the green backdrop of bushes. Gage didn't recognize the park's setting; Maury could have plucked her from any park anywhere, real or imagined.

"Juliet originated in the mind of a suicidal dreamer named Barbara," Maury said.

"So, why are you still here? She seems secure in her enclosure."

"After Barbara failed with her fourth attempt to kill herself, her injuries left her in a catatonic state. From what I've heard, she really enjoyed jumping from buildings. Her family contacted me through a referral from her family physician. They feared her dreams had subverted the rest of her mind. I went to their house, transmuted the young woman's demon, and now we have the privilege of displaying Juliet. I left her parents' home only a few hours ago, and they've already called my cell to tell me their daughter has pulled out of it, at least somewhat. She has the mind of a five-year-old, and considering she's a jumper, she's lucky to have that much. At least she's conscious."

"What are they going to do now?"

"To tell you the truth, I don't care. They were going to wait until morning to take her to see their family physician. I can guarantee he'll find her as normal as Barbara can be."

"You didn't explain why you're still here."

"Right, sorry about that. I'm observing. Since Barbara is acutely bipolar, and Juliet is a mirror image of her, Juliet's moods also swing wildly. Right now, she appears to be more manic than depressed."

They quietly observed this dream person that simple logic would exclude from the possibility of existence. Natural light--actual sunlight and not the bleached-out variety emanating from fluorescents--shined through a thin veil of clouds that floated along the enclosure's ceiling. The tiny room seemed without boundary. A steady downpour of tepid rain drenched the girl, pressing the flowered fabric of her dress against her skin, accentuated her small breasts. She was quite stunning, and Gage had to remind himself that she was only a dream.

"I'm thinking of breeding her."

"You're thinking of what?"

"She seems to be a perfectly lithesome and fertile sort of dream. Suppose I introduce a perfectly masculine and fertile sort of male dream to her enclosure. Suppose they mate."

Gage's eyes widened at what he was hearing. "I will not stand for that."

"Think of the raw data produced from such an experiment. Think of the possibilities."

"I didn't hire you to perform perverse acts of dream husbandry. Do I need to remind you that your sole focus should be your work with my daughter?"

"It wouldn't take any time away from Nicole. I see progress with your daughter, and I think it's just a matter of time."

"My answer is no." Gage's voice boomed through the little room, making it seem even smaller. He didn't normally raise his voice, but Maury's suggestion threw him off kilter. Maury didn't say a word and appeared hurt by the exchange.

Juliet turned, as if noticing her onlookers for the first time. Gage caught a glimpse of a revolver in her hand.

"She has a gun," Gage said, backing away from the enclosure.

"Don't worry, it's a dream-gun--her own creation and harmless to us. But this never ends pleasantly."

Juliet smiled at her onlookers before putting the gun barrel between her lips.

"No!" Gage went to the enclosure and slammed his hands against the glass. It didn't matter. Juliet held her smile as she squeezed the trigger. A red cloud burst from the back of her head. The smoke from the gun scattered quickly in the rain. Juliet, drowsily struggling to steady herself on the bench, dropped the gun into the deepening puddle at her feet.

"She's remarkably consistent. She kills herself every twenty minutes or so," Maury said.

"I wasn't expecting that," Gage said meekly.

"I know. That's part of the attraction of this place."

Pink-tainted water funneled from her mouth and painted the front of her white dress. She waved emphatically to Maury and Gage, somehow able to smile after her ordeal. She seemed happy to the point of tears just seeing them.

Maury waved back warily. When Gage looked at him, he was comforted in the fact that he also looked uncomfortable. If Maury had appeared unmoved by Juliet's actions, then he would start to doubt if he was doing the right thing.

The blood-tainted water in Juliet's enclosure began to clear, and the exit wound at the back of her skull began to heal. The rain eased to a drizzle and the sun dipped behind darkening clouds. Juliet's mood had drained. The muscles of her face seemed to sag as she dipped toward the darker depths of her personality.

"It doesn't get any easier to watch," Maury said weakly.

"I need to get out of here." Gage opened the door. He didn't wait for a response from Maury before he exited the room.

Maury jumped from his chair and caught the door before it could swing closed. "That's fine. I can show you what I've been working on with Nicole. I can't wait to show you the dreams I've transmuted from her."

As the door closed behind them, Juliet pressed herself against the enclosure glass. She was fascinated by her visitors, especially the man with the sad blue eyes and pink scars on his face and hands. There was something there, she realized, something she wanted to know more about.

Juliet didn't notice the prolonged interval of her relative peace. The twenty minute interval of her repeating life cycle lengthened to thirty. She didn't yet feel the tingling sensation through her fingertips that represented the beginning of the end of her life. No gun had appeared in her hand as thirty minutes stretched to forty, her mind occupied by thoughts of the man with the sad blue eyes. The outside world and all its variable stimuli had presented her with the opportunity to expand her mind beyond that of her dreamer. Her mind was growing. Evolving.

The thin veil of clouds hovering above her head had turned a grimy black. When the fluorescent lights lining the ceiling winked out, jagged lightning replaced their brightness. The enclosure vibrated under the gentle roll of thunder.

CHAPTER FIVE

Carin woke groggy and unsure of her surroundings. She saw a shelf overflowing with Girl Scout ribbons and cheerleading trophies. She tossed aside the covers and stood reluctantly. For the briefest moment, she expected to see a teenager staring at her in the mirror hanging near her dresser, but she dismissed the notion when she saw the creases forming at the corners of her eyes and her ratty morning hair.

She heard pleasant sounds coming from the kitchen. Kevin's laughter--a noise she hadn't heard in so long--along with her mother instructing Kevin to break the eggs with a short and sharp blow against the side of the mixing bowl. That's when she remembered that the items sitting on the shelf collecting dust were fading tokens from her childhood. She was in her mother's home, once a place providing comfort with seeming permanence, but now only a rest stop before the next stage of her life could begin.

Carin ducked into the bathroom and grabbed her robe from the hook on the back of the door before heading down the hall to the kitchen.

"Rise and shine!" Kevin said, his laughter becoming a giggle. He was standing on a step stool, towering over his grandma. Flour and cinnamon dusted the front of his pajamas, and he wore a paper chef's hat that was too big for his head.

Her mother turned to Carin, "Sleep well, dear?

"Good enough, I suppose," Carin said through a back-arching yawn.

"We didn't want to wake you, but Kevin practically begged to make you breakfast in bed. We were having too much fun and I guess we ran late with the finished product. You'll just have to eat at the table like any normal person."

Carin looked at the surprisingly well-organized table. Hot tea steeped in a mug at her place at the table. A plate steamed with bacon, none of it burned like her own bacon would turn out. A glass vase holding freshly cut roses from her mother's garden acted as the centerpiece. All that was left to complete the meal was the French toast that Kevin looked well on his way to finishing. He was dipping homemade wheat bread in the batter. Everything looked like it was running smoothly, so she sat down at the table and watched Kevin acting like a kid for the first time in a good while. Carin sipped her tea and noticed a cinnamon stick resting on the saucer's rim. She twirled the cinnamon in her tea and let out a long sigh.

This was starting to feel like her home again. The only thing preventing Carin from completely giving in to the notion was Kevin's nightmare. Even now as he danced around the kitchen, playing the part of the little chef, his eyes were drawn and fatigued. His skin was too pale, and she was afraid he was losing weight. Boys his age didn't lose weight, they packed it on like it was going out of style.

She had planned to wait until Kevin went back to school to find a new job, but from judging his mood this morning, maybe he was okay enough for her to start looking. The chance to get out of the house would do her some good. Daytime television made her want to throw the T.V. through a window.

No harm would come to Kevin if he was with her mom, but she didn't want to impose on her any more than she already had. Her mom would never admit to any imposition, and it was sometimes hard for Carin to read her. Carin didn't want to disrupt her mom's peaceful retirement with all this mess, but she didn't know what else to do. Her mom had already made up the two beds for their arrival before the tragic events at the bus station. They were going to stay with her for a short while anyway, until things with James improved.

Her mom touched the back of Carin's chair, and then sat down next to her. She had been blind since Carin was Kevin's age, but she got around with few difficulties. An extremely rare form of macular degeneration robbed most of her sight by the time her mother was seventeen. Her fear of doctors had prevented her from seeing an optometrist right away, not that it mattered with the aggressive variant of her disorder. It was incurable. By the time her parents took her to the doctor, an empty black void covered most of her central vision.

"You know, the older he gets, the more he reminds me of you." She danced her hand along the table until she could place it on top of Carin's. Her hand felt warm and smooth. "He's going to be tall and leggy. He should run the hurdles on the track team when he's old enough."

Carin looked at Kevin as he tidied up the chaos of dirty dishes. He still seemed in a good mood, but his smile had become muted and the circles under his eyes had darkened. She was glad her mom couldn't see him like that, but in her own way, Carin figured, her mom sensed his emotions without being able to see him.

"Like James," Carin said quietly. His name felt foreign on her tongue, as if she were reading it out of a magazine.

"Oh, I'm sorry, dear. I didn't remember that about James."

"It's okay. Really. Just shows Kevin has some of his father's qualities. There's nothing wrong with that." She felt helpless. Carin never believed their marriage was truly over, even during the ride to the bus station and facing their impending separation. Their marriage was unquestionably on the rocks, but not irreconcilable. Their relationship hadn't been close to ideal since the year Kevin was born, but it had been her marriage, and had been hers to deal with.

Her mother leaned over the table and spoke in a quiet yet strong tone, "You need to put up a better front than that. Wipe that expression off your face, or Kevin won't see any point in trying to recover from this." She squeezed Carin's hand for emphasis.

Her mom was right. She could feel an added gravity pulling at her skin. She perked her eyebrows and felt the tension that had built up around her eyes.

Kevin came over to the table, carrying a platter stacked high with perfectly golden slabs of French toast. Carin gave him the biggest smile she could muster, and squeezed her mom's hand back in thanks.

Their small family enjoyed a well-cooked breakfast, and when Carin mentioned to Kevin about going down the block to play at the baseball field, he didn't shrug off the idea.

Lunch was over and Kevin had already helped his grandma with the dishes. He walked from his bedroom, his baseball glove on his left hand, his right hand smacking thick leather sounds into the glove's pocket. His grandma was tending to her lilies in the backyard, and his mom was in her room, the droning sound of an NPR show murmuring through the closed door. Kevin was so bored he could scream.

He opened the screen door and went out to the front porch. The sun was hot, and the slight breeze smelled dry and florid. The wide wooden porch was peeling and the sloughing white paint made it look like a dormant and decaying creature resting at his grandma's doorstep. He kicked at the paint, sending flying chips into the air.

His grandma's neighborhood felt more like back home than he thought it would. There were blocks of brick homes, complete with small yards and driveways. He always thought of the city as having tall buildings where everyone lived in apartments. But it wasn't anything like that. At least around here. He could hear kids playing ball at the park down the block. He kept his eyes fixed on the paint as he kicked it away, exposing the bone-colored wood beneath.

"You should go to the park," his mom said from behind him.

He looked up to see her smile softened by the door's dark screen.

"I'm kinda tired." Which was true. Kevin hadn't slept well last night or any other night for quite a while.

She opened the door and joined him on the porch. She looked down the block to where she could see the tall chain link ribcage of the baseball backstop. A short kid charged around the bases while the other kids yelled with excitement. The blur kicked up a cloud of dirt as he slid into home plate safely, just under a tag.

"When I was a kid, those ball fields were all woods. You can still see some of the trees past the soccer field way in back. I used to have a tree house in the woods, but the park looks just as fun."

"I guess."

"You guess? You know, if you're not going to go down there and play, then I just might go myself. Think they'd let me play?"

"Mom, come on."

"Okay, fine." She reached into her pocket and pulled out a five-dollar bill. "Here, you go down to the park, play ball, meet the neighbor kids. When you get thirsty, get a Coke down at the ice cream shop on the corner." She stuffed the money into his pocket and put her hand on his shoulder. She gave him a little push.

Kevin took a couple tentative steps down the porch steps. "But... Mom."

"No buts. You go. I don't want you home until dinnertime. I'll be right here on the porch swing reading a book. I won't be too far. Have fun."

Kevin looked over his shoulder and was about to protest further, but it wouldn't get him anywhere. His mom was stubborn. His dad had always told him he was just like her. Well, this time he would let her win. No sense beating his head against a wall. Besides, he wanted to play. He just didn't want to talk to anyone, let alone meet anyone.

He kicked rocks off the sidewalk as he walked, forgetting his mom and her stubbornness and now wondering how he would break the ice with these new kids. He felt in his pocket for the money she had given him and was considering going straight to the ice cream shop instead of the park. She didn't say he couldn't go there right away. He really was kind of thirsty. He could get an ice cream float and figure out a way to meet the other kids. But she could still see him; he could feel her gaze from where she sat on the porch swing. She was liable to yank him out of the ice cream shop and cause a big scene if he didn't go straight to the baseball field.

Kevin didn't hear the crack of the bat, but the movement of the foul ball caught his attention. When he looked up, the ball was skipping in the gutter next to him. Suddenly, a dozen pairs of eyes were staring at him. He came close to crossing to the other side of the street with the ice cream shop, maybe act like he didn't see the ball rolling toward him.

"A little help!" the big kid who hit the foul ball said, holding a taped-up wooden bat in one hand.

A bow-legged kid wearing a catcher's mitt came through the gap in the chain link and was on Kevin's side of the fence. He had his mitt up in the air. "Little help?"

Kevin scooped up the ball with his glove, crow hopped like his dad taught him and rifled a throw back to the catcher. It was a dead-solid throw, making a thwacking noise in the thick leather of the catcher's mitt.

"Thanks," the catcher said then wobbled back through the gap in the fence. He chucked the ball back to the pitcher, and the game returned to normal. No one was staring at Kevin. He walked the rest of the way to the aluminum bleachers behind the dugout, the ice cream shop pushed to the back of his mind. He took a deep breath, rubbed spit into his glove until it gleamed, waited.

When a kid even smaller than Kevin struck out for the third out about five minutes later, the big kid who hit the foul ball jogged over to the bleachers where Kevin sat.

"That was some throw," the big kid said. Up close, Kevin noticed dark peach fuzz on his upper lip. Greasy hair crept out from under the rim of his little league cap.

"Thanks. Need another player?"

"Sure. You can be on my team. We're one short anyway."

Kevin could see the other players waiting for the big kid to finish talking to him. The infielders were tossing a ball around.

"Come on, Reid, gonna play or just sit over there like a cheerleader?"

A short black kid called out from the pitcher's mound.

"Hold on Lucy, don't get your panties in a bunch. I think we got another player. Now we got even teams," Reid said in a wavering, half-man voice. He turned back and asked his name.

"Kevin Dvorak. I just moved in up the street."

"I'm Reid. That bow-legged guy you threw to, he's up to bat now, that's Stephen Rose. He's an all right guy. The loud mouth on the mound, that's Lucius Harper. We call him Lucy because he catches about as good as a girl, but man, can he pitch. They're starting to look pissed. You'll meet the others as you go."

Kevin followed Reid to the diamond. The tall kid trotted over to the vacant first base area. He kicked the surrounding dirt until he erased the tread marks from the previous inning.

"Can you catch?" Reid asked while sizing up the other members of his team.

"I like the infield the best," Kevin said.

"You sure?" Reid said, doubtfully.

"Yeah, my dad used to… I mean, he hits grounders to me all the time."

"Tom, you go to the outfield, and play short center, Jimmy… shift over to left," Reid barked out orders, and his team moved without raising an eyebrow. "Leave right empty. No one hits 'em that way anyway." Reid shifted his attention to Kevin. "Go take shortstop. We'll see how you do."

Kevin went to his position, scooped up a handful of dirt, and dumped it into his glove. He dropped it out slowly, the dust barely stirring as it tumbled back to the baseball diamond. Most of the kids looked to be Kevin's age, and most seemed bigger than him. A couple of kids were a few years older, like Reid. They wore faded baseball and skateboarding shirts, cargo shorts with heavy, weighed-down pockets. Scabs in various states of healing covered their knees and elbows like badges of honor.

Bending at the knees, the other infielders leaned over slightly on the balls of their feet, waiting for Lucy to throw a pitch.

Lucy was as short as Kevin, but his arms were remarkably long and thin. He hid the baseball in his glove as he looked in on the catcher for a sign. The kid behind the plate wiggled his fingers uncontrollably for a moment then lowered his index finger. Fastball all the way. The catcher took a deep breath as he awaited the pitch.

Lucy lifted his left knee until it nearly touched his chin, his chin tilting skyward. He paused at the top of his delivery, and then his motion became a whirling mass of arms and legs as he stepped forward into his release. The hitter, some redheaded kid, had either an unusual grouping of dark brown freckles on his face or had missed his bath for the last three weeks. He stood at the plate, an oversized wooden bat twitching above his shoulder. Kevin heard the baseball exploding into the catcher's mitt before the redhead started his swing. He threw the bat around in an arc so hard he almost left his feet.

Kevin looked over to Reid in astonishment. The older kid nodded and smiled knowingly.

"Hey, Mikey, just wait until I'm warmed up. You'll be swinging so hard, you'll be cooling me off out here," Lucy said. He snatched the return throw with a downward thrust of his glove.

Mikey was understandably quiet. He looked at the next pitch and the catcher called a strike. Mikey didn't argue. The third pitch he failed to nab with a bunt attempt. Mikey took a right-handed turn back to the dugout, his head hanging low.

The inning went by quickly. Lucy mowed down the other team in a couple more minutes with most of that time dedicated to Lucy's taunting.

Kevin sat on the bench next to Reid as they waited to bat. Reid seemed like the center of attention, but he didn't act like a big shot. They watched as Lucy stood at the plate, a baseball bat resting on his shoulder.

"So, did your dad get transferred here?" Reid asked as he watched the pitcher wind up.

Kevin, thrown off by the question, remained silent.

"Oh, I get it. Divorce. I know what that's like. My dad's been divorced twice and my mom's remarried. The whole divorce thing's a bitch."

"Yeah, no kidding," Kevin said quietly. He absently tested the laces of his glove, pulling one tighter. Lucy swung meekly at the first pitch.

"They say it's all right because you get more Christmas presents, but that's all bullshit, too." Kevin noticed how naturally Reid swore, almost like he didn't care if any adults could hear him.

Lucy swung at the second pitch, missed badly, and then slammed the bat into the ground.

"Hey, Lucy, don't blame the bat, blame your game," Reid shouted out to the batter's box.

Lucy looked over his shoulder and gave the whole dugout the finger.

"My dead grandma can swing better than that guy, but he was the first guy I picked for my team."

"I never seen a kid pitch like that," Kevin said, hoping the subject of the conversation had changed.

"They also say divorce is cool because whenever you're around, they want you around, but believe me, when you come for a visit, you're just in the way."

"That's not bullshit," Kevin said, feeling awkward at the words and their context.

Besides good-natured taunting, the dugout was quiet for the rest of the inning. By the time Kevin went out to shortstop when they switched sides, he felt like he belonged. No one gave him weird looks, and better yet, no one understood what was going on inside his head. He wasn't going to let anyone find out, either.

Lucy took the mound, threw a couple warm up tosses, and then stared into the dugout. "Just to let you guys know, I'm retiring the fastball for the rest of the day. From here on out, it's the curveball, the big bender, the knee-buckler."

"Hey Screamer-Screamer-Screamer," the second baseman chirped at the batter.

"Go home and fuck your mom," the boy called Screamer said before settling into his stance.

"Hey Screamer-Screamer-Screamer..." the second baseman continued. The outfielders joined the chant.

Lucy paused at the top of his wind up before unleashing his curveball with the same movement as his other pitches. The only thing that was different was the motion of the ball. It started out fast and letter high, and then by the time it reached Screamer, it dove until it nearly scraped the dirt. Screamer took a huge upper cut, fanning hard. The second pitch was an instant replay of the first. As he readied for the third pitch, Screamer dug in deep with his heel, putting most of his weight on his back foot, and waited.

This time he made contact. The ball skipped on the rocky ground like a chip of granite on a crystal cool lake. It was shooting through the middle of the infield. Kevin took two strides and went airborne--his only way of reaching the ball before it hit the outfield grass. Kevin barely saw the ball leave the bat, but somehow he nabbed it before it could get through. He bounced up to his feet and threw hard to first base before he could get his feet planted. The throw was high, but Reid was tall. The throw beat Screamer to the bag by a step.

"Holy shit! Better luck next time, Screamer!" Reid said, throwing the ball back to Lucy.

Kevin slapped some of the dirt from his clothes, but not all of it.

Leaving some of the dirt would let everyone remember that play every time they saw him. He acted as casually as he could.

Screamer's face turned red, almost purple. He fell to his knees and covered his face with his hands. His voice was shrill and ear shattering. "No! No! God damn it. That was a hit. That should've been in the outfield. And I was SAFE! God damn it! I was SAFE!" Screamer carried on, and as he purged the anger from his system, the infielders tossed the ball around in a zigzag pattern. Everyone was all smiles, and they threw the ball hard, the ball smacking the leather until Kevin's hand hurt.

Everyone ignored Screamer until he was done with his tantrum. He sulked back to the dugout and the game resumed as if he hadn't said a word.

With the sun still warm but falling toward the distant trees, Kevin's winning team came out of the ice cream shop. He felt bad about going home on a full stomach, but he felt incredibly happy as he parted ways with the others. He was going to go back out tomorrow. They were going to pick new teams and start fresh. It sounded like fun.

He was kicking rocks off the sidewalk when he realized how late it was and how soon he would have to go to sleep. Mr. Freakshow would undoubtedly visit his dreams. Every time he woke, the nightmare faded but left him with fear gripping his heart. He thought the nightmares couldn't get any worse, but they always did. And there was nothing he could do about it.

His good mood slipped away completely as he reached the front porch. Inviting light poured through the screen door. Even with a full stomach, his mouth watered when he smelled the roast beef and mashed potatoes wafting from the house. Kevin's stomach grumbled and turned sour. He wanted to go back to the baseball diamond. He wanted to be there with Reid and Stephen and Lucy, and even Screamer, tossing a baseball around. He wanted to play baseball and have the sun high and overhead, and didn't want it to end. But it was getting dark and he was afraid to close his eyes, and even more afraid of what he might find there.

CHAPTER SIX

As night descended, the activity buzzing through the museum died to an afterthought. The carpenters had left for the day. Nearly finished with their work in the old Carnegie Library, they were happy to be home with their families for the weekend. They had finished erecting the display enclosures, and by now, little of the building resembled its former purpose. Someone had removed the packaging material from the new ornate chandeliers, and their warm light cast spidery shadows across the gray marble walls.

With the museum set to open the following Friday, Maury Bennett now spent most of his time here. More befitting the excitement surrounding the opening of an amusement park, Lucidity would open on the Friday night before Labor Day. There would be a write up in the Chicago Tribune's Weekend section, and Nolan Gage had mentioned renting giant lights to pan the sky like at an old-time movie premier.

As Maury headed for the elevator at the far side of the foyer, he caught a glimpse of a red light splashed across the floor leading into the Serenity Wing. He was about to investigate when the memory popped into his head. Rocky. He always imagined the dream cat would come for him. Not long after his brother's burial, Maury had heard the first murmurings. Rumors. Gossip. On the news or in three column inch stories hidden at the center of the newspaper. People would see a burning cat near their home. A little girl would come across a cat covered in flames stalking a field mouse.

Feeling foolish, Maury ducked into the Serenity Wing, and felt even more foolish for the cause. He had been scared by an illuminated exit sign.

He chuckled to himself as he walked back to the elevator. As he pressed the down button, the memory of his brother became his focal point. Dale, his constant shadow growing up. The little pest could get on his nerves in a split second or bring out Maury's sensitive side with his unrelenting devotion. He missed his brother.

Dale pulled the tent flap closed, carrying yet another blanket from their mother just in case a blizzard might chase away the Indian Summer warmth of late September. It was closer to winter than the boys wanted to admit. It was the dying days for everything: the sun's warmth, the trees holding onto the last of their withered leaves, the last peaceful days for their family.

"They're drinking wine," Dale said. He had brought enough equipment for a week of camping down by the river, instead of a night in their backyard. There wasn't a single square inch free in the three-person tent.

"So, what's wrong with that?"

"They never drink wine. It's like they don't want us in the house. They're celebrating."

"You're crazy. Gimme your canteen."

"Told you you'd be thirsty," Dale said with his bunched up *I told you so* face. He tossed him the canteen anyway.

"Aw, I'm not thirsty. I just need to take a wiz." Maury put the canteen between his legs and pretended to unzip his fly.

Dale lunged for his canteen, but Maury held it at arm's length.

"Gimme it back."

"It's mine now." Maury let the canteen fall within easy reach of Dale's hand and then yanked it away. He sat on the canteen, grabbed Dale by the arm and peppered his shoulder with punches.

Dale squealed in pain, but after years of roughhousing, Maury knew his brother's pain threshold.

"Say uncle, little boy. Say it." Maury increased the force of his punches, focusing his knuckles at just the right pressure point.

Dale weaseled from Maury's grip and jumped onto Maury's left side. His little brother had never turned the tables on him, and thus had no idea of the rules for administering a beating.

"Ah ha! You say uncle, you little prick." Dale began pounding Maury's left arm without holding back anything.

Maury screamed himself hoarse as he felt pain tear through his permanently damaged left arm. Dormant scar tissue sprung to life.

Frayed nerve endings showered his arm and torso with jarring impulses of electrical current. Dale didn't know that he had stepped beyond their game. He was finally pounding on his brother and didn't seem to want to stop.

"Uncle, damn it, uncle! Lay off," Maury whined through gritting teeth.

Dale let loose with one more roundhouse into the bony area near Maury's shoulder blade. He was panting and wearing a goofy grin as he leaned back against a mountain of blankets.

Maury slumped over and cradled his arm. He closed his eyes and it was all he could do to try to make the flashing pain in his arm disappear.

"I didn't hit you *that* hard," Dale said defensively after Maury hadn't moved or said anything for over a minute. Dale's breathing slowed, but sweat dripped from his face and his cheeks were flushed. He pulled the canteen from under Maury by its strap and took a long, victorious drink.

Through his blanket of pain, Maury heard the sliding door at the back of their house creep open. "Hey, keep it down out there, or the neighbors are going to think someone's getting murdered," their mother said. She shut the door before they could answer.

"I never knew you were such a wimp."

"That's my bad arm, asshole." Maury sat up, cradling his arm, but the pain had begun to subside.

"Oh, poor Maury," Dale said mockingly, but his face revealed that he truly was sorry. Maury guessed it was the closest thing he was going to get to an apology.

Maury dug through the blankets and duffle bags next to him until he uncovered a wrinkled brown paper lunch bag. He pulled out a package of pop rocks and tossed it to his brother. "Take this. I was going to keep them as a surprise, but you always seem to ruin all the fun anyway. Eat 'em up, but don't talk to me," Maury said.

Dale tore off the top of the black packet and tossed a few of the tiny pebbles into his mouth. They snapped and bit into his tongue, but Dale looked about as sad as a kid could look.

"I'm sorry, Maury. I forgot about your arm. You've been better for so long, I don't even, you know, see the scars no more. It's like there weren't no fire."

Maury held a packet of pop rocks in his hand, but hadn't opened it. In his mind he replayed what his brother had just said, and was instantly sorry for getting so pissed off. It was the first time since the fire that he could remember someone treating him like a normal person. At school he felt like an alien fallen to earth. At the playground, kids would walk the other way when he approached. In the grocery store, parents would embarrassingly whisper to their kids to stop pointing at him.

Instead of embracing his brother like he wanted to, Maury tore the top off his pop rocks and dumped the whole packet into his mouth. He let the candy foam from his lips and he bugged out his eyes like he was about to die. Dale let out a snort that turned into a giggle. He followed Maury's lead and emptied the rest of his candy into his mouth. Maury could barely contain his laughter, and for the briefest of moments, he was completely happy and had forgotten why he was so mad in the first place.

The tent was filled with the sound of popping rock candy and the last ragged jags of their laughter. Maury suddenly stopped laughing when he noticed a globe of blue light illuminating the tent wall by the zippered exit. He slapped Dale's arm, and his laughter died in his throat.

"Mom and Dad are trying to scare us for making so much noise," Maury whispered, inching closer to the door.

"Don't open it."

The light grew and brightened until the light shining through the thin material of the tent was nearly blinding.

Maury's mind raced, but he opened the zipper anyway. Blue light flooded the tent, throwing spastic shadows over every surface. Heat gushed through the opening like a breath from hell. As Rocky jumped through the slit opening, Maury fell to his back to avoid the cat. Dale began to scream again, and Maury was soon lending his voice to his cries for help.

Their parents were inside polishing off a second bottle of wine and didn't respond to their screams. Their neighbors, however, did end up calling the police. As it turned out, someone *was* being murdered.

The elevator slowed to a stop as it reached the basement. Maury stepped out and turned on the hall lights as he walked from one snaking hallway to the next. He took a cursory look around to make sure he was alone before entering one of the many doors leading to the rooms storing the dreams.

He had waited until the last of the workers had left and he was sure that he had the museum to himself. Last night he couldn't sleep after thinking up his little experiment, and then he had to wait through an entire day to begin. He felt like a kid waiting for Christmas morning.

When he entered the room, Juliet didn't seem surprised to see him.

48

Rain pattered across her pale skin, plastering her auburn hair against her cheeks, nearly hiding her blue eyes. She gently placed the loaded dream-revolver on the park bench and walked barefoot through ankle deep rain puddles to the front of her confinement. Her sheer dress clung to her skin and a thin strap had fallen from her shoulder. He could see her breath condense in the chill air. Gooseflesh covered her arms.

The seemingly natural sunlight shining through the black-tinged clouds was disorienting so far from the surface of the real world. For all of the anticipation and excitement that marked his day, Maury was unsure of himself. He didn't know why he felt this way. Palms sweaty, temples pounding. He always thought of the dream-people as beings as dumb as cattle. They did what they were told. They went where you guided them.

Juliet placed first one hand then the other palm-flat against the enclosure glass. Maury hesitated, but approached the glass, copying her display. Without thinking, he nearly stumbled as he backed away. He felt something he should have expected, that he should have prepared himself for. Warmth. The simple process of energy conversion and the resulting dispersal of heat had made him as jelly-legged as a freshman at his first dance.

Juliet was grinning at Maury as a child would look at a puppy at play. She pursed her lips and lightning tore through the dream clouds above her, small vibrations trembling through the basement walls. She breathed a circle of fog onto the glass and traced her index finger along its surface.

Hi

Thrown off by Juliet's seamless humanity, Maury began to question why he had come down here in the first place. It seemed so childish to him now. So childish and wrong. He had planned to enter her enclosure. He was going to instruct her like the simple-minded thing that she was to strip herself naked, and then he was going to... why he was going to do whatever he damn well pleased. And now, the simple act of feeling warmth through the glass, feeling warmth emanating from this specter of the mind, this embodied psychological enchantment, made him feel something totally foreign to his nervous system. Guilt.

"How are you?" He stepped closer to the glass, feeling slightly less jelly-legged.

He put his palms against the glass and she mirrored his movements. He felt the warmth, expected this time, and when she looked him in the eye, she didn't flinch. When her eyes wandered from his eyes to his cheeks and neck and his burden of marred flesh, she didn't shy away or look sickened by his appearance.

She met his eyes and now he saw pain below the surface. Not the bleak, depressive pain she normally carried, but something different.

"Sorry, poor boy." Her voice was thin and melodic, on the verge of breaking. A bare silver tear, a speck of crystal in the flowing rivulets of rainwater drenching her, filled her eye, fell from her heavy lashes.

He pulled his hands away. Pulled away from the trance she seemed to have on him. He sat on the edge of the battered desk and suddenly hated her, this dream-woman. He didn't want her pity. He wanted to enter her enclosure, tear the clothes from her and mount her like a wild fucking animal.

"Fuck you," he said, mostly to himself, defeat in his voice. "I did this to myself." He touched the familiar brown and pink scars on his cheek, the smooth surface that was his living torture.

Juliet retreated to the park bench and covered her face in her hands. He could hear her sobs through the glass. When the clouds broke and the rain eased, he jumped to his feet.

He had forgotten about the time. He had been in the little room for at least ten minutes. Juliet picked up the gun and placed the barrel against her chin.

Maury opened the access door to the small hallway leading to the entrance of her enclosure. He fumbled with his keys, finally found the right one, and fumbled with getting it into the keyhole. He threw open the door, splashed through the cold rain puddles and grabbed Juliet's forearm. His actions deflected the gunshot and the bullet sheared through her cheekbone, split her eye socket, exposed a swath of brain matter through her shattered skull.

"Why? Why do you do this?" She slumped into his arms and he cradled her. He could feel her quake as shock settled in. Blood flowed freely onto his shirt and down his pant legs.

"Thank you," she whispered.

Juliet's body fought to hold onto her fleeting life. A seizure gripped her in its fist, and spasms shook her wildly in his arms. Soon, her breathing slowed. Maury held her until she died. Then her wounds began to heal, to disappear altogether. The crimson glow of life crept back into her cheeks, human quality spreading once again throughout her body. Blood soaked, but without a wound to show for it, Juliet opened her eyes. She had changed, somehow through her interaction with Maury, she had broken her cycle of death and life. The clouds reformed and a chilly rain began to fall, washing most of the blood and gore from their bodies.

Maury leaned over, kissed Juliet's forehead.

Maury didn't know about the immortality of dreams until after Rocky killed his brother.

His parents were never religious people, but they were wearing their Sunday best the day they signed over Maury as a ward of the state. He sat in a secretary's office, in an orange vinyl chair that had foam busting through a split seam. The secretary peered over what she was typing, looking at Maury over the fat brown rim of her glasses.

"You want some water? Or some coffee? Ha, who am I kidding? No coffee for you. Too young for that. I can get you some water though. It's kinda rusty from the pipes being old, but that shouldn't do no harm." Her eyes lingered on his face, and she couldn't help but shake her head.

"No thanks."

Maury didn't know why he was in this cramped office on the first Thursday afternoon after they buried Dale. But he had done what his dad had told him to do. He washed up after school, put on a suit his mom had bought for him for Dale's funeral, and he kept his mouth shut. The day they buried his brother, Maury had pleaded to keep his cap as they entered the church, but his mom had taken it from him. He couldn't concentrate during the entire funeral, not with so many eyes investigating his singed, pink scalp.

The dark gray suit didn't really fit, especially when he bent at the elbow. He had been preoccupied with trying not to bend his arms at the funeral, hoping no one would see his scabby wrists. When the priest had told them to kneel and pray for Dale's soul, his dad had nudged Maury with a sharp elbow for not clasping his hands together in prayer. He didn't like the suit in the first place, and now he was wearing it for the second time in a week.

His healing arm still itched as if festering insects were burrowing through his bones. He snuck his right hand up the sleeve and scratched until he felt pain in his skin. It didn't feel good, but at least he felt something in his arm. The doctors had told him he may never feel anything--that he would need to be careful not to put his arm in any danger. They had told him to keep it away from open flame (he told them he had learned that lesson already). They had also recommended keeping it away from extreme cold or prolonged sunlight. That seemed like an awful amount of responsibility for someone who had torched his family's home on a whim. If they had only known.

He didn't know how long his parents were in the office with the frosted glass door with that Mr. Smelzer guy, but it seemed like forever. Twenty minutes ago, he noted the time on a wall clock that looked just like the one from his homeroom at school. A stark white circle with thin black numerals. It seemed like time went by slower if he was ever in the presence of such a clock. He sighed in boredom, but at least boredom kept his mind off his dead brother.

When they had entered the waiting room, his dad had told him to sit quietly and to not touch anything. Not that he wanted to touch anything in the dust and cigarette smoke stained everything of the waiting area. So, an eternity plus twenty minutes equaled forever, at least in Maury's estimation, especially when you're wearing a Sunday best suit that doesn't quite fit.

The secretary, who seemed as uncomfortable as Maury in his suit, wore a brown woolen blazer. She kept looking from Maury to the frosted glass door. He was about to ask if she knew anything about what was going on (and he figured she knew something since she seemed so twitchy and nervous), when Mr. Smelzer's office door opened. His parents emerged, his dad with a consoling arm around his mom's shoulder while she stared blankly at the floor. They had the door to the hallway open before Maury could even stand. His mom cried into her hands while his dad mumbled something in response as the door shut behind them.

Mr. Smelzer stood in the doorway to his office. He waved for Maury to follow, and when Maury entered the cigarette clouds of his office, he was sitting in a big leather chair.

"Your parents told me that a cat killed your brother?"

Maury still didn't know what was going on, or why his parents were no longer in the office. His theory was that Mr. Smelzer was some kind of counselor. Like the Jung guy he had read about. Counselors seemed so cool.

"Yes. A burning cat. Blue flames, like the ones coming from a kitchen stove."

Mr. Smelzer jotted something in a notebook as Maury spoke.

"And, your house burnt down not that long ago?"

"It was an apartment. We didn't get a house until people felt sorry for us and gave us donations after the apartment fire."

"There have been other instances, is that correct?"

"Instances?"

"Yes. Of fire."

Maury thought back to the time he had set his bedroom on fire. It had been nothing big, just a burn hole in the carpet when he was playing with matches. And that had been so long ago.

"Well, one time. I guess."

Mr. Smelzer looked at the notebook, flipped through a few pages of notes. "And then somehow a burning cat scratched apart your brother's chest."

"He had monster claws." He realized how crazy this sounded, but couldn't help telling the truth.

"Did you try to help your brother?"

This conversation wasn't heading in the direction he figured it would, and he didn't like it one bit. "Right away. I loved that little prick," Maury said. From his tone, it sounded like this guy believed everything had been Maury's fault. Well, maybe some of it had been his fault. No one had forced him to torch that poor cat, but Dale... he had nothing to do with that. It was an accident, totally out of his control.

"And what happened when you fought off this burning cat?"

"Not much, really. I thought it would hurt if I touched him, but he was barely warm, just like any other cat. He hissed at me and swatted his paw through the air, but he already had Dale's blood on his whiskers. Dale died pretty quick."

"So, like you said, you didn't get burned. Can you explain more about that?"

"It's simple. Rocky is a dream-cat. He does what he wants. I guess he wanted to kill my brother."

"Do you have any idea why Rocky would want to kill your brother?"

"I have no clue." He did have an idea of why Rocky killed his brother, but it was only a theory. If a dream person could kill the person who dreamed it, then perhaps it would be free to do whatever it wanted. Immortality. Why else would Rocky return?

"I need to have you understand, Maury, this is for your own good. Your parents feel like they can no longer protect you from yourself. They want to get help for you. That's why they brought you here."

"When are they coming back?"

"I'm afraid I don't have an answer for that one. Your parents feel like they can't let you out of their sights, even for a second. It's a matter of trust."

"Are they coming back?" Maury asked, his voice cracking.

Mr. Smelzer didn't answer and was saved from any more questions when someone knocked on the door. When the door opened, Maury could see the twitchy secretary in her itchy woolen blazer peering inside as two burly men entered the office. Mr. Smelzer told Maury to follow the men, and he did as he was told, and he kept his mouth shut, and he didn't touch a thing.

The sun had set and Maury was sitting on a lower bunk bed in a sterile white room with one of those super-slow homeroom wall clocks. A dozen bunk beds stretched in either direction. Shortly after an eternity had elapsed, the door opened and white-clad kids with dour expressions filed into the room. They climbed into their bunks. Maury rested his head on the paper-thin pillow and closed his eyes. No one said a word to him. He could only marvel at the mess they must have gotten themselves into in order to end up in a place like this.

He kept his thoughts to himself, kept the pain buried deep inside. The loss of his brother, followed by the rejection of his parents. Cast off like an old suit that doesn't quite fit anymore. He thought of Dale, the only one who really mattered anyway, and tears seeped from his closed eyes.

CHAPTER SEVEN

Kevin removed the crumpled packaging material from his new backpack. The blue bag had red straps and pockets all over the place. His mom had left it on his bed as some kind of present, but all it did was remind him that school was approaching much too quickly for his liking. After playing ball with the kids from the neighborhood, going to a new school wouldn't be all that bad, but still, he wondered why everything had to change all at once. Why couldn't he wake up every morning, grab his baseball glove and disappear until the sun dipped below the trees?

He had made it through dinner, but barely. He didn't want to let on that he had gorged himself on ice cream so close to dinnertime, even if his mom had given him the money. He ate as much roast beef and mashed potatoes as he could manage. He told his mom and grandma about how his team had won, and about Lucy's inability to catch a ball or swing a bat and his God-like pitching arm. He left out mentioning Screamer's swear-laced tantrum or how Reid had assumed Kevin's parents were divorced. It was like the kids from down the block and his family came from different worlds and he didn't want them to mix.

But now his heart raced as night overwhelmed everything it touched. The day started slowly, with an enjoyable breakfast with his family. Then the hours at the ball field slipped away as leisurely as maple syrup dripping from a bottle. The sun had set, having taken shelter from the coming night, leaving him alone in his room. It felt like time was accelerating, shoving him down a road to the inevitable and painful crash of sleep and the ever-present Mr. Freakshow. He didn't want to think about falling asleep. Maybe he was just being a chicken. Maybe he should just grow up.

I bet Reid isn't afraid to fall asleep.

Kevin thought of his new friend, and wondered if he could call him a friend at this point. Probably not. Reid probably hadn't given Kevin a second thought after the game split up earlier tonight. Kevin would probably have to reintroduce himself when he went back tomorrow. Reid seemed so confident and grown up that he didn't need to know anyone. He didn't need to go out of his way to know anybody when everybody already knew who he was.

Kevin tugged the zipper all the way open on the biggest pocket of his backpack and held it open like a lion tamer ready to stuff his head into a lion's mouth. The bag had enough space to carry just about anything. He glanced from the bag to his dresser (or rather his Uncle David's old dresser), and knew he wasn't nearly as confident as Reid. He couldn't face another night of nightmares, couldn't face the pain straining every chest muscle as his heart throttled against his sternum. Even if it meant he was a chicken, he didn't want to ever sleep again.

He opened a dresser drawer and took out a clean t-shirt, and then grabbed his windbreaker off the back of his desk chair. His mom had also bought him a new dictionary and thesaurus, placing them on his desk. He couldn't imagine a future where he would soon spend hours on end sitting at the desk, looking up vocabulary words or reading a history textbook. He couldn't wrap his mind around the idea of tomorrow.

His old Boy Scout flashlight was in the bottom of the closet. He glanced at the band stickers his Uncle David had left on the closet's back wall: Kiss, Yes, Boston, and absently wondered why people named their bands such stupid names. He filled his backpack with gear he might need. Clothes, check. Flashlight, check. The pocketknife his mom didn't know about stashed in his sock drawer, check. The blade was dull, but the point might do some damage if he needed it to. He looked around the room and couldn't think of anything else he should bring. That only left going to the kitchen before he would leave.

Running away like a chicken.

He pressed his ear to the door, but didn't hear anything. It was fully dark out and his grandma was almost certainly asleep. She was a light sleeper, but would usually turn in early and listen to the day's soaps on the soap opera channel, falling asleep in the process. His mom was another story. She was unpredictable and could be just about anywhere in the house at this time of night. She could be in taking a bath, or washing the last of the dinner dishes, or possibly in the living room doing a crossword. It was much to his relief when he noticed her bedroom door closed and the light of her T.V. flickering under the door. Kevin hefted his backpack to one shoulder and closed his bedroom door as quietly as possible.

Once in the kitchen, he eased open the zipper to a medium-sized pocket of his backpack and tossed in a couple cans of Coke from an open case sitting on the floor. He took a bag of cheese puffs from the pantry and grabbed a couple packets of toaster pastries as long as he was there. He was nearly out the back door when he went back to a cupboard and took out a jar of Sanka instant coffee. He snatched a teaspoon from the drying rack next to the sink, and then stealthily slipped out the back door, tightly closing and locking it behind him. He couldn't help feeling like his life was about to change.

When he first started scrambling for supplies, Kevin imagined leaving his grandma's house and heading north to Canada, and still farther, to whatever was beyond that. He had heard that if you went far enough north, there was no night, just daylight and high skies. So now he would walk all night, every night, and maybe hang out during the day, playing pickup baseball, or reading Ray Bradbury novels from the local libraries. Anything to stay awake.

His plan all but evaporated by the time he reached the grass of the back yard. Running away, or in this case, walking away, would do him no good. He realized he needed to take this one night at a time. Scaring his family by running away to Canada didn't seem like it would help any. He imagined them finding his bed empty, and the guilt the images conjured wasn't very pleasant.

Cool air rose from the damp grass as he cut across the lawn to the garage. He tried the side door and found it unlocked. He quickly entered and closed the door, leaving the lights off.

The garage smelled of motor oil and ancient saw dust. His grandpa's old workbench sat along the far wall, his woodworking tools hung on pegs and resting on shelves, held in place by a decade's worth of dust and disuse. Kevin never knew his grandpa. His mom carried a wallet-sized photo of her father holding Kevin at the hospital after he was born, but even in the picture, with his drawn, tallow skin and sunken eyes, it was obvious he wouldn't hold off his diabetes much longer. Even without ever having met his grandpa, Kevin didn't need to see the picture to remember what he looked like. Seeing the picture only a single time would have left an indelible image in his mind.

He slung his backpack onto a high-backed workshop chair. The workbench had been left untouched, and inarticulate scraps of pine from his grandpa's projects littered the bench like a tumbled over city.

He unzipped a pocket of his backpack and pulled out a room temperature Coke. When he opened it, the psst-sound made him jump. The warm soda stung his throat, but focused his sleepy mind.

He hefted a sizable wood plain, and wondered if his fingerprints were now meshed with his grandpa's. Pushing aside tools and scraping away piles of sawdust with a triangle of pine, Kevin started piecing together a mound of wood, and it soon took shape. The front wall was a little off, slightly too big, but the whirling brown knots in the wood looked like windows. He took out short, pin-like finishing nails from a cardboard box, and tapped on an overhanging roof--a bit too wide, but who's to know? He built the garage off to the left, a solid brick of wood. When he was finished, Kevin stood back. He could imagine his old house if he squinted enough. He could barely hold off sleep and sipped from his Coke to stay awake.

He was searching the workbench for paint, something in a light shade of green to match his old house, when a garbage can tipped over outside the garage. He just about jumped out of his skin, but after a moment, he figured it was just a tomcat in search of an easy meal. His mom and grandma, even if they heard the noise, would probably think the same.

But then the long bar locking the garage door folded into its open position. Whatever was outside, it wasn't a tomcat. Kevin resigned himself to being caught outside in the middle of the night. While his mind raced for a good explanation to tell his mom, the garage door creaked open.

The first thing he saw were the polished black oxford dress shoes. Then the solid crease of the freshly ironed dress pants. Kevin could see his dad's black leather belt then his white office work shirt then his warm, shaven face. He was standing just outside the door with his arms folded, as if he had been waiting for Kevin to open the door for him.

Kevin dropped the half-empty Coke to the dusty floor, while his heart pounded like it was a sick, mistreated animal. He wanted to jump into his dad's arms.

"Hi, Kev. I missed you," his dad said casually, moving his hands to his hips and looking down at him with that dad-smile of his, that smile that said he was proud of him and that he honestly and truly missed him.

The thought was in the back of Kevin's mind, drifting like smoke. He tried focusing it, but every time he grasped at the thought, it pushed through his mental grip. He couldn't move; he just stood looking up at his dad, wanting more than anything to jump into his arms and smell his aftershave and cigarette smell. But the thought suddenly crystallized.

His dad was dead.

When the thought solidified in Kevin's mind, his dad's expression changed. He looked upset, as if he had somehow hurt Kevin.

"Kevin, I'm sorry I had to go, but I had an important mission."

"Really?" Kevin imagined his dad going away on a mission for the government, wearing his black suit and having one of those earpieces with the wire disappearing into his coat.

"No, Kevin, it was nothing like that," his dad said, reading his mind. "I'll tell you more about it later. But the real reason I'm here is for your help. I need your help with my mission. I could think of no one more qualified to help than you. So here I am."

Kevin gave his dad a puzzled look. "But, you're..." Kevin said and the animal in his chest bucked as if hammered with a rusty nail.

"Yes, I'm dead. But I'm still here. In your dreams. Protecting you," his dad said, extending his arms to Kevin.

Kevin shook his head, trying to clear the fogginess. A dream. If all of this was only a dream, then maybe his dad was alive for real. Maybe he was alive and sleeping in his bed back at their house in Warren Cove. Maybe Kevin was asleep in his own bed, and none of these crazy changes had taken place. His dad was alive, they had never moved, he wouldn't have to go to a new school. Kevin jumped into the air and his dad caught him before he could touch the ground again. He could smell the cigarettes and aftershave, but there was also an underbelly odor. Like old garbage. No, not quite. And no, his Dad could never smell so bad; maybe the stink leached over from the tipped over garbage can outside the garage.

"Are you ready to help me?"

"Sure I am!" Kevin said and wrapped his hands around his dad's neck.

"Okay. Good. What I need from you, Kevin--and this is critically important--what I need is for you to never forget what happened in the bus station bathroom." The whispered words fell to Kevin's ears as if floating on a slight summer breeze.

Kevin looked at his dad at arm's length, as if he had misunderstood. His dad had also changed somehow. His face had cracked along the lines of his deep dimples, and there was a hint of something unpleasant beneath.

"You watched me die, Kevin."

The wind died to nothing and the smell hit Kevin again. Seafood rotting in a month-old diaper pail--that came close to the smell, but not really. And it was coming from his dad.

Kevin strained his elbows into a locked position, holding his dad as far away as possible.

"Every time you blink, I want you to see me gushing blood. With every sound you hear, I want you to hear an echo that is actually my internal juices gurgling through my lungs. Can you do that for me, Kevin? Be a good son and remember how your old man was murdered."

Kevin was struggling now, trying to get out of his grip, a grip that held him fast and cut off his circulation. His arms grew cold and started tingling from lack of blood. This stranger's skin--because there was no way this could actually be his dad--had disintegrated and was now falling in pulpy clumps to the floor, like oatmeal gruel on a winter morning. Somehow, the whites of his eyeballs were peeling like a snake losing its skin.

"Let me down," Kevin cried, kicking his legs out against the stranger.

"Can't do that, boy. But oh how I can tell you how much I care! I want us to become friends, you and I. I want you to open your heart to me. Let me feel your pain, your fear. Let me see the mutilated remains of that gruesome day at the bus station painted in your every expression," the stranger mouthed through his melting lips.

Kevin was kicking the man as hard as he could, but it didn't seem to matter. He simply spread his lips in a ragged-toothed smile.

"So that's your mission, my boy. Listen. Listen closely and hear your precious dad's last heartbeat. Take a deep breath and smell his spilled blood staining the bathroom floor."

Enough of the stranger's outer shell had crumbled away that Kevin could see what was hidden beneath. Pale blue skin pulled taut by ridged muscle, tattoos littering his chest and arms like a tortured artist's spoiled canvas. His dad's pants still encircled this monster's legs, but from the waist up it was Mr. Freakshow staring back at Kevin.

Kevin lunged at Mr. Freakshow and took hold of the wooden splinter piercing his left nipple. He tightened his grip and pulled down hard, initially meeting resistance. But then came the sickening sound of tearing flesh. Mr. Freakshow screamed and Kevin was able to slip through his captor's hands, his shoes hitting the driveway gravel. He stomped on the monster's foot and backed away until he was in the murkiness of the garage.

"You're not my dad!"

"I never said I was."

Kevin looked around, but he had no other way out. He ran for his backpack and fumbled out his pocketknife. He flipped the blade open and waved it in front of him. Mr. Freakshow was not impressed and laughed quietly as he entered the garage. He held one thickly clawed hand against his chest, grimy brown blood spouting from between his fingers. Kevin was seeing him now for what seemed like the first time. Purple veined wings twitched at his sides, stirring up small tornados of dust near the workbench. The shackles hanging from his wrists and neck jangled as he walked.

"Leave me alone!" Kevin screamed.

"No. That's not how this relationship of ours is going to work. *I'm* in control. Every step of the way. I'm the one who started it all. You are simply the chalice holding the precious Eucharist. But soon, very soon, I will drink from the holy chalice. I am fear and rage. I am the dirge of your soul."

Mr. Freakshow's wings flooded with blood and aroused in full splendor at his sides. Nothing was left of the man who had appeared to be his father. He was a beast wearing the shredded remains of a once presentable white-collar uniform. He moved closer to Kevin, blocking out the moonlight. Mr. Freakshow took hold of his shoulders and pulled him into his enveloping wings. Kevin couldn't say another word, but he could still scream…

Long after he woke he still screamed, a sweaty, agonized mess. Every time he closed his eyes he saw his dad dying on the tile of the bus station bathroom. He smelled his father's spreading blood, and heard a faint echo that was the gurgling in his father's lungs. Upon waking, Kevin brought every minute detail of his nightmare with him. He had woken dripping with sweat, his coherence drowned out by fear. With every breath he relived the memory of his dad's final moments.

Carin was sleeping deeply when Kevin's screaming roused her like a face slap. She ran to his room when she heard his cries, and still fighting sleep's grip, thought he had fallen out of bed. His bed was empty. But she could hear his voice, his screams. She stumbled around the edge of the bed to the window and pushed the drapes aside. When she saw the open garage door, she bolted from the bedroom.

She stormed through the kitchen and saw that the back door was open. When she reached the garage, her mother was already there. Kevin was sobbing in her arms while mumbling something about his mission to help Mr. Freakshow. And something about the smell of his father's blood.

Carin's heart broke. She felt more sadness now than the moment of discovering James in the bus station bathroom. This was ten times worse. Carin began to cry the first tears she had shed since they moved to her mother's house. Before she lost it completely, she went to her mother and gently touched her shoulder. When she turned, Carin sat on the gravel next to her.

Under a canopy of night pierced with starry light, they held each other and shed tears for very different reasons.

CHAPTER EIGHT

Carin stood with Dr. Edwardson outside an examination room. Her mother's doctor kept his voice quiet so Kevin wouldn't hear from inside. The doctor wore thick bifocals and had wispy fine white hair. His breath smelled like ancient dinner mints.

"Your son is fine. Physically, there's nothing wrong. Obviously, he's still suffering mental trauma over the loss of his father."

"What can we do? We can't go on like this. He sees something, I don't know what, but he sees something in everything he looks at. Something awful."

"I've seen this before. Happens every time soldiers come home. Post-traumatic stress. Unfortunately, I'm not the doctor to help deal with something like this."

"So I need to consult a psychologist?"

"A therapist, yes. I know a good man, a psychiatrist. Dr. Maury Bennett. He even specializes in dream therapy. While I don't know Dr. Bennett's philosophy or practices, I've heard nothing but raves from his patients. From my experience, there's no better doctor for dealing with nightmares."

"When can we see him?"

"It normally takes a couple weeks for an initial consult," Dr. Edwardson said. When he saw the color drain from Carin's face, he added, "Let me make a phone call. Let me see if I can pull any weight and get Kevin in right away."

Carin focused on the road and the bombardment of midday traffic.

The fatigue from a sleepless night was starting to catch up to her and her reaction time felt a second too slow. Kevin's eyes were closed and he hadn't said much of anything since they left Dr. Edwardson's office. They had an immediate appointment with Dr. Bennett, for which she thanked Dr. Edwardson profusely. Now, if only she could find the right address. She wasn't familiar with the neighborhood, but she had a feeling they were getting close.

Since waking this morning, Kevin appeared perpetually nauseated, while his skin seemed pale even after spending time in the summer sun with Reid and the other neighborhood kids.

At a red light, Carin looked at the scrap of paper with the directions to the doctor's office. It wasn't technically an office building, according to Dr. Edwardson. He'd said that Dr. Bennett was also working at a museum, and at least during the initial evaluation, Kevin would have to see him there. She didn't care if they had to meet with him in a junkyard, as long this Dr. Bennett was able to help.

The car behind her slammed on its horn when she didn't immediately react to the green light. "Hold on, I'm moving," Carin said as she accelerated. "What a jerk." A powder blue Fiat swerved around her, cutting her off before she finished crossing the intersection. The sour-looking fat man crammed into the car's tiny driving compartment gave her the finger.

She wanted to scream at the guy, but she took a deep breath and tried to decompress. Kevin seemed unaware of the exchange and was now looking out the window at the passing buildings, mumbling to himself. For the first time this morning, he appeared to be somewhat relaxed.

She heard partial words, but one stuck out in particular.

"What did you say?"

Kevin looked at her, winced at what he saw in his mother's face, but continued mumbling.

"Kevin, speak up, I can't understand you."

"Lu-cid-ity."

"Where did you hear that word? Why did you say that?"

"It's on a sign. I like how it sounds," Kevin said, pointing out the window.

Carin looked over her shoulder and saw the side of a lighted sign on a tall white pole near the street. They were too far away for her to read the sign, so she hooked a quick right and went around the block.

Lucidity, The Museum of Dreams

"What is it, Mom?"

Carin pulled into an open parking space in front of the building.

"We're here. I think." It was an old limestone building with columns framing the overhanging doorway.

"What is this place?" Kevin peered out the window, his nose pressed against the glass. The tension had left his face, at least, temporarily.

"A museum. The other doctor works here."

"Can we go inside?" he asked, his dour expression softened slightly.

"It doesn't even look like they're open." Which was true. A group of men wearing overalls entered through the front door at the top of the concrete steps. They looked like workmen.

"Please?"

Carin realized she didn't want to see Dr. Bennett, at least not quite yet. She didn't want to hear bad news. But thinking of the alternative brought her to her senses. Kevin needed help and as soon as possible.

"Okay, kiddo, let's go."

They climbed the steps to the front door. They stood for a minute, and Carin didn't know what to do next.

"Maybe you should knock?" Kevin suggested.

"I don't know about that. It doesn't look like they're open yet."

"Can I help you?" a man asked from the street level.

The man scaled the steps, and as he got closer, Carin could see pink scars on the side of his face and spiky locks of brown hair escaping from under his Chicago Cubs ball cap. One of his ears seemed larger than the other. When he reached the top step, she could tell his left ear wasn't real. He fit Dr. Edwardson's description perfectly.

"Dr. Bennett?" Carin asked.

"Yes?"

"Dr. Edwardson, he called over from his office. I'm Carin Dvorak. This is my son Kevin."

"Good. Perfect timing. Dr. Edwardson reached me on my cell, and I had to rush to get here."

"Thanks. We really appreciate it."

"What's inside?" Kevin asked as he tried to get a look inside the building through a curtained window.

"Why, dreams of course," Dr. Bennett said.

"Nightmares?" Kevin asked softly.

"Nightmares are dreams, aren't they?"

"Yes…"

"Nightmares are the most powerful of dreams, and we have many that will be displayed."

"I'm sorry, Dr.--"

"You can call me Maury."

"What exactly do you mean, displayed?"

Maury looked at Kevin and his gaze seemed to linger on his eyes, and their evident sadness. "Why don't I show you?"

"Really?" Kevin said with excitement. "Mom, can we?"

She too looked into Kevin's eyes and knew she couldn't deny him the hope of ridding himself of his burdensome nightmares. The three of them entered the museum of dreams.

Carin was astonished at the sudden change in Kevin's demeanor. He still looked like he hadn't had a decent night's sleep in weeks, but his eyes seemed to shine. She walked a step behind her son and Maury, this slightly odd stranger with his slightly odd limp. He had swept in from who knows where to welcome them into this strange building. If workmen weren't bustling through the wide marble foyer, she might have taken Kevin by the hand and made a run for the car.

Kevin was talking to Maury and walking by his side like he had forgotten she was even in the building.

"Maybe this wasn't the best idea. We can come by your office when you have an opening," Carin said, and both Kevin and Maury turned to look at her.

"Mom, look at this place," Kevin said in a pleading tone. "It's incredible."

"Ma'am, it's no bother. I remember being Kevin's age."

Kevin's expression, bordering on dire, broke her will. She waved for him to continue his tour. Maury didn't follow until he was sure that Carin was okay with it.

"So you like nightmares?"

"No, sir," Kevin said. "Not one bit."

"Then, why don't we take a walk through the Serenity Wing?" Maury suggested, gesturing to a far doorway. "It's my favorite place to be. Nothing scary there."

Carin followed a few steps behind. When she entered the hallway with the glassed-in wall, the amazingly detailed mural with it's magical waterfall and shimmering shore, she picked up her pace, as if pulled by a subordinate gravity.

"Look at that!" Kevin shouted, pointing a trembling finger at the glass wall. Carin traced the focal point of his excitement and was astounded. Somehow, the room contained a dense tree line snaking into an S-curve backdrop. A downy purple fluff carpeted the ground in front of the woods. The trees bowed over under the weight of basketball-sized oranges.

"This is what I meant by display. This dream is called 'Gavin's Glade.' It was taken from the mind of a four-year-old boy."

Crystal-clear sunlight shone through the leaves, and a gusting wind rustled the branches, sending puzzle-piece shadows dancing into the ground-fluff. The shadows tumbled over each other, taking on the shape of black-furred squirrels with over-large ears and paws that would normally be attached to the body of a golden retriever. They bit and scratched at one another playfully, and chased about under the lowest branches of the dense copse.

"This has to be some kind of monitor or T.V. screen." Carin touched the glass, but couldn't figure out the trick. It seemed so convincing.

"I'm afraid not. 'Gavin's Glade' is as real a physical environment as this hallway."

Kevin pressed his face against the enclosure with his hands cupped around his eyes to block out any glare from the overhead lights.

He looked up at Maury. "This is pretty neat, Maury."

Maury leaned over to Kevin's eyelevel and stared into his eyes. He seemed to be searching for something. "I can see it, young man. You have a monster haunting your sleep."

"Mr. Freakshow," Kevin said quietly.

"Ah, the powerful ones always seem to have a name. It gives them credibility, and authority, I suppose."

"Dr. Bennett, can I have a word with you?" Carin asked. Kevin looked forlorn, upset over the interruption and the possibility that she might make him leave. Which was exactly her intention.

"Sure."

They left Kevin nearby, walking to the end of the Serenity Wing.

"Dr. Bennett, I don't know what you're trying to pull, but I'm not falling for it. I thought I could trust Dr. Edwardson, but you obviously have him fooled."

"Please, just see what I can do for your son."

"My son is fine, it's his dreams I have trouble with."

"Dealing with dreams is my specialty," Maury said. "I have the ability to perform a homeopathic, noninvasive removal of dreams from the dreamer's mind."

"And what does that mean?"

"You saw the dream, the mutant squirrels."

Carin turned and watched Kevin peering into the glass enclosure.

"This is so crazy. I don't know how you can get away with this... fooling people like this."

"I can help Kevin," Maury spoke solemnly. "I can see it in his eyes. He's dying inside. Rotting from some recent hurt, something so painful that he can't bear to fall asleep. It's to the point that he sees his horror, this parasitic haunting of his mind, even when he's awake."

"That's a good guess, but we're going to see a real doctor."

"Ma'am--"

"Carin. My name is Carin."

"Fine. Carin, a family physician won't be able to do what I can for Kevin. I can take his nightmare away. Afterward, you'll take him home and he'll slowly heal, he'll recoup, and eventually, when he closes his eyes to sleep, he won't see this Mr. Freakshow. His life will extend beyond *just this minute*, this excruciating minute when he can barely hold onto his wits long enough to make it to the next. He will have hopes and dreams that won't scare him, that won't leave him hating life."

Carin's heart ached for Kevin. Her will was bending, but she tried her best not to show it.

"Let me talk to him. I can take away his pain. He can be home in time for lunch."

"And how much would this cost?"

"Nothing. Not a penny. We display the dreams to recover our costs and to not limit this procedure to the wealthy. You have to let me help your son. I won't be able to look in the mirror knowing I didn't do all I could for Kevin."

Carin looked down the hall, and she saw her son--gaunt, weary of the waking world, weary of the world hidden behind his eyelids. "Okay. Just let me know what you're doing. Every step of the way. If anything happens to him... if you hurt my son..." Carin said, and her will broke completely. Kevin couldn't take much more pain.

Carin stood outside an enclosure in the basement of the museum. Gooseflesh traveled her arms, spilled over to her spine. Kevin was in the enclosure with Maury. They were both seated in old wooden chairs, facing each other. In Maury's lap, he had a rubber reflex mallet and a small pocket flashlight. Kevin's eyes were glassy, and he seemed entranced by Maury's gaze.

Maury leaned forward, his lips moving deliberately, rhythmically as he spoke. He placed his left hand on Kevin's forehead. Maury's touch made her son flinch, as if in pain. Carin's fatigue was stripped away. She was ready to charge into the room, but Kevin quickly settled down to his docile trance-like state. Maury was now so close that his breath, his words, blew through the hair by Kevin's ear. Like a small breeze on a fall day and...

...Distant words, torn from the wind, seep into the ruin. A hollowed, broken shell. A form crumpled across the bus station floor. Blood trickling, imbuing the air with copper. Life spiraling away, struggling for one more ragged breath. Losing all. Through fingers slipped. Away.

And the words, from without this sullen boy's mind, break through the barrier, break through the fragile bones grown round his mind; Mr. Freakshow's fist gripping him, tightening. And still, the blood spreads across the bathroom tiles, with its sad meaty stench drowning the cinnamon disinfectant stench drowning the urine and shit stench of his father's dying place. These words like rumor twice removed. These words prodding for answers, torn from the wind.

Kevin answers with a mumble. Maybe words. Maybe a whimper of pain. Someone from somewhere far away shines a beacon of white light into the whites of his eyes and the pain pulls the Freak's hand into an even tighter grip. Someone from somewhere far away taps below Kevin's kneecap, sending a short and quickly forgotten jolt through his leg. It kicks forward, once. Then again a tap, a jolt, a kick. Again the beacon of white light. First one eye and then panning across to the other, sending a wash of pain stabbing through his skull.

Again, he hears words from a distance. Again prodding, again feeding on his mumbled response. Then the white-hot white beacon dims to darkness. The pain stabbing his skull, the Freak's clawed fist, insensate and cruel, slackens.

And the words, torn from the wind, fallen upon the ruin of his mind, coalesce: "Do you want this nightmare to end?"

And Kevin, sobbing, eyes closed to the sight of his father's dying place, his last breath: "I never wanted to hate him. I never wanted to miss him. I just wanted to be with him and be like him. Now I hate him. He's gone, and I love him and miss him. He won't let me forget it. His blood..." *the boy's words become hitching, uncontrollable sobs. Oblivion. Ruin.*

Kevin exhausted, bone-weary, speaking in his withered voice. "Mr. Freakshow... he won't let me go. Won't let me forget. His dying place, his last breath. Him fucking some whore..."

Now the words no longer prodded. They reassured. "Don't worry, it will soon be over."

Kevin took in these words, like a stranger's laundry pulled from a clothesline. As he focused to understand, seeing the fabric of these words, he exhaled some of the pain away. Someone was going to kill him. Take him away from this ruin. An end to it all. Peace and emptiness.

The emptiness of death would be sweet relief. "Okay."

...suddenly with the dexterity saved for mad magicians pulling rabbits from top hats, Maury removed his hand from Kevin's forehead, struggling for control of his deformed arm as if it had a will of its own... and suddenly, in the blink of an eye, without flashing lights, the roar of thunder, or a crowd's raucous clapping, the room held three people.

Kevin slumped in his chair, his eyes closed, the pain etched into the skin of his brow gone. Taken away. Replaced by tranquil repose.

Maury sat up in his chair, wide-eyed and awe-struck. He quickly gained his feet and looked at Carin. She was frantically slapping the glass until her palms stung and throbbed.

In the far corner of the tiny room, a slumped form, dead-gray skin stretched over massive, tattooed arms, greasy hair fallen in tangles over sharply ridged cheekbones to the level of the square jaw line, a beast more monster than man, stirring in his awakening. Her child's nightmare. Mr. Freakshow. In the flesh.

Maury, seeing Mr. Freakshow, pulled Kevin to his feet, and together they stumbled to the doorway. Maury closed the door behind them, nearly panting for breath. He locked the door, then double checked to be sure.

"What the hell is that, Dr. Bennett?" Carin asked, still struck numb by the transmutation.

"Mr. Freakshow. Let's get your son upstairs, to the sunlight."

Kevin wobbled between them, and they worked together to get him down the hall and to the elevator. His head listed from side to side and he appeared to be asleep.

"What did you do to him? What's wrong?"

"He's exhausted. He was exhausted when he entered the museum. After a nightmare's removal, it's not uncommon for the dreamer to sleep quite a bit for a few days. Once he gets plenty of rest, he will be back as good as new in a week."

"So this is normal?"

"Certainly." Maury watched the elevator lights above the door. They reached the ground floor and the doors opened.

They struggled as they walked Kevin toward the door. A kind-looking old lady rushed to open it for them as they approached.

"Miss, don't you worry," the old woman said. "Maury helped me, and I couldn't be happier. He's a genius. A gift from God."

Carin thought she could be just one more crazy person in the population of crazies that seemed to fill the building. She was covered in different shades of paint, and her eyes were filled with joy. Joy. Carin couldn't remember ever feeling the emotion. It was foreign to her. All she knew was pain and anguish and loss. Anyone so full of happiness must be crazy.

Carin nodded, taking Kevin from Maury.

"Everything should be fine from here on out. Let me know if there is anything else I can do for Kevin, or anyone else troubled by their dreams." Maury gave her a smile that warped his features. It wasn't a friendly smile, and she wanted to be free of this place. Kevin was starting to walk, one foot awkwardly thrown in front of the other. His eyes rolled to whites, fluttered, and finally opened.

"Maury... thank you. It's gone. The blood, it's gone. Thank you..." Kevin said, weeping softly, his eyes fighting to remain open.

Carin half-carried Kevin down the concrete steps to the Explorer. Adrenaline still coursed through her system. She wanted to speed away, but took a deep breath and forced herself to drive the speed limit.

CHAPTER NINE

Nolan Gage thanked Nika's day nurse, Shirley, as she left the museum for the night. After watching how gently Shirley cared for his Nika at the hospital, Gage had hired her away at double her salary. He felt better knowing someone with such a kind spirit was keeping an eye on her. Gage closed the door to the basement room and was alone with his daughter.

He turned to face her as she drifted through her endless sleep. His heart caught in his throat. Every time he saw her, he had the same reaction. A thick throb in his chest, self-loathing gripping his every breath. His daughter, his once angelic cherub, now a husk of bones and sunken skin hooked up to prosthetic machines that stimulated her heart to beat, forced air into her lungs, monitored her brainwaves. Her lips, once full and apple red like her mother's, now two dried earthworms coated in petroleum jelly. Her eyes--warm, brown eyes that Nolan Gage could barely remember--shut from the waking world, sealed with medical adhesive against the desiccant air. His little Nika, her mind trapped in a dead body. Her mind remembering the carefree whimsy of her childhood. A time before Gage forced her away.

He had brought her to the museum basement a month ago. When she was still at the hospital, Maury had insisted that he was making progress, that he was constantly locating and transmuting increasingly complex dreams from her mind. It had grown more difficult to hide his work from the doctors and staff. They had started to question Gage about Maury and what exactly his specialty was. They didn't understand why a woman in her condition would need a psychiatrist. But Gage still had his faith. If he couldn't believe in Maury and his enticing promises to bring him happiness, what else was there to live for? Soon enough, he would transmute a full-scale dream-Nika.

He reached into his inner coat pocket and pulled out a small pink teddy bear. It was holding a smaller version of itself in its stubby stuffed-bear paws. He placed the bear in the bony crook of Nika's arm and pushed a wisp of lank, straw hair from her forehead. His poor Nika; today, her nineteenth birthday. She didn't look nineteen. She didn't even look human anymore. Nika had always had an adorable kewpie doll face, but now her skin looked like a wet napkin draped over a toy plastic skull.

Whenever he closed his eyes, imagining his daughter, she was the enchanting girl captured in Sophie's mural on the wall of the Serenity Wing. Eight years old. Pigtails and scabbed knees. Sun-dappled freckles and a grin showing off her missing front teeth. Not so long ago, really, but a lifetime ago in actuality. A short lifetime, a lifetime that Gage felt responsible for bringing to such an abrupt close.

He had met her mother at a black-tie fundraiser for urban renewal. He hated those things. Men with enough money to bring about guilt gathering to congratulate one another, and women without any shame for seeking such men circling like vultures. The banquet hall was set up with enormous circular tables spread out like an archipelago of millionaires. Michelle's golden hair fell to shoulder length, but her smile is what captured Gage's heart. She sat at a long oak table near the doors, seeming so small and fragile, a stranger set adrift in the upper crust menagerie of her surroundings. She didn't look up from the pile of papers spread before her when he inquired about making a bid on a tilting slab of red clay that they were trying to pass off as art. The clay was not kilned, and a name brand shoeprint was visible on the side of the solid slab. A shoe kicking over a structure somewhat building-like. How symbolic.

She hadn't lifted her head to look at him. Just her eyes. Gage, looking down the slope of her face--the gentle bridge of her nose, and the delicate curve of her lips--had quite suddenly fallen in love. Her smile and upturned gaze set him off balance. He stammered. She explained how to fill out the form for the silent auction. She smiled, and he made an outrageously high bid for the piece of junk art without realizing it. He stammered and asked for her name. She told him, *Michelle*.

He had never expected to meet someone at a stuffy fundraiser. He was only in attendance to maintain his profile in the city's highest social circles. But Michelle was different from the usual gold-digging women in attendance. She had received her degree in sociology the year before, and had been working at a women's shelter in the south side of Chicago since graduating. As they talked, his stammering lessened and the abrasive fundraising hobnobbing became increasingly distant.

They had talked most of the night, and by the time the event was wrapping up, the subject matter of their conversation had continued to get deeper and more personal. They had already parted company when Gage realized he hadn't asked for her phone number. As politely as possible, he wedged back through the exiting black-tied old men with their Versace-draped younger companions. When she greeted him at the table, her papers gathered and her purse slung on her shoulder, she gave him that same perfect smile. She wrote her phone number on a cocktail napkin, and he knew his life was about to change dramatically.

Their age difference had never been an issue. So what if he was eighteen years her senior? Michelle didn't care, and as long as she was happy, so was he. She took him places he had never been and would have never imagined visiting. They walked the crumbling sidewalks of seedy public housing neighborhoods, walking two blocks away to where expensive high rises rose like some new life form set to dominate. She pointed out the gentrified layers of the city. Layers of money pushing away layers of decay, like grasping tree branches stealing the richest sunlight from the underlying ground brush. She pointed out the walls separating the classes and races. The expressways cutting off the projects and their populations of the poor, the disaffected, the drug-addled. Michelle opened Gage's eyes. He'd rarely felt compassion or empathy for others. She proved day after day just how wrong he was for his first impression of her. She was a fighter with a stubborn streak, yet somehow, she was able to care for people she had never met. Her personality was intoxicating.

Their marriage was a civil ceremony a year later. Nicole was born a year after that, a bundle of energy so similar to her mother that they could have been carbon copies.

Sixteen years on, sixteen years in which Gage thought he lived a happy life with his wife and daughter. Sharing moments, making memories. All fallen apart as quickly as he had fallen for Michelle all those years before. It was a trivial morning and Michelle was running trivial errands. Dry cleaning exchanged, a library book returned, tasks that Gage had always told Michelle were simply too trivial to waste her time doing. They had people to do those things for them. But his wife enjoyed her early morning walks, the fresh air, and the quiet streets. Maybe he should have gone with her. Maybe things would have turned out differently.

In line at the dry cleaners, a stranger had taken up a conversation with his wife. Later on, he learned this stranger was an artist. A poet, a pianist, a man who presumably neither shaved nor showered regularly. Gage wondered why such a man would be in line at a dry cleaner's. His clothes would be wrinkled, disorderly, mismatched, his uniform representative of his suffering for his craft. This weasel of a stranger had taken up a conversation with his wife, a trivial chit-chatty subject no doubt, and just that easily, so simply, the woman he had trusted and loved beyond words followed this angst-ridden would-be artist back to his loft. She had called later on, long after Gage had left worrying behind and was heading straight for full-blown hysteria, tears in her voice, scratchy jazz music thick in the background. Between her tears she told him it was over, she'd found someone else. She'd actually used the words *soul mate* when describing her new man. Just that quickly, fallen apart, a family ruined.

He wasn't able to tell Nika right away. The words wouldn't come to him, and if he *could* find the words, saying them would only make them true. Her mother was never coming home. He wished he could hire someone to explain to his daughter that for a reason as stupid as a chance meeting in line at a dry cleaner's, her mother was no longer a part of the family. The night of Michelle's phone call he eventually gathered his courage and went to Nika's bedroom--her boy band posters with their Colgate smiles leering at him, her stuffed animals appearing defensive of their place within his daughter's heart--and he had told her the news. At first, he thought Nika hadn't heard him, that his grief had possibly weakened his voice. But Nika had heard, and even more importantly, she had listened, distilling the knowledge down to its base elements. By the time he had finished speaking, his beard was wet with tears and a dull pain was shooting across his temples, mocking the beat of his heart. For some reason, Nika's lack of reaction hurt more than if she had broken down completely.

Michelle's betrayal had sent Gage into a tailspin of depression. Over the ensuing months, he rarely left his room, rarely left his bed, in fact. His pain was so blinding he couldn't see that even after such loss, life went on. She didn't react as he had expected, but Nicole was just as hurt by her mother's abandonment, maybe more so. During those most trying times, when she needed his support, she hadn't been able to count on him.

While he retreated to his darkened bedroom, his reddish beard getting longer and grayer, Nika took up with new friends. He didn't learn until later, not until after she had fallen into her coma, that she had started experimenting with drugs. Ecstasy and LSD and God knows what else, ingested with impunity. Dancing at rave parties and staying up for days at a time. Hurting herself, using the pain to fill the void where her mother once resided.

The phone call from the hospital slapped some sense into him. They told him someone had dropped Nika off at the hospital's front steps. She was unconscious and near death. Her temperature had skyrocketed and her pulse had dipped to almost nothing. He didn't remember much about the conversation, but the words *brain damage*, and *perpetual coma state* stayed with him. His daughter, having been unable to find reassurance in her father, had overdosed on some rave drug that left her in a near vegetative state.

His future hopes hinged on those few words that crept through the ether of his depression: *near vegetative state*. The doctors told him that on the Harvard diagnostic scale, she was on the better side of the spectrum, if there was such a thing as a better side of being comatose. Yes, she was non-responsive to outside stimuli. He could stab a needle into her arm and pray that Nika would scream; he could pluck the fine hairs from her arm one by one, hoping she would flinch, but all to no avail. The outside world was dead to her. But her mind continued to function. She had thoughts, memories, dreams.

Now, as he sat next to her, wary of blinking in case she so much as twitched a toe, Gage looked at her nearly black hair, a color defying her heredity. Michelle was a golden apple beauty, while he had always shied attention away from his fierce red locks and smudged red freckles. When he first saw her in the bleached out hospital room with the guilt-laden aroma of giftshop flowers, her unconscious roommate's helium balloons swaying over a heating grate like clownish clouds, Nika's hair was streaks of purple and green. Black makeup coated her closed eyelids. Golden flecks of glitter shined along her neck and collarbone, mixing with the remnant bile and blood-tinged vomit the doctors had forcefully removed from her stomach. They'd uncovered a toxic stew of a dozen pills that would need a week to decipher. The doctors didn't think she would live until morning.

Now, almost a year later, her hair stripped of the purple and green dye, and her skin cleansed by Shirley's gentle hand, Gage still wondered if she would live until morning. That's why Maury Bennett's work was so important.

That is what started Lucidity. Nika's dreams. The first experiments had been simple. Gage had brought in doctors specializing in neurology and sleep science. They had shown Gage EEG printouts of Nika's sleep cycles--kinetic scratches of horsehair-thin waves on reams of printer paper. Gage first thought the reports looked like Richter printouts after an earthquake. The doctors assured him that the ideas were fairly similar; a Richter printout showed earth plate activity, while the EEG printouts indicated brain activity. Those first printouts led to a series of countless experiments involving countless scientists. A tenuous job security rewarded success and advancement in the project. Gage discarded anyone without the passion he demanded or the will to create something never before pondered.

In the end, only Maury Bennett remained. His reputation had been shaky at best, but he had a brilliant mind. Even before he was brought on, Gage had heard rumors of his strange abilities. Most respected doctors didn't think much of Maury, but none of that mattered now. Maury could do what no other person could do.

"You look lovely, Nika. Another birthday comes, but your beauty transcends time," Gage said softly, kissing her eyebrow.

He checked the readout screens showing her vital signs, and as usual, everything was stable. He wrapped the consoles, monitors and other equipment with padded blue tarps he normally kept stored under Nika's bed. He then pushed aside the deep recliner where he spent most of his time waiting for Nika to wake.

The floor needed to be clear.

Gage went to a small panel on the wall. When he flipped the switch, a door slid aside. A horde of animated stuffed animal creatures and frilly-dressed porcelain dolls and miniature horses with miniature girl riders tumbled out of the open space left in the wall.

Nika's transmuted dreams.

One stick-thin sock monkey puppet jumped into Gage's arms and wrapped around his neck. It stayed there, as he always did, cooing into his ear.

"Yes, yes children, hello. I missed all of you." Gage was on his knees, engulfed in stuffed animal fur and the rich voices that Nika had leant her dreams. Gage was laughing along with them and enjoying a companionship that he didn't share with anyone in the waking world.

"Now, Rupert, don't squeeze so hard, I'm not going anywhere," Gage said to the sock monkey hanging on him.

The dream squealed and pulled at Gage's face, smacking him a kiss with his sock fabric lips.

"I love you too, Rupert, but love shouldn't hurt," Gage said.

The sock monkey clung to Gage's neck, picking imaginary fleas from his skin and straggly beard. The other dreams were friendly and playful with Gage, but Rupert was the dominant dream of the bunch. Because of that, Gage figured that Rupert was the dream that was strongest in Nika's mind, so he was Gage's favorite as well. Most of the other dreams had gone off to play amongst themselves. Gage had a small audience of Rupert and twin elves that wore matching suede jumpsuits. Their voices were so high-pitched and the delivery of their speech so swift, Gage understood at most one word in ten. They were simple fellows, but they demonstrated a keen interest in Nika, so Gage felt a surge of emotion when he saw them.

Gage checked the monitoring equipment, and nothing had changed. His little family was unusual, sure, but he had developed a level of calm with Nika and her dream creatures.

Rupert left the comfort of Gage's neck and mimicked how he had checked the equipment.

"Why do you always copy me?" Gage asked the monkey.

In response, Rupert hopped in the air and beat his tiny fists into the bed next to Nika.

"Don't get an attitude with me, Rupert. I simply asked you a question. I didn't mean any harm by it. You're just like a little kid, always copying me. Just like Nika."

Rupert took this as an apology and regained his position around Gage's neck. He knotted his sock hands and began to coo submissively.

He tickled the little monkey until the dream jumped from Gage's arms to the floor. He taunted Gage until he went after him. Soon he was rolling on the floor with slobbering puppies and jittering baby possums, while bright red cardinals chirped and swooped overhead. Gage played with his daughter's dream animals for hours. He only stopped after he had completely worn himself out.

Nika's dreams eventually calmed down. Some rested in the folds of Nika's blankets. Others hid under the bed. Still others dozed in Gage's lap as he reclined next to his daughter. His eyelids were getting heavy, and he let them close.

Freakshow. Gaining consciousness, becoming cognizant of inhaling, aware of the taste of it, this corrupt and putrid air, fouled by the presence of humans. His eyes popped open, liquid fire irises glowing in the midnight backdrop of his eye sockets. For the first time, Freakshow felt discomfort--stiff muscles and aching joints--from remaining chest down in a fetal position. As he breathed the air of his enclosure, he felt his lungs burn, felt the oxygen trickle through the air sacs of his lungs.

He parsed at the miniscule particles bobbing through his newly corporeal form, and like an archeologist, he discovered tiny nuggets that represented all he could hope for. Particles of Kevin, his dreamer and former captor. The dust of his skin; sloughed-off dead cells. Condensed droplets from his lungs, a wetness floating in his used, respired breath. A wetness that made Freakshow's mouth salivate; a wetness that was nearly as dear to him as the rich blood pulsing through the boy's heart.

He unfurled, limbs quaking, nerves frayed. The room was dark. His fiery eyes glowed, embers in a dying campfire. He could step three strides in any direction before finding a wall. He coiled his fists and let loose a raging barrage of kicks, punches and scraping claws against the confining walls.

There was no give to the walls and the surface wasn't the least bit marred by his efforts. He only felt something new to him. Fatigue. Squatting on his haunches, his back against one corner of the room, he began to ponder his escape. He would need to use all of his faculties in order to succeed. The humans had control over their environment and he was a stranger to this new land. But the boy was close. He could feel it aching in the marrow of his bones, aching like some human disease. Kevin was near, and he was asleep.

Let the boy sleep. He would need to rest in order to fight for his life. And a fight would be a dear thing. A fight would increase the boy's fear, and would build Mr. Freakshow's strength in the process.

Freakshow took in a gulp of air, and held it shortly before letting loose a shrill scream that seemed to shake the teeth embedded in his jawbone. It wasn't a scream of pain or frustration. Only pure, unfettered anticipation. When his scream was sated and his lungs were empty, his chest still burned with the unfamiliarity of breathing.

Nika's dreams stirred at the sound of the scream. When Gage opened his eyes, he wondered if it was only a dream. Rupert, his spindly arms shaking as he clung to Gage's arm, whimpered in Gage's lap. Soon enough, the dreams settled again, and Gage let sleep take him away from this place.

CHAPTER TEN

It felt like waking from a dream. Kevin certainly remembered Mr. Freakshow and how the nightmare had tormented his sleep since his dad's murder. But now the Freak didn't rule his sleep, twisting Kevin in his ever-tightening grip.

His nightmare was gone.

Reluctant to leave the comfort of his bed for the day--the first day since visiting Maury Bennett that he'd woken before noon--Kevin stared out his bedroom window. He listened to the birds singing their morning songs. He couldn't enjoy it, this relaxation, this laziness. It felt like a part of him was missing. With his nightmare gone, his emotions were exposed to all the pain he'd gone through leading up to his father's murder. The tension between his parents. The way he abruptly learned of his parents' separation. The pain of knowing his family had failed. It was all there, twirling about his stomach, magnified now that Mr. Freakshow was gone.

Kevin didn't remember much about the museum or the ride home from seeing Maury Bennett. When they had reached the sidewalk after leaving the museum, he felt so drained he could barely keep his eyes open. His mom let him rest the whole trip home without asking him any questions about what had happened inside the glassed-in room.

He didn't know what he would have told her if she had asked. He remembered Maury's hand on the skin of his forehead, and his touch felt white-hot, like the inside of a heated oven. Then the heat disappeared, and with his eyes still closed, he heard a whispered voice, a foul breeze lapping at his ear. The voice became silent, and then he felt a pulling sensation, as if his skeleton was being pulled to the surface of his skin, through his skin, leaving him a tumbled-over pile of skin and blood.

He shook his head as if trying to throw off the image.

In the void he now felt, he found pain. Pain like a physical wound. The answer became as obvious as the sun rising. His loss, the focal point for all his pain.

Dad.

If Kevin could have waited to use the bus station restroom, even for just the two minutes it would have taken until he was safely on the bus with his mom, his dad would have stayed back in Warren Cove. He would still be alive.

He pushed away from the bed, feeling sluggish and on edge. Betrayed. A paste of spit caked his lips. He walked to the bathroom in a not-so-straight line, relieved his bladder, washed his face. The clock on the wall outside the bathroom showed it was shortly after nine a.m.

He went down the hall to the living room, plopped down on the couch next to his mom, the pain in his stomach boiling over to anger. The T.V. blared, unwatched, as she unenthusiastically worked a needlepoint, absently pulling the threaded needle through the round canvas, shaping the likeness of a kitten one needle prick at a time.

She noted his appearance with a glance and nod before going back to the slowly emerging kitten.

"When were you going to tell me?" Kevin asked.

"Tell you what?"

"About Dad."

His mom kept her eyes on the needlepoint, as if gathering her words carefully. "What about your Dad?" She stuck the needle through the canvas and placed it on the end table.

"He wasn't coming with."

For a split second, he saw the grief in her eyes, a brittle fatigue that reminded him of the day of the funeral.

An image popped into his head. A rare detail from one of his countless visits from Mr. Freakshow. Amber Winstrom. "And you let that woman come to the funeral." He rolled the words to her, a ball in her court.

"I... how...?" his mom stammered.

"Why didn't you tell me?"

"I don't need to justify anything to you Kevin. We were leaving. That's all there is to say."

Kevin thought tears would come to his eyes, but they didn't. He didn't cower; he felt strong, willing to fight.

81

His mom looked like she was about to say something, but was interrupted by the doorbell.

"I'll get that," she said, rising from the couch.

Kevin muted the game show on the T.V. and perked his ears.

"Hello?"

"Mrs. Dvorak?"

"Yes? Can I help you?"

"I was hoping you could answer some questions."

"What is this about?"

"Mrs. Dvorak, it is my understanding that your husband was the last victim of the so called Steak Knife Killer, Jeremiah--"

"I'm sorry, I don't want to talk about this." She leaned outside and closed the door against her body to block out the conversation.

"If this is a bad time…"

"Yes, it is. Any time would be a bad time for you to come knocking on my door."

"But Mrs. Dvorak, I'm writing a book about--"

His mom struck like a prodded snake, "I won't have you bothering my family about this. You goddamn vulture… swarming around like you belong here, like in some sick way you're necessary. Go, just get out of here. Get out of here!" She stepped outside, closing the door behind her.

Kevin jumped up from the couch and pulled aside the front drapes and watched his mom chase after the reporter, chase him all the way to his rusted-out Chevy parked on the street.

Her voice carried, even as she trailed after the defeated reporter down the sidewalk. "I don't want to tell my story. Nobody needs to hear my story. Telling it won't bring back my husband. All you want to do is glorify some dead psycho…"

The squealing of tires broke through his mom's tirade. The reporter's car spat a plume of black smoke and seemed to disappear into it, like some magic trick.

His mom slowly walked back to the house. He could see her chest heave as she took in deep breaths of air, trying to compose herself. When her hand turned the doorknob, he quickly un-muted the T.V. Someone on The Price is Right just won a dining room set. Kevin acted like he was entirely consumed by the game show and didn't acknowledge her return.

She took her seat on the couch and picked up her needlepoint, but it remained untouched in her lap.

"Damn reporters. They're almost as bad as lawyers," she said.

Only a few days went by once they moved to his grandma's house before the reporters found them. They tried phone calls and letters by mail, and occasionally, someone would be aggressive enough to knock on the front door and try to get his mom to spill her guts. They obviously didn't know his mom.

"Sorry, Mom," Kevin said, offering a blanket apology for both the reporter's appearance, and their argument. He felt deflated. Defeated.

"When you're older, you'll understand."

"I hope so." He would do anything to bring meaning to such senseless loss. He wanted to just move on, forgetting everything before his arrival at his grandma's house. He would be willing to not have a past, to forget all of his memories, both good and bad, if he could just move on.

She patted his knee and seemed even less interested in her needlepoint than when he entered the living room.

Kevin didn't take his eyes from the T.V. until after the end credits. He tossed the remote to the couch cushion near his mom.

"I'm going to see what Grandma's up to."

"I think she's out back, in the garden."

Kevin didn't make eye contact with his mom, but he noticed the tremor in her hand as she tried to make the next needle prick in the pale blue canvas. He headed out the front door. A pair of black streaks marred the road where the reporter's rust bucket sped away. Kevin hooked a right and followed the narrow sidewalk around the side of the house.

The feeling was deep inside, like the slow lurch of a stomach flu. Things were changing. Maybe it was school starting next week--the end of summer, chasing fireflies in the dusk, playing ball in the morning dew (ignoring the cold damp working into his feet), and a thousand other mindless summer activities--things done during summertime and no other time, those would soon be gone. But was it a summer to pine over and cling to, tasting every last hour of it until it was gone, and missing it when it was over? Kevin's stomach did another slow lurch, and he knew he wasn't going to miss this summer.

He went through the gate leading to the back yard and stopped short of closing the latch. His grandma sat on an old wooden crate, leaning over to pry weeds from the flowerbed lining the fence encircling the backyard. Her hands fluttered in the air, inches above the shriveled blooms of her flowers, as if sensing out the invading weeds. She worked her gloved hands down the stem of a thorny thistle, found its base, and gently pulled until the roots tore free. She shook it free of soil before tossing it over her shoulder, near a pile of other vanquished weeds.

"Come back to help your grandma?" She teased another weed from the ground.

"Sure." Kevin closed the gate latch and walked over to where she was working. The garden soil had a grayish, dry tint where she wasn't working. A moist, black circle fanned out in a semicircle from her improvised stool. The dried blooms clinging to the flowers had remnant traces of color, red turned to rust, yellow turned to mustard, all passed their shining days of early summer.

"Throw those weeds in the paper bag. I need to get this done before they stop picking up lawn waste for the year."

Kevin tossed the weeds into the tall brown bag. Her hands passed over the flowers, hesitated upon reaching a weed, and then carefully yanked it from the ground.

"Another reporter, huh?"

"Yeah. Mom chased him off."

"Good. I don't know how those people can stand being in their own skin. Some are good, reporting on things fairly and without causing additional damage with their questions. But they sure make it difficult for people to get over things."

"Yeah," Kevin said simply.

"Excited about school starting?"

"Sure," Kevin lied. He was glad for the change in subject.

"Starting in a new school is hard, but in a week or two it won't be so much. Soon you won't realize it's a new school." She stood and arched her back, groaning at her sore muscles.

"Grandma?" Kevin said, then hesitated.

"Yes, dear?"

"I was wondering... um, why do you spend so much time out here, if you know..." he said, unable to finish the question.

"Why do I bother with my garden when I can't *see* my garden?"

"Well, yeah," Kevin said, embarrassed. "Because your back hurts and your hands get stiff."

"When I'm complaining about my back or stiff muscles, that's just an old lady talking to make sure she's still alive." She took off her gardening gloves and left them near the flower bed. She placed her hand on his shoulder and together they walked over to the lawn chairs by the back door. "Truth is, Kevin, your grandpa was a country boy. He grew up on a farm. He didn't like the city one bit. Wasn't enough nature for him. But my doctor was in the city, in that old granite building on Westmont, and the doctors at Loyola were close by. I guess I knew he loved me when he said he would live in the city if I would marry him."

"So you couldn't see back then?"

"By that time, all I could see were little bits on the outside of my vision. You know when they say you see something from the corner of your eye?"

"Sure."

"It was kind of like that. By the time I met Howard, that is all I really saw, just glimpses. He didn't like the city, so we put up those high fences, and I planted as many green plants as possible. At least our property would seem like a little island he could escape to after work."

"Do you feel like you miss out on anything?"

"With my vision, you mean?"

"Well, yeah." He hoped he wasn't prying too much. No one in the family talked about his grandmother's condition. Everyone just accepted it as fact. He couldn't help a little curiosity.

"Seeing is subjective."

Kevin didn't say anything because he didn't know what she meant.

"How can I say this... well, I guess you could say I can still see, to a certain extent. Like you for instance." She turned to look at his face. "You, Kevin, are a royal blue in a black backdrop. Your mother's an emerald green, slightly darker than her father."

"You see us as colors?"

"The doctors always looked at me like I was crazy, so after awhile, I just stopped mentioning it. If I concentrate hard enough, I begin to see the shape of things. Not all things, just living things, people mostly. The shapes are small clouds of color. I call it the 'hidden color.'"

"What does royal blue mean?"

"Oh, I long ago gave up trying to put meaning to either the colors or why I even see it in the first place. It's just a blessing to see anything at all. The colors tend to stick to families, I know that much. Twins are the only ones with identical shades. Figures, since they're a part of one another, even down to the DNA."

"What color are you?"

"I'm a slightly lighter color of blue than you."

Kevin thought on this for a while. He imagined his grandma getting up in the morning, and seeing a blue-shaped cloud staring back at her in the mirror. He wondered why his mom never mentioned this before. "Can Mom do it?" Kevin instantly thought of a family of witches, passing on their talents from generation to generation.

"See the hidden color? I've never mentioned it to her. Around the time she was your age, the doctors were acting like they thought I was crazy for even mentioning it, so I gave up on mentioning it to anyone. Howard knew, of course, but now no one else knows but you."

"Is it a secret?"

"Just for you and me."

"Okay," Kevin said, happy to be a part of something secretive. His grandma's coolness factor just ratcheted up a few notches in his estimation.

They sat on the lawn chairs, and the only sound was the traffic that was starting to pick up a couple blocks over at the busy intersection. Kevin looked out at the backyard, with the horseshoe shaped garden, and the tall oak tree, and tried to see the "hidden color" of things. After a few minutes of fruitless effort, all he saw were the same old colors he saw every day.

"So what's wrong, Kev?"

"I can't see a thing. Nothing more than I usually see."

"That's not what I mean. You came back here for a reason. I could tell the moment you stepped foot back here."

"I don't know," Kevin said, feeling like he was caught doing something he wasn't supposed to.

"You know if you need to talk to someone, I'm always here. Even if you need to keep a secret."

"Thanks, Grandma." Kevin waited until he could leave without his grandma thinking it was because she asked how he was doing. Because he didn't know the answer to that ever-present question. "I'm going to go wash up."

Kevin was flipping channels, not keeping a steady channel for more than a couple seconds. His mom was back at her needlepoint, and for all the time she put into it, she didn't seem to be getting anywhere. Neither one of them mentioned their earlier argument. He figured they had both decided it was better to just forget it and move on. His grandma had come in after another half hour, and she patted Kevin's hand as she walked by, a gesture that his mom probably didn't understand. She then went into the kitchen to start dinner.

A knock at the door broke the silence. When he looked up, his mom gave him a questioning glance on her way to the door. He heard murmuring voices, but couldn't place them. He hoped it wasn't another nosey reporter.

"Kevin, it's for you," his mom said. She walked back to the kitchen to help his grandma, leaving the screen door closed. From the brown head of hair showing through the screen, he could tell it was Reid.

"Hey, Reid. What's up?"

"We thought you were coming back to play."

"Sorry. I've been sick."

"Well, we were wondering if you'd be out tomorrow. Lucy has his cousins over for the week and we need all the help we can get to beat them."

"They can't throw like him, but they sure can hit," the catcher, Stephen Rose, said from off to one side. Both boys had their gloves with them, and Reid had a nicked-up bat resting on his shoulder.

"Tomorrow?" Stephen asked, hopefully.

"Yeah, about ten in the morning. We can get in a full game before lunch," Reid said.

Kevin was going to tell them no, that he was too tired. He had ducked out of playing since his visit with Dr. Bennett. He *did* feel tired. The guys seemed so intent on having him play, but his mind had just been... well, a mess.

"Come on, Kevin. We need your glove," Stephen said. He shifted his weight from one bowed leg to the other.

Kevin hesitated, but then gave in. "Sure. Ten o'clock."

"Cool," Reid said, with controlled excitement. Kevin didn't know he had made such a big impression with the other neighbor kids until he missed a couple days at the ball field.

"Yeah, it's probably the last ball before school starts. It'll be like playing in the playoffs or something," Stephen said.

"See you then," Kevin said, ready to close the door.

"Later." Stephen left the porch in the direction of the baseball field.

Reid stayed on the porch for a moment before speaking. "Hey, everything okay? We were wondering what was up."

"Yeah, I think I had a summer cold is all. Wiped me out. I'll make sure I'm there tomorrow," Kevin said.

Reid looked over Kevin's shoulder to make sure no adult was around. He lowered his voice, "I know how things can get. I've been there. You need anything, just let me know. It's shitty when your parents are fighting."

Kevin was going to say something about his parents, that he only had one parent, but when he just nodded, Reid took off after Stephen.

CHAPTER ELEVEN

Maury feared he wouldn't get the door closed before Kevin's nightmare woke up enough to lash out at him. The beast seemed to fill most of the room and gave off a stench that made Maury's eyes water. But he was able to get the boy out of there, and then his mom had practically carried him to her car without much of a thank you or good bye. When they left the museum, and he returned to Mr. Freakshow's enclosure, Maury knew immediately that he had discovered the star that would make him famous, someone who mattered.

Now, he was just waiting for Gage to show. Maury lounged as comfortably as he could at the old library desk he kept in the basement room that once housed Juliet. The room had become his makeshift office. It wasn't a practical working space, but he didn't like being around the rowdy workmen that were finishing up the last of their work above ground. Gage spent most of last night in Nika's room. Maury knew this from spending most of last night in this same office chair in the room adjacent to Nika's. Gage left sometime after dark, and hadn't returned. Maury wanted to bring his boss in to see Mr. Freakshow right away, but he guessed it would have to wait.

He thought of the boy, Kevin. He was ten, maybe eleven. In a way he sympathized with him, since at that same age he had gone through his own turmoil with the apartment fire, the months of recovery and rehab, and the death of his brother. Of course, he had secretly started the fire, and had been responsible for his neighbors' deaths. And by all accounts, the Steak Knife Killer had killed Kevin's father--a random act of violence. So it was a matter of semantics, but he still felt a connection with the boy.

Those troubles of Maury's youth were decidedly unpleasant, even depressing, but they didn't compare with his worst childhood experience. The white cinder-block room with the dozens of bunk beds. The emptiness of knowing his family had abandoned him. Knowing they would rather go on living without him. It was a dividing point in his life, even more so than the apartment fire. On the one hand, there was Maury's life with his family, and the other, his life on his own, a life of loneliness and painful introspection. The second half of his life continued. He dozed, thinking of his former family, and how he met his new family.

Maury was off by himself, reading the comics section of a Sunday paper. Well-dressed couples circled the room, yearning to make a special connection with one of the thirty or so kids in the playroom. This was one of the first weeks he was brought out for this procession of potential new parents. He'd been in therapy for months, and was now deemed mentally fit to move on with his life. His parents, his real parents, had never even called to inquire about him, at least as far as he knew.

No couple paid particular attention to Maury, not even the people with dollar signs for eyeballs that just wanted another check from the state. Couples would look at him, quickly avert their eyes, and continue their tour of the playroom. He was definitely not pretty to look at, and after awhile of seeing those averted glances, he didn't even bother meeting anyone's gaze. He imagined himself as a forty year-old cast off, still reading the newspaper, still waiting for someone to look at him with warmth.

Miss Harris, his caseworker since his arrival, approached him with a couple in-tow. She tapped a finger against the newspaper for him to lower it. When Maury reluctantly set it aside, a young blond man and a Hispanic woman were at his side. They both beamed with genuine happiness. Their eyes were strange. Maury looked around, but no other children were near him. They wanted *him*. The couple pulled up child-sized chairs, and the three of them chatted. Time slipped by. Miss Harris quietly left, wearing a delighted smile that wouldn't go away. They came to an agreement. Maury would come home with them and be their son. In return, he would have a new family, a fresh start.

The Unger's lived in a middle-class suburb of Chicago. Robert was a construction foreman on the new expressway. He made a decent living that allowed Eliza to be a stay-at-home mom. During their chat, Maury learned he would have a foster brother named Gabe, who was six months younger than him. Once school started, they would be in the same class. Maury didn't want to share a family with another boy, especially another foster kid, but he couldn't be choosy. No other family had spoken a word to him since he had become a ward of the state.

"This is your room. You'll share it with Gabe. You're lucky. He's a bit of a neat-freak. Just make sure your belongings stay on your side of the room and you should be fine," Robert told him, showing off the 12'x12' box of a room. With bunk beds in one corner and a large dresser in the other, there wasn't much space in between.

"This is great. Thanks again, Robert."

"No problem, son," Robert said, trying out the word. Paternal pride deepened his voice.

Maury ignored him, but continued, "So, where's Gabe?"

"Out back in the pool. You should go out and say hello. There are trunks in the dresser for you. I think we got the sizes right, if not, let us know. We'll make sure you get whatever you need."

Maury was hesitant to wear just swim trunks, especially when he would be around people who were providing him food and a roof over his head.

"What's wrong? Can't you swim?" Robert asked with a concerned look on his face. He furrowed his light brown eyebrows. From his peeling red skin, it was obvious that Robert enjoyed the pool a great deal. "Gabe isn't the best swimmer, so don't worry about that."

Maury considered telling him that he couldn't swim, but didn't think that would be a good idea. Someone like Robert would probably sign him up for swim lessons thinking it would be a nice thing to do. Then Maury would have to flail in a public pool in front of all those other kids. All those watching eyes. "No, I can swim."

"Then put the trunks on," he said, his tone finding a sharpness Maury had never heard from Robert. "If you don't want to swim, at least put your feet in. It's nice. Gabe's been waiting all week to meet you."

"I'll be out in a few minutes."

Maury thought he looked ridiculous in the red Hawaiian shorts that he found in the top dresser drawer. They fit just fine, and he supposed if he kept a t-shirt on, he could get through the ordeal.

The Unger's house was nicer than the new house his parents bought from all the donation money after the apartment fire. It wasn't large or particularly ornate, just comfortable. Knee-high bushes lined the concrete walk that spilled out to a wide concrete patio. Eliza was pouring Robert a glass of lemonade, and when they both saw Maury, they smiled. There was a lawn furniture set, complete with a sun umbrella and an ice chest full of soda.

"Help yourself," Eliza said.

"He's waiting," Robert said, hooking his thumb in the direction of the pool.

"Maybe later," Maury said to Eliza, indicating the soda. He climbed the metal steps to the lip of the pool. When he reached the top, he saw a shimmering blob underwater as someone swam across the pool bottom. As his foster brother broke the surface of the water, Maury nearly fell down the steps. He had to steel himself so he wouldn't gasp.

"Hi, I'm Gabe. I'm gonna be your brother!" the boy chirped. The right side of his skull was shaved bald and was noticeably sunken. It looked like a sinkhole. When Gabe braced his arms on the lip of the pool to pull himself out, Maury was seeing the left side of his face. Perfectly normal. But then Gabe stood up, dripping water all over the place and Maury was faced with that caved in skull.

"I'm Maury," he said, extending his hand. He erased any reaction from his face. He couldn't let Gabe know what he thought of his appearance. Who was he to say or think anything about someone's appearance?

Gabe readily took his hand, although he looked more like he wanted to give Maury a hug. "Nice to meet you. I fell from a window. My skull broke. Do you like to swim? I just learned and all, but I like it. Dad got me lessons," Gabe rattled off quickly. Before Maury could answer, the boy jumped back into the pool.

When his new foster brother broke the surface again, Robert was on his feet. "Gabe, what did I tell you about diving? Do you want to hurt yourself?"

"Sorry, Dad." His foster brother had a guilty smirk on his face, happy to have someone looking after his well-being.

"Wanna come in? We can play Marco Polo, or tag or Johnny Quest?" Gabe asked, hopeful.

"I'll just sit on the deck. I don't really want to swim right now."

Gabe dog paddled over to Maury, and when he stopped to tread water, Maury was uncomfortable with how close he was. Gabe had no sense of personal space. The boy whispered, "So what's your deal?"

"My deal?"

"Yeah, you know, you're all fried up."

Maury wanted to get out of the pool, and go... well away, anywhere but here. He looked over his shoulder and Eliza still smiled, her white teeth as straight as headstones in a new cemetery. Robert was talking into her ear, his face buried in her black hair, making her laugh. His hand squeezed her knee, and then it crept higher on her leg, the tips of his fingers just under the hem of her white shorts. She continued to laugh at whatever he was saying, but seeing Maury, she slapped his hand away. His foster parents seemed giddy, and for that reason alone, he didn't immediately leave the pool. "Apartment fire."

"Is that what made you an award?"

"Award?"

"You know, like a prize for new families. An award."

He was about to tell him no, that his parents only gave up on him after his younger brother turned up dead, his heart mysteriously devoured by a dream cat that only Maury was witness to.

"Yeah, I'm an orphan."

"My mom smoked crack. I fell out a window, broke my head. I got patched up, but they might have to split me open again to even it out. I don't mind though. I get to shave my head."

"So how long have you lived with the Ungers?" Maury asked. He stood up and went across the deck to get a beach ball.

"Next week'll be a year. They're going to adopt me, change my name like theirs."

"Do they want kids of their own then?"

"Yeah, but Dad calls Mom a baron."

"You mean she's barren?"

"Yeah, like a prince or whatever."

Maury didn't correct him. Dale had seemed sharper than Gabe, and he had been seven when he died. He wondered if they saw Maury as a potential son. He also wondered why they would bother snatching up damaged kids to be their offspring.

"Still don't want to come in?"

"Naw. I'm bushed. All the excitement, you know."

"Later then?"

"Sure. Later." Maury threw the beach ball at Gabe, and his reactions were too slow. The ball bounced off his head and flew into the grass.

"They give you whatever you want, you know. They're nice. They said I'll get to a doctor, get fixed up. When it's fall, I'm joining a soccer team. They said I can go to any college I want, too. They'll pay for all of it." Gabe's lips were turning blue since he wasn't moving around anymore, just flapping his gums. Maury couldn't imagine Gabe ever getting into college. On the other hand, Maury would readily accept someone else paying for his own education. He had already decided he was going to go to the University of Chicago to study psychology. Since his hand hadn't responded to physical therapy, he'd set aside his dream of being a surgeon. The therapists he'd seen had only further opened his eyes. This Unger deal was sounding better and better.

"That's great, Gabe," Maury said, his mind drifting to the possibility of going to college.

Gabe talked his ear off until it was time for dinner. He left the pool, wrinkled and shivering. His lips were darn near purple, but he seemed like the happiest boy alive. Eliza greeted Gabe with a towel. Robert put his hand on Maury's shoulder as they went inside to have barbequed hamburgers and potato chips.

As Maury settled in at the Unger's house, Gabe proved to be a welcomed distraction from his loneliness. It was also refreshing that Gabe wasn't always judging him, staring at him, or trying desperately to avoid eye contact with him. Most of the time, Maury missed his family so much it hurt, but when Gabe was in the room, he did the silliest things just to make Maury laugh. It made their cramped bedroom seem not so small.

"Wanna see me drink water up my nose?" Gabe asked excitedly.

"Again?" Maury was on his stomach on the lower bunk. Gabe was sitting on the floor, leaning against the dresser.

"Come on. It's my best trick."

"No."

Gabe looked defeated. "No kidding?"

"Hey, Gabe, do you remember your dreams?"

Gabe paused, confused. His brain switched tracks and caught up to the change in subject. "Do I!"

"Anything in particular?"

"Let's see... frogs fall to the ground, like rain, then they splat. And there's this mean lady who looks all gray, gray skin, gray hair, gray *everything*, she's got ratty clothes, she's always out to get me, but I'm too fast for her... and... and..." Gabe said, rubbing his chin as if he would uncover a hidden memory by doing so. Maury figured the ratty-looking lady was actually Gabe's mom in disguise. From what he had heard so far, Gabe was in a much better situation living with the Ungers. "...Let me see... oh, I know! Junior!"

"Who's Junior?"

"He's me, but smaller, and with a big round head with no dent."

"Can I show you my best trick?" Maury asked, a conspiratorial tone to his voice.

"A trick, I love tricks!"

Maury hopped off the bed and poked his head outside their bedroom. He listened for the Ungers, but they must've still been outside taking an after dinner swim. He closed the door, and had a serious expression when he turned back to Gabe.

"It don't hurt, right?"

"No, Gabe. But you can't tell a soul. Not even Eliza."

His foster brother's face went through expressions like quickly flipped poker cards--sad to nervous to happy to elated--all in a matter of seconds. "Okay."

"Promise? Not a word to anyone. They might take us away from the Ungers if anyone finds out."

Gabe was quiet for the first time since Maury had met him. Maury motioned Gabe to sit on the edge of the bed. His palms were sweaty. He hadn't done this since Dale and Rocky. He didn't even know if he could still do it. He steadied his hands, not wanting to touch that sinkhole skull. As he reached out toward Gabe's forehead, his foster brother's eyes crossed as he tried to see what was happening. Maury felt a white-hot burning pour through his hand and into Gabe's skull...

Maury woke at the sound of his office door opening. Nolan Gage entered, looking as tired as Maury felt.

"Good. You're here. I have a surprise for you," Maury said.

"Good or bad?"

"Oh, definitely good. I've found our star. Our Shamu. Our King Tut."

"Show me," Gage perked up, the fatigue gone from his face. His eyes were bloodshot but alert as he followed Maury from the museum basement. They took the elevator to the second floor. The nightmares' roost.

Maury held his arm in front of Gage, barring his path. "His name is Mr. Freakshow. Brace yourself." The two men entered the hall.

Maury didn't look into the Freak's enclosure. He kept his gaze on Gage's face, his somewhat beady eyes, his red-gray beard grown wild. Gage blinked several times, not moving, his eyes glassing over as with fever. A grunt and the sound of torn flesh came from within the enclosure, but Maury still kept his eyes trained on Gage. His boss's eyes widened. Something splattered within the enclosure. Gage's face paled. His skin seemed to sag, the invisible weight of gravity pulling it to the floor. Then his lips twitched at the corners. They perked up into a slight, fleeting smile. The sound of the Freak's claws rending, slashing, gouging, brought Gage's hands to his mouth. The enclosure was now silent, but Gage gave off a sick, lurching wheeze.

Gage turned his glassy eyes to Maury and then hurried from the Nightmare Wing, lucky to make it to the bathroom before his empty stomach purged nothing more than hot, acidic bile.

Maury felt vindicated. He had been holding back his hopes until he could get Gage to see Mr. Freakshow. Gage's reaction was confirmation enough to know he had found the creature that would change the world.

Gabe wanted to prove to Maury how good a diver he was. The Ungers would never allow him to dive for fear of him re-damaging his skull. Robert was off to work, and Eliza had gone inside to throw a load of clothes in the wash. They were alone.

"Watch this. A full twist," Gabe said in a hushed voice. Gabe didn't realize he gave off a mad squeal when he dove, and the splashing noise sounded like a giant falling out of a fishing trawler. Gabe leapt into the air, his head leaning to the side. He arched over the water, and came crashing down on his shoulder.

"See, what'd I tell you," Gabe said, speaking as soon as he broke the surface.

"I'm not sure, Gabe. That looked more like a quarter twist, not a full."

Gabe thought about it for a minute, then said, "Come on, Maury, I'm not *that* good." Gabe dog paddled across the water. Maury still hadn't ventured into the pool. He was too distracted. While his body was at the pool, his legs dangling in the water, his mind was in the second floor bedroom he shared with Gabe, focusing on the footlocker at the end of their bunk beds. He listened for a scream in case Eliza opened the locker and found what they had hidden.

"What are we going to do with Junior?" Gabe asked.

"I don't know." Maury didn't know what they were going to do with the pint-sized Gabe. At least the dream didn't talk as much as Gabe. They would without a doubt get in trouble otherwise.

"I'm gonna take Junior in for show and tell when school starts," Gabe said, climbing from the pool. He was measuring another dive, not yet sure which aerial acrobatics to perform next.

"Gabe, what did I say? Not a word to anyone. I mean it. We can get in some serious trouble. I mean, go-to-jail type trouble."

"Fine. Our secret. Can we can go play soldiers with him like last night?" He wondered if Gabe had enough sense to keep his mouth shut. He guessed not.

"Not now. That would look suspicious to Eliza. We have to stay outside, in the pool. We can't open the locker until we're supposed to be in bed, until long after we're supposed to be asleep."

"Fine." Gabe gave him a dour look. He did a herky-jerky waving of his arms and legs, and when he hit the water, a wave splashed Maury's dry t-shirt.

Maury shook his head. Letting Gabe know about his abilities was probably a mistake. It would be impossible for him to keep quiet. Then Maury's chance at having a happy family would be over. And his hopes of going to college. They would take him away. Experiment on him. Try to figure him out so they could exploit him. The government always did things like that. Like the aliens at Roswell, or the X-Men, or any of the other things they kept from the public. Maury didn't want to be a guinea pig. He just wanted a family.

"Hey, Maury?"

"Yeah, Gabe?"

"I got a secret." Gabe climbed from the pool. Water dripped from his trunks like rain.

"Well, then keep it to yourself, like we talked about."

"Not *that* secret. Another one. One about Mom and Dad." Gabe stood with his toes overhanging the edge of the pool. His skin was red where it had repeatedly slapped the surface of the water.

"Can you tell me?" Maury was legitimately curious. He didn't know much about the Ungers yet, but he definitely wanted to know what he was getting himself into.

"No. It's secret. They don't even know I heard."

"Come on, Gabe. I wanna know."

Gabe lined up his next dive, swinging his arms gently at his sides, as if building momentum. "Only if you promise."

"Promise what?"

"We go see Junior after I tell you. I just want to see if he's okay. Maybe he can't breathe in that footlocker."

"Fine. What is it?"

Gabe moved his arms faster and faster, but before he jumped, he looked at Maury. "The Ungers fought some other couple for you. They wanna fix you up like they're gonna fix me up. The other couple only wanted more money from the state for taking 'nother kid. I heard Dad tell Mom he would'a done anything to get that 'crispy critter.'"

Gabe jumped high into the air, straight up, and at the high point of his dive, his head went straight down. His skull broke the surface of the water, and with his trajectory into the four feet of water, he forcefully hit the bottom of the pool. He gave off a cloud of bubbles as his lungs released their air.

Maury saw none of this. He was staring at the house, at the windows, to where his foster mom was washing his clothes. Just when he thought he might like his new family, he instantly hated them.

The bubbles of air from Gabe's lungs popped at the surface. Maury turned to see Gabe floating two feet below the surface, no movement to his limbs.

"Eliza!" Maury screamed as he jumped into the water feet first, one of his flip flops flying off wildly. He paddle-walked through the sluggish water to Gabe's prone body. "Gabe. Gabe, come on." Maury lifted his foster brother's head from the water. "Eliza!"

A wicked thought flashed through his head: *What the fuck? Why does shit always happen to me?*

He latched on to Gabe's shoulders, trying to pull him to the metal deck, but the boy was slim, his skin slick with water and sunscreen. Gabe slipped below the surface, and he didn't fight the water covering his face, invading his nostrils.

"Damn it, Gabe!"

Maury lifted Gabe's face above the water. When the water drained from his open eyelids, blood seeped from the corner of his left eye, a pink stain coating his iris. A wave of chlorinated water splashed across his face, cleaning his bare eyeball of the blood. Gabe still didn't move.

Adrenaline must have been pumping hard for Maury to be able to lift both Gabe and himself onto the deck. He felt like his comic hero, The Hulk--enraged, anger clouding his mind and giving him strength. He tilted the boy's head back, pushed aside his tongue and blew a lungful of air into his lungs.

"Eliza! It's Gabe. He's hurt. Hurt bad. Eliza!" Maury shouted, somehow able to count chest compressions.

Something clicked inside Maury's head. An epiphany. The next gust of breath he blew, he blew against the outside of Gabe's cheek. He started chest compressions again, keeping an eye on the house. "Mom! Please Mom, you have to help!" Maury cried. The chlorine of the pool made it easier to cry.

Eliza Unger threw open the back door and ran down the curving concrete walkway. She had grabbed a cordless phone on her way out and was yelling at a 911 dispatcher. "Hold on a sec," she shouted into the phone, mounting the metal steps. Then to Maury, "What happened? Did he dive? Move, move out the way damn it!" Eliza pushed Maury away, and he teetered on unsteady feet, almost falling into the pool.

"I don't know what happened. I went to get the beach ball... I turned when I heard the splash... he was floating, not moving... I don't know..." Maury playacted next to Eliza as she repeated the CPR steps. He paced across the metal deck, his clothes soaked, his hands fumbling through the air as if in uncontrollable frustration. Eliza didn't see the smirk on his face. She was too busy trying to save a life that was already gone.

Later on, while a paramedic climbed on top of Gabe to continue CPR, Maury snuck off to their bedroom. He opened the footlocker at the end of their bunkbeds. It was empty, just as he suspected. He grabbed a couple of towels from the bathroom before leaving the house. He draped one over his shoulders and wrapped one around Eliza as they climbed into the back of the ambulance. The siren soared through the quiet suburban afternoon. Maury put his arm around Eliza's shoulders. He cried against her shoulder, whispering into her ear, "Mom, I don't know what happened. I never should have left him alone... never should have left... never should have..."

CHAPTER TWELVE

On the wall at the top of the curving stairwell, a billboard in simple block letters spoke volumes about what waited inside the Nightmare Wing for unlearned museum patrons:

PLEASE DON'T PESTER THE DREAMS. TO AVOID POSSIBLE DANGER--DON'T LEAN ON THE GLASS ENCLOSURES.

Nolan Gage watched as some people scoffed at the ominous warnings before they entered the Nightmare Wing. From the looks on their faces, most people exiting had gained a measurable amount of respect for whomever printed the signage.

God, this place is an all-out madhouse, Gage mused as he pushed through the crowd. It was Lucidity's opening night, and the people had started lining up outside the doors of the old Carnegie Library shortly after lunchtime.

He walked down the curving steps, hearing gasps of shock and revulsion coming from the Nightmare Wing behind him. The upstairs attractions had the longest lines, but the whole museum was packed to the gills. They decided to allow full access to the media, and anyone else who wanted to bring cameras inside, at least for the night. The more free publicity they could get, the better. What better publicity than the media and word of mouth kind? He felt winded by the time he reached the ground floor and approached the concessions' area. They had six people working the counter tonight. They were moving around like chickens with their heads cut off, and all the while, taking in money hand over fist.

Gage leaned over the counter to speak to his floor manager. "Hey, Peter, how are things going?"

Peter looked up as he finished bagging a t-shirt for a young girl. He worked his way over to speak to his boss. "It's crazy busy, Mr. Gage, but you hired the right people. We're doing fine. We're low on singles and the popcorn machine can't keep up." He didn't look frazzled one bit. He actually seemed to be enjoying himself, totally in his own element, even with customers surrounding the concessions' island four deep.

"Thanks, Pete. I'll make sure you guys get more singles. Just make sure your people get their breaks. I want to make sure they come back tomorrow."

"Oh, I will." Peter turned to take someone's order, and Gage slipped away, making a mental note to bring them more singles. Needing more singles was a good sign for a business. It meant people were turning over big bills and only getting small bills in return. So far, it was the best opening of any of his businesses.

Gage floated through the crowd, simply observing. He watched people's expressions, watched their body language. This was how he did business. Through body language he could reasonably tell if a business model was going to work, even this early into the ballgame. The customers' voices filled the open foyer as they shared their thoughts on the displayed dreams. They held hands, or tapped each other on the shoulder to grab their attention. Lucidity had its fill of the *take a look at this* quotient. People were laughing in awe. People looked terrified.

"I don't know how we pulled this off," someone said from behind Gage. When he turned, he saw Maury Bennett, wearing a new tailored suit (a suit that Gage had happily paid for), and his omnipresent Cubs cap. For some reason, the hat didn't look out of place at all.

"I've been meaning to thank you, Maury." Gage offered his hand. In mid-shake Gage drew Maury in for a back-patting man hug. When he looked at Maury, his dream catcher looked entirely uncomfortable.

"Oh, it was going to work. All of these people, I bet it's the tip of the iceberg," Maury said, shifting from foot to foot. "No way this wasn't going to work."

"That's not what I meant. All of this," Gage said waving his hand over his head, "This is just the icing. I'm talking about Nika. What you've done so far has been remarkable, and I have a feeling it's going to happen any day. You will bring me back my daughter." He could feel tears forming in his eyes, but he wasn't sad at all. He couldn't remember a happier time since before Michelle left him so long ago.

"Mr. Gage... it's my job."

Maury didn't take praise well, but Gage had to let him know how he felt. "Your job stems from your powerful gift. Without your gift, there would be none of this. Or any hope for my daughter. I feel I owe you more than the money I've given you. I just wanted to let you know that if it's in your heart to leave your practice, you will always have a job with me. Even if you want to sit on the side of the road and count cars all day, I owe it to you to let you do what you wish," Gage said.

"But..." Maury said, stammering. He too had tears in his eyes, and all he could do was clench his lips and nod. "Okay. I'd like that."

"Excellent! We have an agreement. Just let me know what your intentions are. I'll get you whatever you need."

Maury kept on nodding, his face bunched like he had swallowed something unsavory. He kept nodding, even after Gage turned and left.

Gage had expected such a reaction from Maury. Most people thought he was an odd sort, but Gage was starting to figure out what made him tick.

The line leading to the Nightmare Wing hadn't slowed one bit, and he could hear cries coming from the patrons upstairs. He thought of the possibility of having a Nightmare-only themed attraction, and took a mental note to investigate the potential of such a business. While taking his mental note, he remembered that Peter from concessions needed singles. Gage meandered through the crowd to the elevator at the back of the foyer. He pushed the button for the basement, where he had his vault--a vault he knew would be full by night's end.

For the first hour, when the humans entered the Nightmare Wing to gawp at Mr. Freakshow, he gave them what they expected. He slit his stomach with a claw and snaked his intestines through the narrow opening, his face contorted in misery. He masticated his own flesh, and then carved himself with rusty dream-blades. He tore off his jawbone and used it to gouge his eyes. The filthy humans ooh'd and aah'd. He was delighted to see one young woman brace herself from vomiting as she hurried away. But everyone else stayed right where they stood. They only pressed closer to his confining cage, fighting for position to get a better look at him. He obviously couldn't shock these pests into leaving him be.

Then he came up with an idea to get rid of them. The idea was simple, but he would need time to observe his quarry. The thought made him sick, but he would need to look into the minds of these insidious beasts and learn what dark thoughts lurked inside. He created a throne on which to sit and observe--a replica of the throne he would assemble once free of this infernal containment. He ran his hand over the curves and nooks of his creation. A thin slime of blood coated the stacked skulls that made up the throne. As he sat down, the bones accepted his weight and he couldn't imagine a more luxurious place to observe. He sat in an arrogant pose with one leg draped over an armrest. He rubbed his chin contemplatively, starting to probe the minds of these sick fucks.

After awhile, a good long while, a small segment of the crowd had dispersed, apparently bored. But Mr. Freakshow was ready to perform. The crowd stirred as he rose from his throne. He waved his hand from floor to ceiling to floor again, and as he moved, a partition formed, separating him from his onlookers. He could see through the partition in a gray tint, and seeing the humans, he found them slightly more palatable to the eye. The gray, gauzy obstruction made them seem like dead things. The Freak smiled.

While the Freak could see them, the humans couldn't see beyond the partition. What they were looking at, or into rather, was the silvery sheen of a full-length mirror. Mr. Freakshow had turned the tables on these sick fucks. As they turned to look at one another, confused, and then back to the mysterious mirror, they had no idea the fun was about to begin.

"I talked to Maury like I said I would," Gage said to Nika while holding and stroking her hand. He had the habit of talking to his daughter as if she could hear him. When he first started doing it, he was self-conscious and couldn't stand to hear his own voice holding down a one-sided conversation. It sounded hollow, false. But he became accustomed to it and soon he was pausing intermittently during his rambling, as if she would respond. He kept thinking, *maybe this time, maybe right now she's going to speak, to wake up. This very instant.* Of course, she never acknowledged her father, but after awhile, he found he needed his one sided conversations. They solidified his sense of hope. As he lost his self-consciousness, he opened up to Nika for the first time. If only she could hear. He talked to her about his life and his hopes and aspirations. His views on politics and religion. He had to believe that somewhere deep inside, she heard his voice. Otherwise, he was just a crazy old man speaking to himself, and he didn't want to concede that as fact.

"Maury accepted my offer like I figured he would. I could always tell he never enjoyed his practice. You need to have a certain amount of self-confidence in order to listen to other people's problems, and then even more self-confidence to offer suggestions on how to fix them. You need to project security, and I'm afraid, Maury projects a solid wall of insecurity even to people he knows fairly well."

Tonight, he didn't bring out her dreams. He wasn't in the mood to see the playful, energetic dream-throng. All he wanted was to be right here, right now, holding his daughter's hand, telling her everything about his life. He wanted her all to himself.

"I think the museum is going to work. We still have lines outside the door, and it's a younger crowd than I envisioned. But you know what they say--target that young demo. You hook them now, you have them for life. And it's all because of you, my sweet daughter." Gage leaned forward and gently kissed her forehead.

As soon as his lips left her skin, he felt a discernible twitch from her hand. Initially, he didn't realize what had just happened. He could only look down at her hand in amazement. Yes, he had definitely felt a twitch. A twitch coming from his daughter's hand.

"Nika… can you hear me? Nika!" he said, patting her hand, trying to get her to repeat that slightest movement that he had almost dismissed as nothing. But if she did it again… If only… if only.

"Please, Nika, move… do the slightest little... *anything*. Do something to let me know I'm not going crazy," he pleaded. As the seconds ticked away, he began to doubt what he had felt. It could have been a phantom twitch amounting to nothing. "Nika, please… I'm so lonely. I have nobody…" he said, pulling her hands to his lips and kissing them as tears filled his eyes and spilled down through his beard. At her bedside, he collapsed to a kneeling position, as if in prayer. Resting his head on his daughter's withered stomach, still clutching her hand, Nolan Gage sobbed. "Please…"

Through his anguish and tears, through the memories of his once happy family saturating his mind, Nika's hand flexed, squeezing Gage's hand in a fierce grip. As quickly as his tears appeared, they halted their advance as he lifted his head to look at her. Her face was unchanged, but oh dear God his daughter squeezed his hand! As if in confirmation, she did it again, her grip so strong it would have normally buckled his knees.

"Nika! You can hear me, can't you? You know it's me, your father. I can't believe this. I have to call the doctor, I have to tell someone--"

The shrill cry of the fire alarm temporarily dulled his excitement.

103

Of all the things... why now?

He looked at the door and then back at his daughter and realized, that even if it was the apocalypse, if the ceiling should collapse in a heap of burning cinders, he couldn't imagine being anywhere else. With the excitement of the crowd upstairs, it was probably a false alarm. Some punk kid showing off to his friends. If the alarm didn't stop soon, he would leave to investigate, but not yet. Not when Nika had just squeezed his hand. As the fire alarm continued to blare, he held his daughter's hand, waiting for that pristine and magical moment when Nika would open her eyes and look into his.

At first, the mirror images amused the crowd outside the Freak's enclosure. Once they understood that Mr. Freakshow was playing a trick on them, they actually seemed to enjoy themselves. Some acted as if they were looking at a funhouse mirror. A middle-aged man made a googlie-eyed face, laughing spasmodically, and then flattened his face against the enclosure glass. Good.

Mr. Freakshow had his first volunteer. And what a volunteer this maggot would be!

From his observance, Mr. Freakshow learned his volunteer's name, Graham. He was married, and had gained five pounds a year every year of his twelve-year marriage. Unsatisfied in his marriage, he found solace during late night runs for bags of fast food burgers. The added pounds stressed his inherently weak heart, and made his wife even less interested in him physically. The Freak slowly changed Graham's reflection, incrementally, until the image the human was looking at represented his wildest indiscretion, a fantasy that he could never act out in real life:

The replica-Graham approached a woman wearing only a leather thong and two straps holding back her overly large dream-breasts. A formal nun's habit held back her hair, and her eyes were like ice glaring out from under the black fabric. She didn't say a word but lunged at him, ruthlessly grabbing him by the tongue, yanking it hard enough to send Graham to his hands and knees. She brandished a well-used school paddle, reminiscent of the discipline paddle used by his fourth grade teacher, some dried up cunt of a nun (Graham's description, not Mr. Freakshow's). The replica-Graham hid his face from the woman, hid his perked smile when he saw the paddle. This hard-as-nails, cold-hearted bitch, so unlike the feeble old cunt that used to paddle him at least once a week when he was a child, went to town on the replica-

Graham. She pulled back, and without holding back an ounce of force, slammed the paddle against his ass. The snap of wood on flesh was so loud that people in the foyer could hear the impact, unaware of what was happening upstairs.

She didn't let up. This dream woman, Graham's darkest inner-most thought, pummeled him viciously. The replica-Graham couldn't hide his pleasure. He fell to his stomach, groaning, wincing at every slap of the paddle, but welcoming more, wanting more, acting as freely as if he had his eyes closed and no one else could see his thoughts.

But the real Graham, the clown who had pressed his face against the glass of the Freak's enclosure, shied away, his face red with embarrassment. The other onlookers had no clue that the image in the mirror had come from Graham's mind.

Mr. Freakshow was only starting.

His onlookers were once again entertained by Mr. Freakshow, and they would draw blood soon enough to get a closer glimpse of his mirror. He could see it in their eyes and smell the thickness of their desperation even through the glass. These sick fucks would get what they deserved.

In the front row, two men sandwiched a woman protectively, one her boyfriend of three years, the other, named Paul, a friend she had grown up with. They were crammed together against the glass, unable to move away even if they wanted to. Would the Freak make them want to move away?

He took hold of their reflections and molded them, taking the darkest thoughts of each of them, and letting their reflections roll with it. The boyfriend-replica smiled over his shoulder at his girlfriend, a snake's smile. He took hold of the girlfriend-replica and pinched the skin of her arm until she winced, until she cried out in pain. But the Paul-replica, the friend who would always be just a friend, had pressed his hand against the girl's exposed thigh, just below the fabric of her skirt. He slid his fingers into the dark recesses, sneaking ever so higher on the tease-replica's tanned thigh, even as she tried to resist her boyfriend's torment. Her boyfriend now used his other hand to slap her face, first with his palm, and then backhanding her. Unable to move away from her boyfriend, the girl-replica leaned against Paul's insistent pressure, inviting him closer, making him pleasure her to take away her pain.

The three real life people could barely look each other in the eye, unwilling to see the truth they found there. They struggled against the crowd, all three of them separately, trying to get away from the awful reflection.

The Freak was starting on the next sick-fuck gaper, some stew-brain numb fuck pedophile, and oh boy would this one set the crowd afire!

But he hadn't planned on the real life girlfriend pulling out a can of pepper spray. Or for her to use it on someone behind her, someone she couldn't actually see for all the clamoring onlookers. This unseen bastard was trying to replicate the reflection and had his hand creeping up her thigh, had the tips of his fingers pressed against the curve of her buttocks. She greeted this violation with several sprays from the can. The pepper spray cut a fine path through the air, and would have been dead on target, hitting this unseen pervert square in the face, but a circulation vent was just overhead. A small vent grate so innocuous that no one noticed the gentle breeze brushing their skin. Not until the thin stream of pepper spray hit the tiny fan's invisible jet stream and showered out over the crowd like particulate matter in a dust storm.

All hell broke loose.

Some woman--who the Freak learned through his mental probing, had won a small lottery and hadn't told her husband--had her pert little nose smashed up against the glass by the build up of pressure from the mob. Her blood smeared against the glass, the cartilage of her nose ground to pulp. The crowd drowned out her cries.

Even as the crowd dispersed, with the excruciating pain attacking their nasal and sinus passages, the reflections carried on their performances. The darkest lurking thoughts from the gray matter of these sick fucks. While not able to use all of the choice information from his observances, Mr. Freakshow was happy with the results.

While the reflections continued to grunt, paddle, lick, and abuse, the humans screamed and stumbled away from his enclosure. Within a couple minutes, the foyer below was also flowing with screams and the sounds of fists striking muscle and bone. The fire alarm blared, an angry noise that the Freak found intolerably annoying.

Mr. Freakshow rose from his throne of human skulls and gave the mayhem he had orchestrated a standing ovation.

CHAPTER THIRTEEN

Kevin hesitated to open his eyes. When he did, he took in his bedroom through squinting eyes, expecting to see his mom next to his bed, as if she had woken him.

His room was empty.

He felt violated and somehow cut off from his family. The full moon was high in the sky, a bright blue disc painting everything it touched with its cool glow. An ink spot of murky shadow first constricted, then dilated, near his dresser in the corner of the room. He strained against his body, against some unknown force that held him motionless. He could control his eyes, but was too afraid to close them, and yet he didn't want to see what was lurking in the corner, either. His heart pounded and the harder he struggled to move an arm, or a mere finger or toe, the more adrenaline churned through his system. He was paralyzed, undeniably, maddeningly paralyzed. His breath shuttered through his lungs as he struggled against blacking out.

The shadow shifted in front of his dresser and seemed to absorb the profuse moonlight. That was when Kevin smelled a nauseating and all-too-familiar smell. Dog shit in a baker's oven. The septic ooze of a backed up sewer. The kind of smell that lingers even under held breath. Mr. Freakshow.

The Freak hadn't disturbed his sleep since Maury transmuted the dream from his mind almost a week ago. This time he didn't bother with a disguise for his visit. During Kevin's countless nightmares the monster's appearance would always change, but what he now saw was without a doubt his full-blown freak self. Knuckles as big as a man's kneecaps, shoulders hunched so his hands nearly touched the floor. Ratty long black hair dripping grease and carrying debris that looked like chicken bones. A network of crisscrossing gray scars covering his forearms.

"Hello, Kevin," Mr. Freakshow whispered. "It's been so long. We need to catch up like old friends. What you and your mom did wasn't very nice, so rudely removing me from your mind like that. But things are better now. I didn't understand at first, but things are so much better than just roosting up in your little kid head. The world is so much larger, and a lot less limiting, and Dr. Bennett, my so-called keeper, is a blithering idiot."

Mr. Freakshow filled the window. The moonlight now shied away from him, leaving his body surrounded by gravid blackness. Kevin still couldn't move. Tears dribbled down his cheeks and left cool trails in their wake.

"It's not too awful. You see, I absorb the knowledge of those around me. They leak information like your daddy's blood pouring from his gut. And these," Mr. Freakshow said, showing him a full view of his whip-scarred forearms, "I no longer have to worry about. Ever since I was released from you, boy, you've no longer been able to torment me. No longer can you fight me, shackle me, lash out at me with your hatred for me. Every time you would close your eyes and willfully oppose me, you would whip me like some wayward animal. Times have changed. And I will have my revenge."

Kevin closed his eyes, squeezed away his tears and tried to wake up from this nightmare.

"Oh, Kevin, you can't wake up. You're already awake. Well, almost. More like, halfway awake. That's why you can't move. When you fall asleep your body is paralyzed to prevent you from harming your poor fragile body."

No... Kevin fought as hard as he could to move a single muscle. Sweat dotted his brow from his effort.

"You can see me, yes, but I remain in my confining cage, but that won't last--it won't last another twenty-four hours. I'm just visiting to let you in on a little secret. Do you want to know my little secret, and hold it dear and close to your heart? You have to promise not to tell anyone. Things can get messy if you do. Your mom is a beautiful woman. It wouldn't take much for me to want to taste her flesh, to wipe away the pooling blood from her exposed bones, to collect her naked skull to mount on my throne. Her skull would ideally accent the end of my armrest, her empty eye sockets unblinking and glorious. Your grammy, she's a whole different story, I'm afraid. I would have to prod and probe. Gnaw some of her gamy flesh, pull off her scalp like a swim cap, you know, to find that inner beauty of which you humans always speak. That might take more time, and she might suffer, that poor old blind bitch, and you know I would give you a front row seat for the whole spectacle.

"That's why no one can know I'm here. You don't want me to hurt your family, do you, Kevin? Do you understand what I'm saying?"

The beast crawled onto the bed, his muscled weight pressing the bedsprings flat with a squeak. He placed his hands on either side of Kevin's head, bringing his face within inches of his. Mr. Freakshow's thick claws ripped into the fitted sheet of the bed. Kevin was willing his legs to fly up and strike the Freak from his bed, but he couldn't even twitch his nose.

"Do me a favor. Blink twice if you understand the importance of silence when dealing with this situation," Mr. Freakshow said, giving Kevin an unpleasant view inside the monster's mouth. His gums were swollen black and his teeth jutted from them at crooked angles, looking like shattered bone. Slick worms slithered through the festering gaps between his teeth. Kevin's throat involuntarily clenched to ward off his gorge.

Kevin blinked once. He clenched his eyes shut a second time and paused a heartbeat or two. When he opened them again, the beast was still pressing down on his paralyzed body, his stench cloying in his nostrils.

"Okay. Good, we have an agreement. My secret, Kevin, is so simple, yet so very important." He placed his broad palm against Kevin's chest, spreading his fingers wide enough to rest in either of the boy's armpits.

The pressure increased on Kevin's chest, and he could sense the enormous force Mr. Freakshow held in his powerful upper body. He was having difficulty inhaling; his lungs could only expand so much now.

"I need you. More accurately, Kevin, I need your heart. I need to drain your pumping heart-blood down my gullet. Then and only then will I be free." He pressed his fingers against Kevin's chest, propping his curved claws directly over his heart.

Kevin barely heard the beast with all the blood pulsing through his ears. His mind raged against the weight on top of him, and in the distance, so far away it couldn't be a part of him, Kevin felt his hand twitch. One solitary twitch. Not much of a defensive blow, but at least he did something. He focused on his finger bones, then the network of fragile hand bones and their connection to his wrist, and could feel the memory of their last movement. A muscle memory. Kevin stared at Mr. Freakshow, while tensing his fingers.

Then there was a pain Kevin had never felt before. A pain so swift and sharp he nearly passed out. It was Mr. Freakshow stabbing his fingers into Kevin's chest, through the soft muscle and cartilage of his upper ribs. The pain brought sweat streaming down his face. Suddenly, electricity bolted through his arm as if a hatpin had stabbed him. With the electricity came movement.

I am moving my arm!

More control; electricity danced over his skin, allowing Kevin to move his extremities.

Mr. Freakshow plunged his claws wrist-deep in Kevin's chest, even as the boy's entire body quivered with pain. In one triumphant second, Kevin regained complete control over his body. He riled against his attacker while his blood was seeping into the sheet and the mattress below. He clenched his fingers into a fist and threw a punch at Mr. Freakshow.

But Mr. Freakshow was gone. At the moment his knuckles should have connected with the Freak's face, he disappeared.

Kevin was awake. Fully awake this time.

He jumped from bed and looked in every corner of the room and then under his bed and in the closet. He checked the lock on the window, and when everything seemed clear, he sat down on his bed.

What just happened?

His first instinct was to run to get his mom.

But what if it were true? Everything Mr. Freakshow said about hurting his family. No, he couldn't seek the comfort and reassurance of his mom. What he had just experienced couldn't have been a dream. He remembered every detail of the grisly encounter, and none of it was fading like it always did. Even so, his shirt was intact, and his chest was not bloody and broken.

If it had been a dream, then what Dr. Bennett said had been a lie. He said once he took his nightmare away, it was gone for good. Kevin didn't know what to think or do. He rolled onto his side on the bed and curled up with a pillow.

As he pondered his dream, his fingers absently toyed with a rip in the sheet. He quickly sat upright, ready to call out for help, but he held back his panic when Mr. Freakshow's words returned to him. He felt the monster's claw marks in the fabric and knew he couldn't say a word to his family. Kevin didn't know what he was going to do, but whatever it was, he would have to act alone.

Mr. Freakshow cursed himself for his foolishness and stalked about his cage feeling the weakness brought on by his efforts. His wings hung limply at his sides and his shoulders slumped from the grave internal purging of his energy stores.

Going to the boy had been a test. Even Mr. Freakshow didn't know the limits of his power, but it was a worthy venture considering the knowledge learned during the excursion. He established the fact that he still had a connection with the boy, a connection that would hopefully prove invaluable when he escaped this hellhole. If he still had a foothold within the boy, he was still a part of him. He would be able to discern his location and intentions.

And in a way, he was topping off the boy's fear. Of all the collected dreams, he alone knew his dreamer's fear led to his own strength. One more fright before he escaped, one more fright to add to his own strength.

Once he found the boy, he would dig his claws into his chest. He would spread his delicate breastbone, and pull out his engorged heart and consume it, gleefully relishing every drop of blood. Then the Freak would be free. Immortal. The thought of stealing his freedom from the boy sent a chill of excitement through the exposed ridges of his spine. He would be free and it would be soon.

He shouldn't have wasted his energies on the humans, but he couldn't help his enthusiasm. The whole display of the their reflections... that was merely for the simple pleasure of observing the humans' herd instinct--their trampling and reviling of the weak of their kind, to witness their boundless frailty. They were little more than sentient pests, these clamoring maggots; they had neither fangs to tear with, nor wings to glide upon. As the crowds had grown denser, he knew he had to do something to show his audience what they looked like from his perspective. The whole series of events made him laugh. While they gawped and hooted at the Freak, he simply pointed a mirror at them and revealed the truth. Their reaction was predictable and brought a brief levity to his confinement.

Once he escaped and killed the boy, it would be like looking into a mirror and finding his own salvation. But for now, he needed rest. He would need all of his reserves to make his escape. Once free of this degrading internment, he couldn't afford any vulnerability.

With a small strand of energy, Mr. Freakshow reached out to the boy.

He subtly came upon the boy and wormed into his mind, finding the root of himself still imbedded within him. The Freak closed his eyes and slowly pried open the tightly folded seed he occupied in the boy's mind. He could see through his innocent eyes, see him flitting about his bed, fearful of returning to sleep. To gain consolation and to feel closer to his quarry, the Freak eased into a comfortable stasis just shy of the boy's awareness. He was an unseen voyeur lurking behind the boy's eyelids. The Freak rested and waited for just the right time to make his move.

Furious with the Grand Opening of Lucidity, Gage had given Maury the menial task of clearing the museum of straggling customers. Lucidity had been open for a total of two hours.

Who would've thought there would be a stampede?

The police promised a swift investigation. A pair of officers were still conducting interviews in the foyer. No charges were immediately filed after Gage insured the museum wouldn't reopen until the conclusion of the investigation. At least no one was permanently injured. Maury searched the corners of the museum, feeling like he was being punished for something he hadn't done.

To leave something to look forward to, he didn't visit Juliet's area until the end of his inspection. When he entered the narrow hall of the Nightmare Wing to see Juliet, he was surprised to see Sophie Marigold. She clutched her sketchpad under her arm and greeted him with her welcoming smile.

"Some night," Sophie said.

"The Grand Opening didn't go exactly as planned, no. I'm afraid I'm going to have to chase you out now. Mr. Gage has decided we should close until we can regroup, if that is at all possible."

"That's too bad. Can I come back tomorrow? I'm working on sketches for a new mural Nolan wanted painted in the Nightmare Wing."

"I don't know. With all the craziness tonight, I wouldn't be surprised if he doesn't want anyone around for at least a little while. You know, to let the dust settle."

"How could that creature have come from that boy's mind?" Sophie asked, indicating Mr. Freakshow's nearby enclosure. The glass was cleaned of the woman's blood who had suffered a broken nose in the rush to get away.

112

"I don't know, Sophie. I thought he would be our star. I guess the world wasn't ready for this."

"I better go then before you call the cops on me."

"I would never do that."

"Just teasing. I should go, regardless. I can see you want to see your new friend anyway."

"What...?" Maury looked at Juliet for the first time since coming across Sophie. The dream-woman looked like she had been expecting him. "Oh no, I'm just making sure the museum is empty."

"It's okay, Maury. You can like her if you want. She won't bite. Some dreams will if you get too close, but not Juliet. She's like you and me. Dreamers."

Maury sighed as if resigned to the fact that he was interested in the dream behind the glass. He wouldn't fully accept it though. Something inside him was fighting the urge to let loose and feel emotions as freely as Juliet did.

"You might learn something from her."

"All right, Sophie, I really need to lock up."

"I know, I know," Sophie said, shuffling away from Maury. She paused before returning to his side. She carefully tore a sketch from her sketchpad. "Why don't you take this?"

Maury took the thick sheet of drawing paper. Sophie waved to Juliet as she left the Nightmare Wing. Juliet returned the wave and watched with affection as the old woman left. He was alone with the dreams.

Maury was momentarily speechless. The sketch was of Juliet. Sophie had captured the delicate beauty of the dream-woman. Her soft lips, the gentle curl of her auburn hair. The crazed energy she gave off like sunlight.

He looked at Juliet and could do nothing more than stare. A slight updraft swirled her hair. Low white clouds hovered around her legs. He remembered the night when his lips touched her forehead. She had said she was like him. That's why she had a habit of blowing her brains out. That's why she smiled the whole time the dream-rainwater poured through the hole in her skull. Because she was just like him.

Can she see my violent past just by looking into my eyes?

"Out of all the people to see me today, why are you so interesting?" Juliet asked. Maury didn't see her telltale gun, or the hint that her mood might suddenly plummet. Not since the moment he deflected the gunshot off her skull. Every time he saw her, she seemed more human, more normal and stable. "You don't like your suit."

"It makes me feel claustrophobic." He noticed how tight his tie felt on his neck. He loosened it while trying to place her lyrical accent. He wondered if it originated in the non-dreaming world or was just a fabrication of her dreamer. "So... where are you from?" he asked as if he had just met her in a bar.

She laughed. Her joy was contagious and soon Maury couldn't help but join her.

"Do you know you are a dream?"

"Of course I do. Do you know you are a human?"

"Well..."

"Yes, I know who dreamed of me. A delightful woman from Milwaukee named Barbara."

Maury marveled over Juliet's self-perception. "I've met Barbara, and she's not a delightful person. She's actually rather gloomy."

"Well, even so, she created me. She is, in a way, my parent. I should respect that."

"I never thought of it in that context."

Juliet sat on the park bench, the clouds parting at her presence, and Maury continued the conversation with her. He felt like he was talking to any woman, that is, if he'd had any practical experience talking to women. She asked him about the city, about the things he liked, about his favorite foods. He asked her reciprocal questions, and not long into their conversation, Maury realized she was more than just a physical embodiment of a dream. She was a real person, albeit a slightly flighty person. She had a tendency to speak in a sing-songy cadence, and with her melodic accent, it made for a hypnotic combination.

He didn't know how long he stood outside her enclosure, learning more about this dream-woman. He remembered he was supposed to be making sure the museum was empty. Then he had a meeting with Nolan Gage later on. Maury glanced at his watch. "I need to get going."

"Too bad." Juliet frowned. A smile filtered through her frown. Her eyes glistened.

"Can I come back and talk to you?" Maury asked, as if he needed her permission.

"Why don't you come here," she said mischievously.

"I have to..." Maury stammered. "I just... what do you mean?"

"Come *here*," she said nodding toward the access door in the corner of the room.

Maury looked around--Sophie was obviously gone--and the rest of the museum was, for the most part, empty. He hurried his keys from his pocket before he could have second thoughts. He opened the door and she was in his arms before he had the door closed. Her lips enveloped his, and he clumsily kissed her in return. She pulled off his Cubs cap and ran her fingers through his patchy swaths of hair. He self-consciously pulled away from her touch.

"It's okay. I like how you are." Juliet took his disfigured hand and kissed each fingertip, continuing along the path of his deformity, pulling away his clothes as she went. She kissed every inch of his disfigurement, and even if he shouldn't have been able to feel the gentle pressure of her lips through the nerveless tissue, somehow he did. Like the warmth of swallowed brandy on his skin.

The sight of the enclosure glass and the open hallway beyond still distracted Maury. As if reading his thoughts, Juliet funneled the low white clouds at the glass until they collected like tumbleweeds, giving them all the privacy they needed.

CHAPTER FOURTEEN

His dress shirt wrinkled, and his discarded tie forgotten, Maury left Juliet's enclosure with mixed feelings bandying about his brain. He had never been with a woman before tonight, and had never actually come close. It confused him to think of her. He had never felt this way before. The fact he had to leave her behind and seal her up inside that confining area like a penned animal… he felt like more of an animal for turning the key to keep her there. It wasn't possible to let her out. What exactly would that accomplish? Would he run off with her, go into hiding from Nolan Gage's far-reaching influence?

He imagined looking through a big picture window to a cozy living room. *Their* living room. He saw himself with a trade journal on his lap, Juliet sitting on a sofa across the room from him. On the floor, a child, indiscernible in age or sex (because Maury had never imagined ever having a woman to share his years with, let alone having a child with her), crawled around an oval area rug that covered the floor in front of the blazing screened-in fireplace. His imagined self looked up from the crawling child to see Juliet with a handgun in her hand, her smile unwavering. She lifted the gun ever so closer to her head and…

Maury turned the corner at the top of the stairs, reentering the Nightmare Wing. He had absently wandered through the museum since leaving Juliet, making sure the place was empty. But he couldn't stay away from her. He had to see her again.

What he saw in front of him sharply focused his attention. The sight turned his stomach.

He took an unconscious step back.

"I don't think you should leave right now," a gravelly voice came from inside the first enclosure. Mr. Freakshow's enclosure.

What drew Maury's attention away from the thought of Juliet was the sight of Juliet, her face smashed against the inside of the glass. Fearful, wide-eyed, trembling. Maury took another step back and wondered how any of this was possible. For one, Juliet escaping her enclosure, and two, for her to wander into Mr. Freakshow's clutches.

Mr. Freakshow left the shadows, joining Juliet near the glass. It was now evident that the beast's claws were buried through Juliet's back and had expelled her insides to the floor.

"What the... how the hell?" Maury didn't know what to do. It had to be fake, an illusion of some sort. Juliet hung off the ground, suspended by the Freak's impaling claw, but she was still alive. Frothy blood gathered at the lips he had minutes before fumbled his way through kissing passionately. Her mouth sputtered gobbets of blood-streaked spit against the glass as she tried to form words. Her whole body writhed, struggling against the enormity of her pain.

"I've got an idea. Your friend here, your *lover*, is in immense pain. You know she can't die at my hand, not truly and forever, and so does she. Look into her eyes," Mr. Freakshow commanded in a grating yet soft voice.

Maury looked into Juliet's eyes, and the emotion and longing he saw, the connection he felt for her breeched the glass, the boundaries of their varied existences. This was no illusion. Somehow, however improbable, Juliet had unwittingly put herself in the gravest danger possible.

He must have forgotten to lock her enclosure. Of course. His mind had been so muddled. Still was.

This is all my fault. I can't do anything right.

"Maury, please. He won't hurt me, anymore... he won't hurt you. He just wants his freedom," Juliet said, the melodic lilt of her voice melted away. Only cold edges accompanied her pain-addled words.

"*Let me out of here*," the Freak said, leaning over Juliet's shoulder, his breath steaming the glass. "I'll let her go, and maybe in time, her pain will go away."

The other nightmares were howling in their enclosures. Glancing down the walkway, Maury saw oozing flesh pressed against the panes of glass, bloodshot eyes leering. They all wanted to get a better view of the Freak at work.

Mr. Freakshow turned his wrist and his claws tore deeper. Juliet's legs twitched uncontrollably, her summer dress torn and stained with blood and urine released from her ruined insides. "Time's running out. Choose or lose. She is about to bleed to death. Then, of course, I will have to start this whole process over again."

The tension seeped from Juliet's body. She slumped, hanging limply on Mr. Freakshow's hand. She was gone. Dead for the moment.

Mr. Freakshow whipped her lifeless body into the corner of the enclosure. Her head slammed into the wall before she hit the ground. She didn't move.

"She's going to come back in a few minutes, then I will begin again. I have so many ideas I will try out on her. Each one worse than the one preceding. I have no mercy. You should know this, Doctor. You can insure that I would never hurt her again. Open the fucking cage!"

Maury gave in and pulled out his fistful of keys. His shaky fingers couldn't find the right key, and Mr. Freakshow quickly became impatient.

"Come on, come on!" Mr. Freakshow growled, his face up against the glass.

"Just give me a second." Maury fumbled with the keys. The other nightmares slammed their dream-fists against the glass of their enclosures.

"Fuck your second!"

Maury found the key and unlocked the door, stepping as far away as possible from the opening. The monster emerged from his confinement, shoving Maury into the tiny room.

When Maury steadied his eyes on the interior of the enclosure, Juliet was gone. She was never there. Mr. Freakshow had tricked him.

As soon as this realization sunk in, Maury's brain shifted to figure out how to fix this mother of all fuck-ups. But by then, of course, it was too late. If he hadn't come back to see Juliet... and if he hadn't gone into her enclosure in the first place... his mind wouldn't have been so messed up. There was no other explanation. *I should have known.* Juliet would never be so foolish...

He took a hesitant step toward the door. The last thing Maury saw was the furrowed scars cross-hatching the back of Mr. Freakshow's forearm. The blow connected with Maury's temple, lifted him off the ground, sending him flying into the nearest marble wall. He slumped down in a disheveled pile, and as his mind receded, he didn't even dream.

His ploy had been so easy to execute--so much so, that Mr. Freakshow was surprised it had even worked. Why didn't Bennett realize he would have done a lot worse to that little dream-nymph if she had really entered his enclosure? Gut her and wait for someone to show up? Come on.

The repulsive stench of humans was overwhelming as he strutted down the stairs. He lifted his nostrils and breathed a lungful of soupy human misery. If his senses were accurate, there were currently four humans in the building. The largest concentration was below ground. How typical. Damn sniveling vermin--they *would* cower underground. Blood coursed through his veins, and when he glanced at his swaying wings, he could see the purple rushing fluid filling their thin skin.

He quickly descended the steps, and when he reached the basement, he paused, sniffing at the air. He followed his senses down a hallway, through a couple of twists in the underground tunnel. When he reached a dead end with three doors, he kicked the first one. A human let out a surprised cry.

The room held two humans and a horde of dreams. The dreams scattered like shot marbles as he pushed through the battered remains of the door. He was enraged and wanted to tear apart every dream he came across, every dream willfully coming in contact with a human.

All in due time.

The old man with the graying red beard threw himself atop the unmoving body covered by a drab pink blanket. Nolan Gage, the man who had earlier sized up Mr. Freakshow like he was some piece of meat and had run away, gagging. The dream creatures hid in cubbies and shadows, but the Freak could sense beady little dream-eyes still trained on him, frightened little dream-eyes that he would gladly pluck from their pathetic little heads if he had any say in the matter. And did he have a say in the matter? He chuckled to himself.

Mr. Freakshow closed on Nolan Gage, a malicious smile parting his lips.

"Please don't. I'll give you anything you want... just... just, please don't." Gage's face flushed crimson. He was trying to cover the girl's face with the blanket, but it was useless; the Freak had already seen her, and had known she was in the room even before he charged through the door.

"Who is this senseless mass of human decay?" Mr. Freakshow kicked the frame of the bed.

"Don't you touch her!" Gage stood up, trying to meet his gaze. The Freak snatched him off the floor by the back of his neck and held him with his curled claw mere inches away from tearing apart his spine.

"How adorable." Mr. Freakshow caressed the girl's cheek with the back of an extended talon. "What's wrong with her? Why does she not stir? What are these machines?"

"She was in an accident. She's in a coma. Harmless," Gage said, trying to rationalize with the Freak.

"Ah, you simple twit. She's gone, dead. Can't you sense that; smell the death on her skin? Can't you just let her finish moldering away to dust and bones?" He waved his free hand over her prone body as if vacuuming up details of her condition with his palm.

Gage groped at Mr. Freakshow's wrist, trying to pull himself free. "She's... alive. She still dreams. These dreams all around you, they are my daughter's dreams."

"In that case, I shall take pleasure in ending their lives as well." Mr. Freakshow glared at the wooden headboard, and two elfin creatures skittered out of hiding, skimmed down the side of the bed and then squeezed under an equipment cart.

"No, you can't! She did nothing wrong. You don't even know her. She may seem dead to you, but my Nika is still somewhere inside. Tonight, she even squeezed my hand." He was crying, struggling in Mr. Freakshow's grasp.

"She's not alive. If she were alive, she would fight for her life." Mr. Freakshow went to a bank of machines and smashed Gage's face through one of the monitors. He was conscious, but deeply cut. His scalp spread in a wide smile across his forehead.

Mr. Freakshow threw him into the chair where he had spent countless hours watching his daughter. The chair pushed back a couple of feet, and Gage's head was tilting from side to side, spilling blood into his eyes.

"Oh, I'm sorry. I almost knocked you out. What a shame that would have been and you wouldn't have seen the grand finale!" Mr. Freakshow went to the first cart of machines and tipped it over. He watched Gage's blood-filled eyes widen with his every move. A monitor shattered and broken glass slipped along the floor like thrown ice cubes, making a mound of dream-puppies dart away, whining. The Freak laughed. He destroyed the other machines just as easily, one actually shooting sparks as he yanked the cord from the wall.

He then grabbed the back of Gage's head and forced him nose to nose with Nika. "See how she has failed to struggle for her life. She doesn't even convulse. Those damn machines offered more of a protest when faced with their own destruction."

With an almost gentle hand, Mr. Freakshow took hold of Nika's neck. He pressed his fingers into her flesh, and still she didn't move.

The monster locked eyes with Gage while he tightened his grip, strangling his daughter.

Nika continued to breathe, but it was shallow and getting weaker. From his hiding place under the bed, Rupert lunged at Mr. Freakshow and gouged at his eyes with his sock-puppet hands. As he had no fingernails and no bones in his hands, his attack was a minor irritant.

"You useless rag of shit." Mr. Freakshow grabbed the sock monkey and threw him across the room. Rupert cried out when he hit the wall, but was soon back on his feet and charging the bed. Anger creased the permanent smile from his fabric lips.

"You're a feisty little fuck, aren't you? Killing you will almost be as gratifying as killing Mr. Nolan Gage," Mr. Freakshow said, still looking into Gage's eyes. Rupert closed on the beast, and for every step, his body seemed to fade, becoming less substantial. In one last surge of energy, Rupert leapt into the air, but there was nothing left of him. Mr. Freakshow stood facing Rupert's attack, but he had disappeared. All the dreams had disappeared. Quietly, and without fuss, Nika was gone, taking her mind's creations with her.

Mr. Freakshow turned his attention back to Gage.

He succumbed to the beast without even blinking, waiting for the moment of serenity when he would once again see his daughter, but this time awake, alive and able to love him as he loved her. The old man held Mr. Freakshow's gaze even as his heart beat for the last time.

Mr. Freakshow had spilled all the blood he could within the halls of the basement. He ventured through the ground floor of Lucidity. One by one, he opened the enclosures. Some of the dreams came out hesitantly, wary of such an easy exit. Some didn't leave the security of their enclosure at all. They were either too weak a dream to realize their own existence, or they didn't want to walk a single step closer to Mr. Freakshow.

His anger deepened when an entire hall was free to leave and few dreams appreciated his kindness. At first he thought he could possibly find common ground with these miscreants, but now he knew how entirely wrong he had been. These timid shells of human thought and emotion could never be his peers. He would have to rid this world of them as well as the human detritus that lingered like caked blood under his claws. He would deal with the humans first, then in time, he would turn his sights on eliminating the dreams unworthy of existing at his side. He kicked over a dream the size of a child. His fluffy orange lion's mane fluttered as he fell to his soft suede-skin knees. Mr. Freakshow snatched a handful of his orange locks and dragged the deplorable mound of dream-stuff to his feet. The dream gave off a blubbering moan from his red licorice lips.

"You make me sick. What exactly are you supposed to be?"

The lion-child shook his head and a flow of tears accompanied his moaning.

Mr. Freakshow tossed the dream aside and stood at the end of the hall. He was a star and carried himself like one. There was a moment of silence as the Freak waited for full attention. He broke the brittle tension with his gravel voice. "Be free my pitiable brethren. Your time upon this earth will end soon enough. Join the horde of human vermin if you must; seek out a life and soul of your own if you have it in you. It will not last. I will bring an end to you all soon enough. But for now, live with and live like the animals that you are."

It was like an order given by a holy man. Mr. Freakshow could have flipped a switch and not seen such an instant change in the malingering dreams. His brethren rose from the sanctuary of their confinement, and as one big wave they fell upon the ground with hungered hearts and empty minds to fill. The dreams left Lucidity to encounter the human world--a world still asleep to too many things once thought incomprehensible. Mr. Freakshow was the mirror revealing and releasing the reflection of a society's conscience.

Mr. Freakshow bowed deeply to the departing dreams and then turned on his bare heel. He headed to the upstairs enclosures, an area where he would find more sentient and aggressive creatures--creatures he hoped more akin to himself.

No one offered to help the helpless dream woman--she was The Object and was created for exploit, and all the other dreams knew it. Viktor's initiative started the whole spectacle once Mr. Freakshow let the dreams of the Erotica Wing free. Viktor was all Id, and once free, he shoved his way through the milling crowd of newly freed erotic dreams and waited outside The Object's enclosure for her release. Then he had claimed her as His Object; he grabbed her by her pale blonde hair. He had bronze flawless skin, a long blond ponytail and was hung as only a dream-man could be. They were freakishly different sizes and forcing her flat to the floor was no problem. Getting his cock into her was another story. After a momentary struggle, Viktor was inside her, ramming her with all his built up aggression.

She was fighting, pushing Viktor, trying to cover her small breasts, but she was not nearly strong enough. The other dreams were pushing their gapers-circle closer. His Object's smooth, featureless face jerked from side to side. As the other dreams pushed in closer, it was obvious that His Object had feigned innocence through her struggles. In truth, she was enjoying her fucking. All the other dreams could see of her now were her dainty hands grabbing hold of Viktor's shoulders. Her razor-sharp nails deeply tore into his flesh. He pummeled her harder, enraptured, even as in her pleasure, she dug her nails deeper, past the knuckle.

The shit hit the fan when a greedy dream-man with a spiked silver collar and black leather pants grabbed His Object's foot. He was trying to take her for his own. Viktor pulled himself free from his conquest, and struck the other dream with his brick-like fist. The arousal of the other dreams had been growing with every fevered thrust of Viktor's hips, and now that he had taken on the task of brutalizing the spike-collar dream, they fell in, enveloping His Object, making her their own, making her a part of their collective engorged lust. They grabbed and spread limbs. Heat poured off the orgy like a sauna, and screams and grunts filled the room.

Mr. Freakshow watched the performance from a distance, an enervated smirk pulling at his cheeks. He knew he would get a more lively reaction from the erotic dreams if he presented them with their freedom. Freedom to an erotic dream meant unabashed sensuality, voyeuristic consumption, and sexual release. Oh, and the occasional dream-orgy. But Viktor's initial penetration was only the prelude to the overall mischief that ensued, the proverbial firing of the starter's pistol.

The Freak let the twenty or so dreams fuck and share partners and fuck and switch again before interrupting. He wanted them to get a taste of the freedom he had given them. Once they knew who had given them their freedom, he would be free to twist them to his will.

"Be free to consume," he said, focusing their attentions. "Do not limit yourselves to your current excesses, your current partners or desires. There are bountiful treasures just outside this building to fill your incredible need. So, seek your release among the humans. They are lower forms than you and I, and I have no doubt they would consent to any of your wishes. If at first they resist, simply remember that these creatures are coy by nature."

Mr. Freakshow left the Erotica Wing, knowing they were his servants. He could call upon them if he needed, but for now, he would slink out on his own. Tracking down the boy would be easier alone.

Kevin jumped awake as if an alarm clock blared next to his ear. There was no noise in his room, and judging the darkness from his window, no one would be awake yet. He had the sudden feeling that something was wrong. He looked about the room, but he didn't see anything unusual, and he didn't get the sense that Mr. Freakshow was here. But the unsettling feeling had something to do with the Freak, that much was certain. He thought back to when Mr. Freakshow breathed his hot rancid breath against his sleep-paralyzed face. He hadn't been able to move a muscle. Then he remembered. Mr. Freakshow said he would soon escape. He said he was coming for him.

Coming to drink the blood beating through his heart.

He grabbed his clothes from the closet, shrugged them on and then leaned over to slide on his shoes. His mind was going in a thousand directions, and he didn't know how much time he had. If Mr. Freakshow was loose, the first thing he was going to do was come for him.

Why can't he just leave me alone?

He wanted to wake his mom and grandma, but knew he shouldn't. No one could know what he was doing. The Freak said he would kill his family if he told them of his intended escape. Kevin couldn't risk their lives after already losing his dad. He finished double-tying his shoelaces, grabbed his backpack, and was about to run out the door when he saw his windbreaker. His mom would have a cow if he didn't have it with him, even if the weather was clear and warm. If she noticed his windbreaker was gone, she might realize he was okay, that no one had taken him in the middle of the night and that leaving was his own doing. She would still be a wreck when she discovered he was gone, but he couldn't help that now. Right now, he had to get out of the house, get as far away from his family as possible. Before the Freak found him.

Running away from sleep had been one thing. All he had to do was avoid that inevitable pull to close his eyes, to shut his mind from the waking world. Running away from a beast like Mr. Freakshow was fear on a whole new level.

His shoes striking the pavement seemed incredibly loud as he ran down the street. He was a block from his grandma's house and already gasping for breath. *Slow down, slow down, or you won't last an hour on your own.*

He took a deep breath and eased into a trot as he approached the baseball field. With the moonlight obscured by clouds, the chain link backstop looked even more like a giant set of ribs half buried in the infield. He stepped through the entrance to the infield and went over to home plate, his face burning from fear and sweat. For the first time since he woke little more than five minutes ago, he wondered what time it was. He sat cross-legged on home plate, trying to collect his thoughts. His mind kept drifting to the other day when he was playing ball at this very field. It seemed so long ago. Everyone had been happy.

"You seem stressed out," a familiar voice called out from the darkness near the aluminum bleachers.

Kevin jumped to his feet, ready to run in a split second.

"Chill out." The voice was familiar, but his mind was such a mess he couldn't place it. "Hope you didn't piss yourself." Reid stepped into a small patch of moonlight, a cigarette dangling from his peach-fuzzed lip.

"I didn't see you," Kevin said, catching his breath.

"Things are fucked up." Reid came closer. He had a swollen lip seeping blood. "You know."

Seeing Reid's face looking like a raw steak pulled Kevin away from his own thoughts. He couldn't take his eyes from Reid's battered face.

"Hey man, take a picture."

"What happened?"

Reid took an awkward drag on his cigarette, and then did his best to hold the butt on his swollen lip as he spoke. "Sometimes people get mad. Not like *angry* mad; I mean *mad* mad. Just... crazy, like some kind of monster."

Kevin thought he knew what he meant. He did his best not to stare, tried instead to act like this meeting was the most casual thing to ever happen.

"You want one of these? I swiped them from my step mom."

"Yeah, sure." He didn't really want one, but didn't want to look like a chump in front of Reid.

Reid floated him the cigarette, and Kevin put it to his lip. When Reid struck a wooden match, Kevin saw his friend's left eye had taken some damage, too. Luckily, the lit cigarette in his mouth was enough to distract him from Reid's face.

"So where you off to?" Reid asked, giving Kevin's backpack a small kick.

"Not sure yet." Kevin felt a strange surge of confidence, as if he were an adult. Then he took a drag on the cigarette, and all the false bravado left him just as fast as the smoke expelled from his lungs.

"Take it easy. Not so much," Reid said with a chuckle.

"Where you going?" Kevin imagined the two of them running away from their problems together, tramping the countryside like Tom and Huck.

"Back home."

"But what about..."

"This?" Reid said, pointing to his face. "This is nothing. This is two hundred dollars and missing the first week of school."

"He gives you money for that?"

"If I don't tell my mom. It's not like he drinks or nothing. He just goes mad every once in a while. Once he calms down, he's an all right guy."

"That sucks."

"It could be worse. Now this," Reid said as he lifted up his shirt. Even in the obscured moonlight a section of his ribs jutted out, almost like he was carrying a chunk of rock under his skin. "This got me almost the whole summer with no hassles. I played ball all summer, went to the pool day or night, had as much spending money as I wanted. I guess my luck ran out."

"Haven't you told anyone?"

"And ruin a good thing?" Reid said. They were quiet for a couple of minutes. Not even a bird's chirp broke the silence. "You'll keep it quiet, right? You've got your shit to deal with, too, right? I don't see any marks on you, so I'm guessing what they do to you is much worse than I get. But that doesn't mean you go off and tell anyone."

"Yeah, no problem." Kevin had puffed on his cigarette until it was down to the filter, keeping the smoke from entering his lungs. He was shocked that Reid would think someone abused him. Once and for all, he wanted to set him straight. He wanted to tell him that a monster was coming for him, and that it wanted to kill him.

And another thing, I created this monster in my own head.

It was easier letting Reid think what he wanted.

"Old man's probably as cool as a cucumber now. If things settle down for you, I guess I'll see you when school starts next Monday, that is, if this shit's cleared up," Reid said, pointing to his face. "Otherwise, it's been..."

"Yeah, I know. Later."

Reid nodded goodbye and left the brief halo of moonlight. Kevin was once again alone, but now more scared than when he left his grandma's house. Inside were people who loved him and would never do anything to harm him. But he also knew he could never go back, not as long as Mr. Freakshow was coming for him. He watched Reid disappear into the night, and for a fleeting moment, Kevin thought his friend was brave for going back home. Knowing that his dad was probably going to beat the crap out of him again, and then to simply take it like it was just another nuisance of life... if only life could be that simple.

Kevin hefted his backpack squarely between his shoulders, and headed for the thin row of trees beyond the baseball field. His mom told him she once built tree houses there. Maybe he would find an old tree house--one possibly built by his mom when she was a kid--and hide out long enough for Mr. Freakshow to forget about him.

CHAPTER FIFTEEN

Maury regained consciousness covered in blood. For a moment, he wondered where he was and what had happened, but then an image flashed through his head--Mr. Freakshow's broad forearm flying into him, sending him crashing into a wall. Maury's head cleared, and he picked himself off the floor. He checked his body for injuries, but only noticed a few scrapes and bruises, nothing fatal, no broken bones. He took in his surroundings and realized he was still in Mr. Freakshow's enclosure. Bloody pools stained the floor and walls. He touched his face and felt a patch of dried blood from a shallow gash on his cheekbone.

The floor had shallow grooves dug into it. They were widely spaced and didn't make sense. Maury spread his fingers over some of them and suddenly understood that they were from the claws of one of the dreams. He shuddered as he pulled back his hand and looked at his surroundings in a new light.

At some point during his unconsciousness, the glass wall had been shattered. Glass he and Gage thought would never break. So much for state of the art. An odor permeated the air. Most likely something he didn't want to consider. With the door to Mr. Freakshow's enclosure thrown wide and the glass wall shattered, anything could have happened when he was unconscious. He approached the shattered glass clinging to the frame of the enclosure. He didn't want to look outside the room, but he had no other choice. Careful not to cut himself, he braced himself and slowly leaned his head through the opening.

At the far end of the hall, a squat creature the size of a German Sheppard sat on four spidery legs. It was tugging at the remains of what once could have been a person. The lighting was too dim to tell from this distance exactly what the nightmare was toying with.

Just outside the door, something had pulled up floor tiles and tooled sharp chunks of concrete from underneath, making the hallway look like a potholed street in a sketchy neighborhood. The overhead fluorescent lights hung lopsided, and their ballasts gave off an occasional dying flicker. Maury stuck to the shadows near the wall as he left the enclosure. Judging by the condition of the hallway, he had to get to a phone as soon as possible. Mr. Freakshow had obviously set the dreams free. He couldn't imagine all the chaos they would cause once free of Lucidity's walls.

When he was close enough to see the sparse green hair on the spider-creature's legs, Maury could also see that it was tearing apart Peter. Of course, Peter-what's-his-name. The concessions' manager. Maury had never really met the guy. He was just someone who ran a cash register and little more.

"Peter..." Maury whispered. He still couldn't remember his last name. He approached the spider-creature cautiously, the scientist in him curious about the natural mechanisms of this dream. One of Peter's arms was missing and the other was a stunted stub just above the elbow that continued to stubbornly shake like a deflating balloon. One eye was bruised shut, while the other remained stationary. His pupil was a distorted cloud shape. His legs were intact, but the dreams had attacked his groin area, and a good deal of it was gone, making it appear as if his legs were literally as high as his ribs.

Maury didn't know how Peter was still alive. There was no reason for it. The remains of his limbs twitched randomly, the last vestiges of life spastically leaving him. The spider-creature growled at Maury, and it hunkered down on its thin legs, burying its velvet fangs into its prey.

Peter was beyond help. Maury needed to get to a phone. He left the Nightmare Wing, but stopped at the hand-carved railing that encircled the marble stairs. The foyer was in shambles below. Smoke swirled from small fires. The concessions stand was in tatters. He ran down the steps, and when he picked up the phone, it didn't have a dial tone. If only he had his cell phone with him. The wooden front doors were open--one hung at an odd angle on its bent hinge--and sunlight lit the opening like a waiting mouth. The museum of dreams was destroyed. Empty.

He could hear sirens in the distance, and people screaming. Shocked voices, pained voices, violent grunts mixed with languid laughter; it was all one jumbled mess. Somehow, his mother of all fuck-ups kept getting worse. He was lamenting his inability to make one good decision in his life, when it dawned on him. When he thought about it, the situation worsened yet again.

Juliet.

The one person he thought he could love. She was somewhere out in that craziness. With the stupidity that allowed him to open the Freak's enclosure in the first place, Maury Bennett charged blindly into the waiting mouth of the open door, one word subverting all other thoughts: *Juliet.*

Mr. Freakshow found solace during his night's escape among the shadows. Hiding never crossed his mind; his arrogance was far too great for that. He had no fear of humans. No one would dare hunt him like an animal, and if they did, he would snuff out their lives like cigarette ash. If he rendered Kevin nearly catatonic before the extraction, the boy would just about drop dead if he saw him now in the flesh, unimpeded by shackles or walls or panes of shatter-proof glass. The nightmare's hatred had only grown after the extraction and it had sharpened his focus and left him a more prudent creature. There was no sense in making a lavish, attention-grabbing foray down major streets. He would never find the boy if he took such a path. He stayed in the shadows in an attempt at anonymity.

He tried to rein in his form to one more suited to human eyes. His hatred tempered his ability to completely change his form into something gentler. He fashioned a boring ensemble from what he'd seen a human wear outside his enclosure. Changing his clothes didn't change his hulking size, so he slumped down as far as possible to conceal his height. A single set of headlights blazed through his path of semi-darkness. A rush of brightness lit his way, allowing him to stare into the bleary whites of the obviously drunk driver. So close, he thought, so close, but it's still too early. He wouldn't risk his immortality for a little fun of feeding on an unaware human. The car snailed down the block, lucky to hold the curb as it turned the corner.

Mr. Freakshow was on the edge of the city, walking by houses shielded behind wrought iron bars. Even after visiting the boy during his paralyzed semi-sleep state, Mr. Freakshow only had a vague idea of his home's location. Since the boy didn't know the city's layout, Mr. Freakshow's knowledge was just as limited. He started in the direction his instincts told him was correct. By first light tomorrow, Mr. Freakshow would have his freedom.

The wish-fulfillment dream, Johnny Flower, walked in his oh-so-cool manner, swaying his flared jeans like it was as natural as the clouds in the star-studded sky. He was an amalgam of his dreamer, an unemployed cyber geek, and the outward persona of John Lennon. The dream's tight fitting paisley shirt was unbuttoned down to his breastbone and the shirt cuffs flared out similarly to his jeans. It was the deadest time of night and Johnny Flower still wore his rose colored granny glasses. His thin lips highlighted his oval face, and his long, center-parted hair was a shade lighter than chocolate. The residential neighborhood he wandered through was a real bore. He looked at the horizon and could see lights like a halo over the city. That's where he needed to be. That's where he would find people of his ilk and acumen. After his inhumane and utterly barbaric imprisonment, Johnny was craving a lively conversation. Politics, the War, artwork--the topic didn't matter, just as long as the person he was interacting with had a well thought-out idea to offer.

After an hour or so, Johnny found himself in a shady-looking neighborhood. Trash littered the street and graffiti covered the buildings. Half the streetlights looked shot out. He was going to push on to the next neighborhood, but Johnny could hear music--beautiful blues guitar and throaty lyrics pumping through cheap amplifiers. The shanty bar on the corner was like a magnet to Johnny. The name, Pop's, was styled in fancy curlicues on the small neon sign in the barred window. Pop's was the only part of the block not boarded up.

Johnny entered the building and realized he once played his own style of music in small dive bars like this. It was before he grew his hair long. Before the hysteria and drugs. Before he found his true calling: Peace. Johnny hid in a dark corner of the bar, the atmosphere leavening his mood. He let the blues pour through his body like a soul enriching lifeblood. No one took note of his presence. When a down on her heel waitress came over to ask for his order, he mumbled for a glass of water, saying little more the rest of the night. He closed his eyes, and remembered a time when people could make a difference by just voicing the truth.

Esmeralda was a beautiful young lady. Her hair was cut to a short bob, but it only made her high cheekbones seem more pronounced and revealed her slender neck to full advantage. Her almond-shaped eyes were exotic and dark. She was also completely aware of her surroundings, not like most of the other dreams set free by Mr. Freakshow. Her only problem was the fact that she was naked. Naked, unless an ever-flowing mantel of beady-eyed rats covering her body was considered clothing. Yes, she was naked, excluding the fabric of furry rodents covering her womanly charms. They didn't bite her; they simply annoyed her, whipping her with an errant tail or squeaking loud enough to blot out her hearing as they scurried about her body. Esmeralda had tried any number of ways to make the rats disappear, but with no luck. After waiting for the other dreams to take their chaos outside, she had made her escape as well. She didn't want to be swept up in the tide of violence and depravity unleashed by the Freak, so she had waited. She wasn't that sort of dream. Esmeralda thought of herself as normal as any human.

She just had the one little problem.

She walked down a flight of concrete steps after exiting a vacant alley. When she reached the bottom, she realized she had entered a subway. The booth was empty and she hopped over a metal railing. The triple pairs of rails arched around a curve, and the concrete benches around the subway stop were empty. She could see a couple of people in the distance, but no one was close enough to see her *little problem*.

The roaring of an approaching train shook the ground before the lights appeared from around the corner. Esmeralda didn't know what to do. She stepped behind a concrete pillar. She was thinking about an escape route when the train pulled up with screeching brakes and a rumbling growl. A handful of bleary-eyed travelers disembarked from the train, and most appeared to be sleepwalking through the subway as if they had walked through the dark cavern a million times.

She felt a bond with these city people. Maybe they would accept her into their society. But they seemed to act like watched prey, quite aware of the danger of hidden predators. Esmeralda, feeling a strange surge of panic, waited for the unsuspecting humans to discover her.

When the small pack of people rounded the pillar, Esmeralda was the first to scream. The humans quickly joined her, mixing with the chorus of squealing dream-rats. Everyone screamed a long, seemingly cathartic scream, but after Esmeralda ran out of sight around the curve of the subway, she didn't feel better for it, and she assumed no one else did either.

The following day at the watercooler, the first rumors of a Queen of the Rats would start. The rumors would become myth, then become legend. People would write stories with her as the subject. Eventually someone would create a comic book starring the Queen of the Rats and the curse of her ever-flowing mantle of vermin. But her end would come soon enough. Once the police figured out how to contain the situation, Esmeralda would be one of the first dreams recaptured.

Juliet stood in the parking lot in front of Lucidity, wondering where Maury was, and if he was still alive. If Mr. Freakshow got his hands on him, there might not be anything left of him. She felt a strange, nearly overpowering sensation deep within her chest. It didn't make her exactly forget her desire to place a gun to her chin and blow her brains out, but it was a distraction from it. The sensation was a throbbing need. When she thought of Maury, and his penetrating eyes, the gentle touch of his fingers, it only intensified this sensation. She left the parking lot, searching out with all her senses for the man that made her feel so… feel so real.

Before setting her free, Mr. Freakshow had run a claw gently under her chin. She had backed away from the beast and slumped down behind the park bench in the center of her enclosure. Her hair had been slick with rain, but the clouds had parted and the sun gleamed high in the sky.

"What nature of dream are you, fair one?" Mr. Freakshow had asked, only his head visible to Juliet. "I see no abnormality, no weakness, weirdness or blight, and still, you are housed with the nightmares. I will enjoy finding out."

She covered her face with her hands, waiting for an attack that never came. After a long time, she opened her eyes. The Freak had left her alone. The enclosure stood wide open. She was reluctant to leave the cell, but soon the noise and commotion of the other dreams faded. Juliet hoped the nightmares had vacated the museum as she tentatively gambled a few steps outside her cell. She quickly learned the truth. Lucidity was empty, destroyed.

She had found the clothing the women wore who came to see her fascinating. The different styles and colors were astounding. No one person could come up with such beauty. From her memory, she was able to morph her simple summer dress to approximate a hodgepodge of the styles that she liked the most. She wore slacks in a splendid purple color. Soft green ruffles waffled the bodice of her blouse. She doubled a brown scarf around her neck. She felt so human. Hopefully, no one would notice her.

She stopped at the edge of the parking lot, the last step before entering the human world. Her feet felt rooted to the asphalt parking lot. She had to get going, but was torn as to what she should do. She wanted to find Maury, wanted more than anything to be in his arms once again. She also understood the cold fact that Mr. Freakshow would want to track down her dreamer, Barbara. He would eventually track down all of the dreamers and destroy them. He wanted a world where he alone could bend and change its physical laws.

Police lights flashed in the distance. She put her hands in her pants pockets, kept her head down, and quickly moved to join the people milling on the sidewalk. There was confusion in the air.

Much to her relief, no one gave her a second glance. For the moment, she put aside her thoughts of Barbara, and focused her attention on finding Maury.

CHAPTER SIXTEEN

Agnes woke early like she always did (six hours of sleep was a blessing these days), and listened to classical music on the radio while waiting for her coffee to brew. The house was chilly and she rubbed her hands together for warmth. The summer's heat was leaving quite abruptly, and it was most noticeable during the mornings when the house was quiet. She prepped her coffee, a small dose of half and half and a squeeze of honey from the plastic bear bottle, and took a sip. Feeling more awake, she went to see if Kevin would help her make breakfast. Agnes had always wanted a helper in the kitchen, and growing up, Carin had proven both disinterested and without skill. She was delighted to learn that Kevin was usually happy to lend a hand.

She would be able to tell how deeply he was sleeping by the way the room felt. If he was close to waking, she would nudge him along, maybe tickle his feet some. If she sensed a deep slumber, she would leave him be. He was finally getting the sleep he needed since Carin took him to that doctor. Even if that Dr. Bennett wasn't her own Dr. Edwardson, whatever he did for Kevin's nightmares was obviously working if he was getting his rest.

When she eased open Kevin's bedroom door the room had no feeling to it at all. It felt as empty as before he moved in. She was suddenly reminded of the haunting moments when she discovered her husband of thirty-seven years dead of a massive stroke. Howard had fallen over in the garage, obviously in some pain. When she had gone out to tear him away from his wood working long enough to grab a sandwich, she first thought the garage was empty. Howard had probably gone off to talk to a neighbor, or shoo away a squirrel from one of his bird feeders. Trusting her instincts that Howard was not in the garage, she slyly went in to run her fingers over his latest creation. While thinking she was getting away with finding out what he was making her for Christmas, she nearly tripped over his legs. She would never forget how cold his cheek felt when she touched it with her trembling fingers.

Kevin's room felt that empty.

"Kevin, honey, are you awake?" Agnes walked over to the bed. She didn't want to find him dead, didn't want to reach out to touch his cold corpse tucked under the blankets. Expecting the worst, she ran her hands across the comforter. The bed was empty and wasn't even warm. She sighed with relief that he wasn't there. But then a chill swept over her, and Agnes pulled her terry cotton robe tighter.

"Carin!" She was hoping she was simply overreacting, hoping that Kevin had slept in Carin's room last night. "Carin, wake up. Come here, dear."

"What is it? What's going on?" Carin immediately noticed the empty bed. "Where's Kevin?"

"I don't know. I thought he was with you."

Carin became instantly alert and rushed from the bedroom. She yelled for Kevin, searching every nook of the house, but he didn't call back. She ducked her head out the back door and the sky was still predawn purple. She ran to the garage, but that too was empty. She hurried back inside.

"Call the police," Carin said while switching out of her nightgown and into yesterday's clothes.

"Okay." Agnes picked up the phone on the kitchen counter. "What are you going to do?"

"I don't know what I'm doing. I never know what I'm doing," Carin snapped. "That's why my son is missing."

Agnes was not used to her daughter raising her voice at her, but it was forgivable under the circumstances.

Carin grabbed her car keys and headed for the door. "I'm going to drive around, see if I can figure out where he might be. I have my cell with me. Let me know whatever you find out."

Just that quickly, Carin was out the door. She dialed 911, trying to keep her dark thoughts at bay.

The brooding stone mansions seemed to lean toward Kevin as he cut through another unfamiliar neighborhood. One house looked the same as the last, all that changed was the breed of yappy dog that would charge the fence, baring its nubby yappy dog teeth. He kept a watchful eye on the houses, but luckily he didn't come across anyone looking out, questioning why a lone boy wandered their street so early in the morning.

Focusing his eyes on the sidewalk in front of him, he tried to plow through the neighborhood as quickly as possible. The roots of the towering trees surrounding the houses had grown under the sidewalk. The uneven concrete looked like the spine of a mile-long slumbering dragon. A growling Yorkshire terrier pulled back his attention. The little dog seemed so angry with Kevin for walking in front of its house. It was in the process of expanding a hole under the wrought iron fence. Kevin glared at the dog for making so much noise. A man wearing a plush purple bathrobe and sleep-wrestled hair stepped outside. The man paused when he saw Kevin. Their eyes met briefly and Kevin instinctively quickened his pace.

"Gertrude... come on back, honey. Come get your breakfast. Gerty... come on girl..."

Gertrude sniffed the air as if insulted by Kevin before trotting back to her master.

He had to stop worrying about the neighborhood dogs, and instead, focus on the possibility that Mr. Freakshow could come from around any corner at any moment. He crossed a cobbled street and soon left the old homes with the little yappy dogs behind. The buildings transitioned to glass-fronted office buildings surrounded by empty parking lots. The stately oaks and elms of the mansion neighborhood transitioned to efficient, bony-looking shrubs housed in slotted metal skirts buried in the sidewalk.

People started to dot the sidewalk--men in suits, women in skirts or slacks and walking shoes. While Kevin remained a face in the morning commute crowd, the crowd became a wrinkled, depressing blur he could never trust, even if someone offered a welcoming hand. He was on his own, and on his own he would have to figure out how to defeat Mr. Freakshow. His options seemed hopeless. The more he thought about it, the more it seemed like his nightmare would get his wish and steal his immortality by killing Kevin.

An extensive garden opened up at the end of the next block. The sidewalk wound through flowery carpets of red and white carnations dancing in the slight morning wind. The path wound clear out of view. A fountain was in the center of the park. Crystal water sputtered down an array of concrete channels, eventually regrouping in a shallow pond at the fountain's base. The garden was empty, and for this Kevin was grateful.

He sat on the ledge circling the pond and immediately felt the strain draining from his feet. He had been on the go at a good clip since two in the morning. When everyone's day was just beginning, fear had been pushing Kevin's every step for six hours. He dangled his fingers through the cool water and was trying to come up with a destination for his journey (or, in the back of his mind, even a stopping point for a last stand). A green leaf twice as wide as Kevin's hand floated over to his fingers. He snagged it from the pond and wiped it dry against his jeans. Its strong veins spread from its core like the branches of the tree from which it came. He opened the front zippered pocket of his backpack and carefully slipped the leaf inside.

Kevin was intelligent, and in some cases, his teachers even labeled him as gifted, but he was still a ten-year-old boy. He collected things. The pocket in which he stashed the perfect leaf held a collection of oddities that only a boy would find fascinating. From his parents' driveway, he had taken stones that looked as if they were carved by hand. He had a blackbird's feather that was as long as his forearm. There was also a wide rubber band that he hoped to one day fashion into a slingshot, and an oblong chunk of metal that he had once thought was gold, but still was intriguing enough to lug around. At the bottom of the pocket, safely sealed inside a Ziploc baggie, he'd hidden a picture of his family at their last Christmas together. His mom wasn't in the picture since she was holding the camera, but Kevin knew she was a part of it. Kevin was in the center of the picture and his expression was of utter joy. Of course, he would be happy, he had just opened a gift from his grandma, an Albert Pujols model baseball glove. Kevin had jumped up and down and had temporarily lost the ability to speak.

He originally carried the Christmas picture because of the happy memory of opening the gift. Now, he kept the picture close at all times because his dad was off to one side, stooped over to kiss his grandma on the cheek as she clapped in excitement over her grandson's reaction. The picture was perfect, capturing a perfect moment. It had become one of his oddities. Something that represented something else. It stirred something deep inside him that he wouldn't fully grasp until he was older. Just like the rubber band and the black bird feather.

When he turned his attention back to the pond, a few coins

glimmered in the sunlight. He had only seven dollars in his pocket, so he hiked up his pants to his knees and took off his windbreaker. The water was refreshing on his skin but was deeper than he expected. It licked at his rolled jeans and he nearly slipped on the slick bottom. He scooped up a handful of mud, and when he sifted it, he counted seventy-four cents. Not a bad haul. He dried the coins on his shirt and pitched them into his pocket. He kicked at the mud, trying to unearth more booty.

After about half an hour, Kevin climbed out of the pond. His clothes were soaked, but his pockets were weighed down with what felt like a limitless treasure. He gathered up his belongings, and went behind the fountain to change into a dry shirt. He had his new gym shirt with him, and it would have to do. He didn't have a change of pants, so he squeezed as much water out of his pant legs as possible.

He wanted to count his money, but knew he should at least wait until his clothes were dry and he was clear of the park. As Kevin left the park, he noticed the traffic had thickened on both the roads and sidewalks. People seemed on edge, even more so than any normal morning.

"Can I help you, son?"

A hand grasped Kevin's shoulder and he knew that when he turned around he would see Mr. Freakshow's slathered mouth.

Actually, it turned out to be a policeman, but a policeman was almost as scary as Mr. Freakshow. The policeman could have seen him take the coins from the fountain. A policeman would ask questions. A policeman would take him home to his grandma's house, making his whole family sitting ducks. Kevin's chest constricted.

"I'm fine, sir." Kevin tried to turn away, but the policeman's hand seemed as firm as Mr. Freakshow's claws.

"Where's your mom? Did she go into one of the shops?" The officer looked around to see if any stray parent was coming to claim him. Kevin could see the man was just trying to be a nice guy. "You know, it's not safe out, especially this morning, all that shit going on."

"What's going on?"

The policeman looked at him as if Kevin had just crawled out of a cave. "That damned museum. They let wild animals out, or whatever they had displayed. Been all over the news. Been causing all kinds of havoc."

"I turned in early last night. We left early to shop. We don't even own a TV," Kevin rambled. He didn't need to hear anymore. He thought Mr. Freakshow would have escaped alone, but it made even more sense to let all the dreams loose. It provided him with a perfect cover.

"Where did you say your mom is?"

"Well... I think she's..." Kevin had never been good at lying, so he did what he had seen in any number of movies--he stomped on the policeman's foot. To his surprise, it worked and the policeman went down to one knee and his hands went to his injured foot as he cried out in pain. Kevin didn't think twice. He charged between two women, and after nearly stumbling over a baby stroller, turned a corner and into an alley. His backpack jostled around on his shoulders and his back started to ache, but he kept sprinting down the alley, across an intersecting street and through to another alley, dodging errant garbage and dumpsters, before he allowed himself to look back. He took a deep breath. It had worked.

The city was strangely quiet, as if it had collectively paused to ponder Kevin's indiscretion with the officer. Then he noticed the sour smell of the alley. Spilled beer and spoiled food. He approached the next cross street cautiously, just in case the cops had set up a roadblock for him. He felt like a fugitive, which wasn't necessarily a bad thing in his mind.

When he figured the coast was clear, Kevin casually walked out of the alley, his hands in his pockets, jingling his stolen coins. He felt like an adult, or maybe an older kid, like Reid--doing bad things just because he could. He felt like he could pass for twelve years old.

Sophie noticed Kevin from a block away. There was no way she would forget his face, not after seeing what he looked like after Maury Bennett had taken that monster from the boy's mind. He'd been woozy and unsteady on his feet, and his poor mother had barely been able to keep him upright. Seeing him now, he no longer had dark circles under his eyes. At the museum he had looked half-dead, now he looked half-scared to death.

He looped his thumbs through the straps of his backpack as he gawked at the skyscrapers. He looked entirely vulnerable, either to Mr. Freakshow, or anyone else who might prey on a child's weakness. She closed in on him, gripping her purse tightly. With him still looking to the sky, she let him run into her.

"Excuse me--" a woman called out after Kevin had run into her.

"I'm sorry, ma'am." Kevin wanted to get by the old lady, but she pinched the sleeve of his gym shirt with her doll-sized hands. He probably hadn't seen her as he walked since she was barely bigger than him and was out of view when he was staring at the buildings. He noticed her small canvas bag was heavy with canned goods. Her gray hair fell out from the corners of her wide-brimmed summer hat.

"It's perfectly okay, young man, but you might want to be careful walking around like that. People will think you've never seen the city before. Some people would want to take advantage of that."

"I've been to the city before." Kevin felt like he was lying to his grandma.

"I didn't say you haven't. I've just been around a while and I've seen the bad side of people. Since you're a big strapping fellow, would you mind walking with me? I would feel safer that way."

Kevin didn't know this woman, but he already liked her. She had called him young man, and she thought he was strapping, whatever that meant. She also had a friendly, inviting face.

"Sure I will."

"If you need to be somewhere, I don't want to take you away from it."

"I don't have any plans 'til tomorrow," Kevin said, trying to sound like he had control over the direction of his life.

"I guess that's good for me. I would greatly appreciate it, especially with all the happenings in the city," she said, staring at him. "There's been all sorts of fires and looting on the far side of town. Even heard of rioting tearing apart whole city blocks."

"Sounds bad. Must be that museum I've been hearing about," Kevin said.

"Yeah, that's what I heard, too." They walked for a while before the woman spoke again. "You know, I once read a newspaper article about a group of forty monkeys escaping from a zoo in Austria."

"Really? What happened?"

"Well, I can't remember what kind of monkey they were, but just that they didn't come from that part of the world. They only recaptured about a dozen of them. Another dozen died because they couldn't adapt to their surroundings."

"What about the rest?"

"That's the interesting part. They didn't come from that part of the world, but that also meant they didn't have any natural enemies. They adapted to their new surroundings. They blended in, and now they're thriving."

"Wow. That's cool. I wonder if that's going to happen to the dreams that escaped..."

"Looks like we're going to find out soon enough. By the way, I'm Sophie Marigold."

They continued walking, and Kevin apprised this woman from the corner of his eye. His grandma had told him that she trusted her instincts when it came to people. Sophie could well be Mr. Freakshow in disguise. But his instincts told him that she was just a nice old lady. He concentrated on the outlines of her face, waiting to see the illusive "hidden color" that his grandma had mentioned. He didn't know why he trusted Sophie, but he did know he felt safe in her presence.

Eventually, Mr. Freakshow found the house. The city was larger than it appeared and he strolled up the front walk with the sun already warming away the morning dew. He had been cautious with his route; he made sure he wasn't near any of the chaos inflicted by the other dreams. He would have enjoyed watching the humans struggle with the dreams, but the boy was priority number one.

The house was an old ranch. He knew the layout intimately from the boy's memory. He went to the front door and glanced around, before twisting the doorknob apart in his hand. It was made of brass, but it crumpled under his grip like tinfoil.

Knock, knock, anyone home? he thought, chuckling to himself.

The boy's room was at the end of a hall, and he immediately headed in that direction. He could smell one human in the house, but it wasn't his prey. He stopped and listened to the sounds of the house.

"Carin, that you?" a voice called from the kitchen.

The Freak heard clinking noises, and then the smell of coffee hit him.

"I made extra coffee for when the officers get here, do you want any?" The voice was closer, in the hall.

The Freak turned toward the brittle old woman. "No thank you. I don't like coffee. It gives me heartburn." He closed the gap with the woman. She was acting strangely--as if she were straining her ears for every nuance of his voice.

The old lady almost fell over as she backed away. "It's you... How did you get here?"

"My, my. You know me, but we haven't been formally introduced.

Let me guess, you must be the boy's grandma? He sure is kind to you in his dreams. You don't look nearly so broken down and old when he dreams of you. That boy of yours, so kind to his dear, dear grandmother."

"I want you out of this house, now!" she raised her voice, but there was little conviction behind her words.

"Oh, I will. But I just need to know where to find the boy." Mr. Freakshow towered over her as he cut the distance between them with every stride. She stood with her arthritic hands clenched at her sides. He could see her vacant eyes.

"You *will not* touch a hair on his head."

"If you insist. I've always tried to respect the old and near dead, so I won't touch a hair on his head. Now, the rest of him... the rest of him will probably have to bleed some. How else am I going to kill him?"

"God damn you," Agnes said under her breath.

The Freak stooped low and turned toward her ear, and growled, "No, Grandma, God damn you!"

She flailed forward as she tried to cover her ears. "Just leave him alone... he's such a nice boy. And he's been through so much." Agnes fell to her knees and started rocking forward and back.

"He's been through so much because I have demanded it of him." He paused to let his words seep into her head. "I will leave him alone when he is good and dead." He pushed her over with his heel. She fell as easily as a bag of autumn leaves.

"No..." the old lady moaned. "Kevin... You'll never find him. He's too clever, and you... you're nothing more than a bully."

"Hmm, interesting. I never knew that. A bully? Okay. I'll accept that, as long as I get what I want. And you know what I want, right? You have information in that sweet gray head of yours. I just have a few questions for you, and then you can go back to your coffee. Agreed?"

"Go to hell..." Agnes said.

It took a few minutes to get any real information out of the old lady, but true to human nature, she eventually reached the point where she was babbling on senselessly about her grandson. Mr. Freakshow learned that she had given the boy a baseball glove for Christmas last year. The most interesting tidbit came when she blurted out about boy's father cheating on her daughter. Of course, Mr. Freakshow already knew this information, but she explained the details with such passion and unveiled anger toward her dead son-in-law. She obviously needed to get the information off her chest before she died.

He pressed her for more dirt on the boy, and he pushed long after she had anything more to give. The Freak enjoyed watching how a human would break under enough pain. At least she had given him a lead or two to follow up before her heart gave out. With the information so tantalizing and dancing through Mr. Freakshow's mind, he headed for the back door. The piercing sirens of two squad cars cut through his contentment as the cars whipped into the old lady's driveway.

He headed toward a baseball field down the street, having left a little present inside the house for the cops. Mr. Freakshow was glad he wasn't a cop; he was too easily squeamish. He cut through a yard three houses down, returning to the sidewalk. He was practically skipping when he heard the cries of horror coming from inside the house. He patted the inner pocket of his drab human coat. The old lady's skull, cleaned of its withered skin, hung heavily near his heart. The first building block in his mighty throne. Mr. Freakshow smiled.

Not long after Carin went charging from her mother's house screaming Kevin's name, she turned her Explorer around. It all hit her at once.

She was a handful of blocks from the house when she realized she would never find Kevin like this, screaming his name from the open window, searching dark corners and through the windows of cars parked on the street. She didn't know where he was, but she was wasting her breath. She let the car idle through a sleepy intersection. The mixture of terror and parental instinct that had sent her half-crazed in search of Kevin had weakened to glowing coals simmering in her belly. The urge to find and protect and love him was still inside, gnawing at her. She decided she would go back and talk with her mother while they waited for the police to arrive.

Carin's throat was scratchy and she felt like she had eaten something rotten. The morning was quickly warming, but Carin rubbed her hands across her arms as if she were trying to keep out a chill. Not all that far away from home, a number of sirens gathered, wailing awake the rest of the neighborhood.

She sped down the residential streets leading to her mother's house. The block was blanketed by men in blue. There wouldn't be nearly so many police cars responding to a call about a missing child. And from the sickened expressions on the faces of the officers lingering near the opened front door, something was horrifically wrong.

CHAPTER SEVENTEEN

A chain of police cars came barreling down the street with their lights flashing and their sirens crying their desperate cries, weaving through the shocked morning traffic. Maury hoped the policemen would sweep up to the curb where he walked, storm from their patrol cars, and throw him against the wall of the nearest building. Blame him. Arrest him. Take him away from this mess that wouldn't have happened if he hadn't been so mind-fucked, love-struck, whatever you wanted to call it.

It's all my fault. My fuck up. Without me, it would be any other Saturday morning.

Prying drunks off the sidewalks, chasing away the panhandlers, busting the speeders, the swervers, the road-ragers. But now it was a new day, totally new, a new city. The cops kept on barreling down the street, around the corner and away.

His mind was a mixture of guilt--for his stupidity at letting loose the Freak, one more stupid decision in a seemingly endless stream--and of desperation. He needed to find Juliet. He imagined finding her, lost, unsure of her surroundings, skittish at the slightest unfamiliar noise, and wondered if he would tell her right away, before any other words could slip from his lips to mess that up too, *I love you.* But that reaction would only fuck up the situation like everything else. When he found Juliet, if he found her, he would hold her, say little or nothing, let his emotions and the closeness of his heartbeat speak for him.

Where would an eccentric dream-woman go if granted her freedom? She would gravitate to humans similar to her. She would seek comfort in those who would understand her human-like qualities. A library.

Used bookstores. A coffee house. Head shops. There were so many possibilities. And she had no family. Her dreamer lived near Milwaukee. She respected Barbara as she would a parent, but Maury didn't think she would leave her immediate surroundings to track her down. At least not right away. She would want to understand what was around her, the ways people acted, what they talked about, how they lived. She wouldn't move on until she achieved this. Or so he hoped. He had barely met her when she invited him into her enclosure. His guesses were only that. Guesses.

He scrutinized every woman who walked by, looking at their clothes, seeing their faces, and not finding Juliet. He felt like he had lost all control of his life.

The thought of family made him realize that he had his own family to think about. Robert and Eliza Unger. His adoptive parents.

He began searching the street for a payphone. People were pushing by him, palpable tension stiffening their movements, tightening the skin of their faces. Everyone was in a hurry, and the morning had just begun. He realized everyone was seeking out their families.

In times of trouble, our family bonds strengthen. Little conviction accompanied the thought.

Maury crossed the street, navigating through the teeming intersection to a bank of payphones. Just before he could make it to the other curb, the driver of some foreign luxury sedan gave him the finger, and for a brief moment, he thought the driver realized the city was in upheaval because of him. But the driver honked his horn, turned his abusive finger in the direction of the too-slow driver in front of him, and then sped off as traffic picked up. Maury quickened his pace to beat a haggard-looking woman to the phone. She hissed at him like an angered cat, then folded her arms and impatiently tapped her foot.

Too slow, lady. He couldn't help chuckling to himself.

He dialed the Ungers' home. It kept on ringing for a half minute. The haggard woman with the tapping foot pointed at her wrist, indicating the time. Maury turned his back to her, facing the graffiti scratched into the stainless steel phone fixture. He waited.

"Yello--" his dad said groggily when he finally picked up.

"Dad? Is everything okay at home? Is Mom okay?"

"Your mom's in watching T.V. I was sleeping. What's going on?"

"I need for you to listen, Dad," Maury paused. He didn't want to admit he had done anything wrong. Growing up, it seemed like his parents, both sets, had always blamed him for everything. "When Mom tells you about the news, listen to her. I want you two to be careful."

He twirled the metal phone cord while a discernible silence grew in their conversation.

"What the hell are you talking about?"

"Police cars are zipping down all the streets here. Something crazy is going on. I can hear ambulances, too. I think you should stay home today. Watch Mom, stay inside."

"You hear sirens, and you want me to stay home?"

"When the sirens hit your neighborhood, turn off the lights and take Mom to a secure place." Maury had never revealed his abilities to his adoptive parents, even after he was making a living because of them.

"Okay, son… we'll do what we can." His dad sounded perplexed and even slightly annoyed.

"Dad, I have to tell you something about Gabe. It's been bothering me lately," Maury said, his heart hurting, knowing he was going to come clean about everything that had been a lie. His entire life.

Maury could nearly hear his dad thinking, through his wheezing breath, the results of living and working so hard. He finally spoke in his raspy voice, "What about Gabe?"

Another squall of an approaching line of police cars broke his concentration.

Right there on the street corner, with the sky full of sirens, the pest of a woman nagging him for the use of the phone, Maury was going to tell it all. That he hadn't done a thing to stop Gabe from diving into the pool, and that he did nothing to save him once he crashed into the bottom. He was going to tell his adoptive dad that he had been using him for over twenty years. Allowing Gabe to die had eased the burdens of Maury's life, had given him all of his new parents' attention. Later on, when he was approaching college age, he let Robert work hard enough to get the second job at the corner gas station, just out of spite. The Ungers had only wanted him because he was damaged, and had only wanted Gabe because he fell from a window because his mom had been too busy lighting her crack pipe. He was going to tell him everything.

"Son? Are you there?"

The police cars pushed through the congested intersection, slowed by the confused traffic. Maury looked into the second squad car, and did a double take. His luck, his mother of all fuckups, was about to change. Inside the second squad car, sitting in the passenger seat, staring somehow both intently and blankly out the window, was Carin Dvorak. Kevin's mom.

"Gabe… Dad, I miss Gabe. He was such a sweet kid."

"I know, son, I know."

"Be careful, Dad."

His dad let out a pent up breath. Relieved. "We will. You too."

Maury hung up the phone. "I warned you..." Maury said as he turned from the payphone. The haggard woman stepped back, thinking Maury was talking to her, but he was already moving on. He could see where the squad cars were heading. With screeching tires, they stopped curbside three blocks up. One of the men in blue escorted Carin from the car, and even from this distance, Maury could see her looking around, as if searching for someone. The policeman guided her into the police station.

Policemen scurried through the station. The people sitting alongside Carin in the double row of bright orange plastic chairs seemed unsettled to see the unnatural strain on the policemen's faces. Carin had been barely aware of the young policeman with the sad, red-rimmed eyes who had guided her from the scene of her mother's murder to his police car. Now, she was sitting alongside other frazzled citizens, and their protectors were running around, scared. She remembered a cop guiding her to the plastic chairs, and someone gently patting her ice cube fingers, mumbling something about getting her a coffee.

Half an hour had lapsed and Carin was still sitting in the same spot, unmoved, noticeably drained of what little will she had left. A police officer eventually brought her a lukewarm cup of coffee. He walked away without saying a word.

She couldn't let herself think right now--it was too much, too painful. Instead, she repeatedly read the words from a nearby public service poster until they weren't words any longer. They were as foreign to her as seeing her own intestines.

Occasional thoughts pushed through her defenses. Her fragile and imperfect marriage was gone, her son was missing, her mother brutalized. She didn't know if she could take anymore, or if she had already reached her limits. Maybe she had already snapped and just hadn't realized it yet.

The details of the public service poster were starting to cement in her mind. She was seeing the poster and it made sense. The black blobs of ink were words again. The poster showed a middle-aged couple standing on the front step of a neighbor's house. The wife was holding a casserole dish, extending their gratuitous greeting to their new neighbors. The caption at the bottom read, *Meet your neighbors. It's a sure way of ending neighborhood violence.* Carin wondered how a simple, yet savory casserole could impact the violence level of a neighborhood.

She looked away from the silly poster as tears filled her eyes. A man was standing at the main reception desk. Carin couldn't see the person behind the desk, but the nervous posture of the man leaning over for information seemed familiar. Stringy legs in tailored pants and a rumpled dress shirt, patchy brown hair sticking out from a worn Cubs cap.

"Dr. Bennett!" Carin shouted as she stood up. The people in the bright orange plastic chairs shied away from Carin as if she were on fire.

Dr. Bennett came over to the waiting area, sympathy weighing down the edges of his angular features. "Mrs. Dvorak. I saw the policemen bringing you in here." He took both of her hands and tried to squeeze the ice from them. "Are you okay?"

"I don't know yet." They were the truest words she had ever spoken. Her son was out there somewhere. At this point, she couldn't take another shock to her system. It was almost better for Kevin to be out there somewhere and for her to never find out what happened to him. If she never knew what happened, at least there was a possibility that no harm had come to him, that he could possibly even be happy.

"Where's Kevin?"

"I... don't know." Speaking sharpened her emotions and she started to sob into her open hands, her reawakened pain racking her every nerve.

"Did Mr. Freakshow take him?"

"No. I woke up and his bed was cold. He must have slipped out in the middle of the night--and what do you mean, Mr. Freakshow? He's supposed to be locked up at the museum."

"If you haven't guessed it yet, the dreams are out. They escaped sometime last night."

"Then... then that means one of them could have taken him," she said, oddly hopeful.

"I don't think so. If he disappeared, I'm thinking Kevin's trying to run away."

"Run away?"

"From Mr. Freakshow."

"What does Mr. Freakshow want with my son?"

"It would be in his best interest to kill him."

Carin wiped her face dry and did her best to suppress any further tears. "That's not going to happen. I can't let that happen."

"I want to help find Kevin. I know Mr. Freakshow, you know your son. The two of us can work together to save him."

"That's all well and good, Dr. Bennett, but why would you want to help me find my son?" She took a tissue from her pocket and dabbed her eyes dry of tears.

"If we don't stop Mr. Freakshow from killing your son, then nothing could stop him from destroying everything."

As Maury and Carin stood talking at the front desk, they were unaware of three cops escorting a recaptured dream into the rear of the building. The thing was the size of a child, but was obviously a dream creature. It sported a lion's mane crowning its head and had skin made of soft, brown suede. An anonymous caller had alerted the station to the little dream-thing digging through a dumpster in a nearby alley. The caller had mentioned, that at first, she thought the noise was a stray cat. Maybe even a dog. But then the fringe of its mane poked out from the dumpster. Once the woman could stop screaming, she called 911.

The dream thing purred like a kitten, even as they cuffed its hands (or were they paws? they wondered) behind its back. It didn't struggle a bit. It seemed totally unaware of its surroundings. All it wanted was to be fed. Maybe a saucer of milk would do. Yes, a saucer of milk, and a warm fireplace to curl up in front of... and then maybe some sleep.

They closed the dream thing inside an empty, secluded cell. It went over to the hard bunk, curled up into a ball, and began to purr.

The boy had been at the park fountain. Mr. Freakshow knew this before he even found his windbreaker. When he had seen the oasis of lush green amongst all the gray of the city, he was certain the boy would have explored its mystery. Every stride he put behind him heightened his sense of the boy's presence. To Kevin, the secluded fountain would have looked as inviting as a loving maternal hug. Yes, the boy had definitely rested by the trickling fountain for an extended period.

The Freak leaned his substantial form to the water's edge and could feel the coolness climb through the air to greet the claws of his extended hand. He cupped a handful of the coolness and brought it to his feral lips. The boy had been in the water. The Freak's eyes flared yellow with excitement. He laved his palms with his tongue, imbibing the fluid like it was life itself. He consumed it, tasting the boy. He was close. Soon enough his blood would entice his tongue instead of his discarded wash water.

Mr. Freakshow licked his palm dry and stepped into the bubbling fountain. He let the water simmer the heat of his hatred. The damned human form and all its frailty--once he had his claws buried in the boy's chest cavity, the Freak would turn his attention to the next step of his master plan. Gather up those dreams worthy of standing next to him. Build an army worthy of serving him. It would be a more luxuriant time. A time when he could go about his business of destroying the humans in a methodical manner, enjoying every quavering lip and tattered body.

For now, he would soak up the essence of the boy. He eased his body lower until he was submerged past his nostrils and only his eyes were visible above the surface.

A young couple latched at the hip, and looking so tuned to each other that they resembled siblings, wandered over to the water fountain. So caught up in the moment and the artifice of their love, they never saw Mr. Freakshow. He fought his impulse to kill and probed for the dream soul of these two hapless humans. The Freak could see the girl's unwavering devotion to her boyfriend, just beneath the skin, a shadow of her human desires, her petulant and nauseating dreams. He saw the gossamer collage of flowing white wedding gowns, cream colored flowers in piled heaps, and the strong, square-shouldered figure of a man dressed in black. His face was not visible; all he saw was shadow. To this young lady the man of her dreams was all that it really was, a dream man, a shape only. A symbol. Her boyfriend fit the mold. Her devotion in her waking world was to the symbol he represented.

The boyfriend had no clue. When the Freak looked inside him, just beneath the skin, hanging tenuously like connective tissue, was the boy's dreams. He had a spiteful, dark soul, and his dreams mirrored this. The girl was only a depository for his sperm. She was a body, a piece of meat, something to soil and discard. Mr. Freakshow laughed and the fountain water rippled. The boyfriend jerked a look over his shoulder as Mr. Freakshow stood, shaking the water from his skin. The girl screamed.

"I sure love that sound. Like manna from heaven."

The Freak made his choice. The irony of the two lovers loving something other than who they were fucking was not lost on him. The girl fucked a symbolic ideal. The boy fucked a wet hole. The girl was too sweet to let live. He struck, with unfurled claws, without an ounce of sympathy for his victim. The park became a blur of torn flesh and blood-tainted water.

He allowed her to scream, even after he knocked her boyfriend off his feet and against a nearby tree, he let her scream. Mr. Freakshow felt badly for eventually silencing the girl. He shouldn't have gone for the throat so quickly. She continued her struggle, but the only sound she gave off was the blood flowing down her shoulders, spurting from her mortal wound. The Freak brought his prey into the fountain, the essence of Kevin lingering in the water. He slumped into the water, pulling the girl with him. He plunged his teeth into the remains of her neck and held her firmly in his coiled arms. He flipped over violently in the water, his limbs clinging to her dying body, flipped until he heard her fragile human neck snap in his jaws.

He held her under until her skin started to soften. He knew he shouldn't have done something so impulsive, but then again, he understood where he came from. Perhaps he had been spurred on by finding Kevin's trail. A boy's mind had spawned Mr. Freakshow, and sometimes he couldn't help a child's unthinking impulse.

CHAPTER EIGHTEEN

Kevin and Sophie shared an amiable banter while they walked through the crazed streets of Chicago. Everyone they passed seemed to have grocery bags in tow, weighed down with nonperishable cans and dry goods. People strained to carry multiple gallons of water.

"You know my name, but you never gave me yours," Sophie said.

"My name's Kevin." He purposely left off his surname. He didn't know why he was walking with this old lady. He had never met her before and his mom was always harping on him about not talking to strangers. But Sophie seemed different, not scary or threatening. Yet somehow, there was something recognizable in her. Maybe she shared similarities with his grandma. Walking with Sophie seemed to bring him a certain level of calm, and as long as he was fleeing from Mr. Freakshow, he would take it where he could.

"Kevin, I'm glad to have met you."

He made to match her more casual pace. Sophie seemed to be oblivious to the tension in the crowd. She would nod or give some other small gesture to most of the people as they hurriedly walked by, as if in recognition, but she couldn't know all of these people. Could anyone be so nice?

They had gone a few blocks and he was beginning to realize just how tired he was. It wouldn't be dark for quite a while, even with the days getting shorter, but Kevin was getting hungry and he would have to start thinking about where he was going to sleep. When he found a safe place, he would rest his eyes for a couple hours, get off his feet and try to relax. If relaxing was possible anymore.

Sophie spoke as they walked. "So, Kevin, what are your big plans?"

"I was thinking about heading out to the country, maybe hook up with a farm or ranch or something like that."

"That sounds wonderful. I grew up on a farm."

"You did?" Kevin had never met an actual farmer, but he had an idea they were a different kind of person, almost like from a foreign country. Farmland surrounded his hometown of Warren Cove, but it always seemed far away. "My grandpa was a country boy," he said, remembering what his grandmother had recently mentioned. "He didn't like the city, and I don't think I do, either."

"A farm is a nice place for a kid to grow up. I sure enjoyed it. I milked cows and split logs all the time."

"You split logs?" He sized up Sophie with a quick glance. He couldn't imagine her being able to lift an axe, let alone use one to split logs.

"When I was younger I was as fit as you. And I was always strong for my size, even though I'm a girl."

They didn't talk much after that. Occasionally, Sophie would point to where she wanted to turn. Kevin didn't want his words to ruin this respite from fear. He was glad Sophie wasn't asking about his parents or trying to turn him into the cops as some kind of juvenile delinquent. He was sick of people asking about his parents. And from now on, he had to accept the fact that he didn't have any. Distancing himself from thoughts of his mom--thinking about her frantically searching for him, crying over the loss of him, his grandma trying her best to console her-- none of this could bother him anymore. He was on his own, and it would stay that way, for his safety and the safety of his family.

"This is my stop, Kevin." Sophie stopped at a corner. They stood and looked at each other for what seemed like a long time. "I've enjoyed talking to you, Kevin. Would you like to stop in and have some chocolate chip cookies and talk some more? You can meet my husband."

"Well..." Kevin said, looking at his suddenly antsy feet. He liked Sophie, but if Mr. Freakshow was close, he was putting her life in danger as well as his own just by standing there.

"I baked the cookies not more than an hour ago. I just stopped down to the store to pick up some supplies, what with all that's going on."

His stomach grumbled its emptiness, as if it had its own set of ears and was eavesdropping on their conversation. "Well, okay. But just for a little while."

"Wonderful!" Sophie held her hand up high in the air, her palm facing Kevin. "Aren't you going to high-five me, or do young men not do that anymore?"

Kevin laughed and slapped Sophie's hand. Her apartment was in a washed-out building in an equally washed-out neighborhood. The buildings looked like they were from another time, a time when there weren't cars or planes, let alone museums displaying the nightmares of traumatized children. Sophie looked younger than Kevin's grandma, and she was light on her feet and moved like someone even younger. She had her hair pulled back, and he saw traces of black hidden within the gray. He was surprised that someone like Sophie would live in such a neighborhood. He didn't want to judge the area too much, but it was a wreck. Sophie was nice. Sophie was intelligent. Bad people lived in bad neighborhoods. She unlocked the door and stepped inside, holding the door open for him.

"This is my tiny apartment, and the man sitting on the stool is my husband, Andrew," Sophie said as they entered her studio apartment. She immediately lowered a heavy steel bar across the closed door, flipped a deadbolt in place and chained the door. So she did know just how bad their neighborhood was.

Sophie left Kevin to get a plate of cookies and a pitcher of milk. Andrew didn't seem to notice him right away. He crouched over from where he squatted on a foot-high stool, dabbing a paintbrush against the wall. All of the walls and most of the ceiling was a big canvas, and Andrew was busy filling up the bottom corner of one of the walls to complete a country scene. The mural was frighteningly similar to what Kevin had in mind when he thought of his venture into the country.

"Hello?" Kevin mumbled.

Andrew turned away from the mural, his expression as inviting as Sophie's had been after Kevin had run into her. He had a mustache as big as the Yorkshire terrier Kevin had laughed at this morning. *What was her name... Gerty?* Gerty the yappy little Yorkshire terrier. *Had that been just this morning?* The day seemed like a whole week or longer.

"Why, hello there. My name's Andrew. And you?" He was wearing old gaudy clothes that Kevin would have snickered at if he saw Andrew on the street, but he bit his tongue. He couldn't laugh at someone Sophie cared about; his parents had taught him better. Andrew's shirt had a wide collar and a strange red check pattern. His pants were rough brown polyester and fit snuggly on his thin legs.

"I'm Kevin."

The walls seemed like windowpanes peering into another world.

155

Golden brown wheat fields seemed to sway in an imaginary wind. Cotton ball clouds cast their long shadows on the fields below, and then he saw them converge and coalesce, merging into larger and larger white puffs of cloud. Kevin shook his head. The painting was as still as a rock when he looked again.

"What do you think? Is the sky too blue? It's been so long I can't remember what the country sky looks like." As Andrew looked at his mural, he turned his head on axis like a dog straining to understand.

"No. I think it's good. Looks better than the real sky."

Andrew made a soft clucking noise with his tongue. "That's the problem. It needs to look like the real sky, not bluer or deeper or cloudier. No sky is perfect. The sky in my memory has flaws, as any sky does."

Kevin studied the wall. Different textures revealed themselves in the paint layers. At first the fields were the same simple golden brown that he had originally seen. Then he saw the layers of red and green underneath it all. The coarse fiber of the plants looked as real as a photograph. Kevin saw beyond the first stalks of wheat, and soon it felt like he was becoming lost in layer upon layer and row upon row of the field. Somehow, the tiny studio apartment smelled earthy and the closed-in air carried with it a certain heaviness, as if it would soon rain. But the vaporous paints quickly overpowered, and everything snapped back into focus. Kevin was only looking at a wall again.

"Here we go. I even warmed them for a few minutes in the oven. You like your cookies warmed I bet?"

"It's my favorite. My grandma... well that's how I like to eat them anyway."

"Good enough. Come on over and sit down. I'll pour you a glass of milk."

While Kevin finished off his third milk-dipped cookie, he felt guilty for eating in front of Andrew without offering him any. "Andrew, aren't you going to have any?"

"I'm not all that hungry. I want to keep on painting as long as I have my inspiration," he said and turned to Sophie. They shared something with their eye contact, as if they didn't need to speak to communicate. Andrew must have been twenty years younger than Sophie. His hair was mostly dark brown peppered with gray, while his thick mustache had no trace of gray at all. His wrinkles looked new, also. It was hard for Kevin to judge people's ages, especially when they were older than sixteen or so, but it looked like Sophie had robbed the cradle. Maybe that's why she was so spry and exuded such happiness all the time.

Kevin and Sophie continued talking for a long time. It was hard to tell how late it was in the windowless apartment, but Kevin had a feeling it was getting dark by now. Kevin learned that Sophie and Andrew had moved to the city almost twenty years ago. They had both been teachers in their hometowns after growing up as farmers' kids. Andrew had been a high school art teacher, while Sophie had taught the sixth grade. Kevin thought that he would love to be taught by Sophie, and that he would be going into the sixth grade soon--next week, if he lived that long. The thought that he might never go back to school popped into his head. He thought about Reid and all the other kids from the baseball field. It was like it was finally sinking in. He wasn't going home. He wasn't going home, and he would never make any friends. Who would he spend Christmas with, make snow forts with, and go fishing with in the springtime? All of these thoughts deluged his mind, and he had to block it out, or he might start crying.

"You must have enjoyed my cookies because there aren't even any crumbs left."

"Yes, ma'am, they were delicious."

"You're dragging a little around the edges. Why not stay awhile? You could take a short nap, if you like."

"I shouldn't have stayed this long. I should get going." Kevin got to his feet. His toes felt raw in his shoes and it wouldn't surprise him to look down and see hot metal rods poking his thighs. He was wiped out.

"Really, now. Do you think you'll get far as tired as you are?" Sophie said.

"I think she's right, Kevin. You look beat. Why not take a load off, and rest up. We have room enough for you to catch a couple Zs." Andrew had gotten up from his stool for the first time since Kevin arrived. He stood next to his wife and put his gangly arm around Sophie's shoulders. He was a good foot taller than her, but they seemed to fit in some odd way. Apart, they were imbalanced, but together they became a steadier whole.

Kevin took a couple steps toward the door, but he realized they were right. He was exhausted and it didn't help that he had slept no more than a few hours the night before. Once outside, he didn't know where he would go, just away and as quickly away as possible. Once outside, fatigue would weaken his defenses. He could barely keep his eyes open as it was.

"Okay. I guess I'll stay a little while. Not more than an hour or two. I need to be on the move." Kevin felt betrayed by his body, by the warmth and security provided by these strangers. He wanted to be mad at them, but couldn't summon the effort.

Sophie opened a folded cot and brought over a handmade quilt and extra pillow. Kevin sat down on the cot, and was glad he could see the whole apartment from his resting place. Andrew was back to his painting, and as Kevin pulled his legs onto the cot, Sophie went over to be with her husband. Their eyes met again and they shared a moment as they had earlier. They were happy despite their meager apartment, and had enough happiness to share with a stranger they had just met.

Sophie took up a long wooden paintbrush, and as a couple, they added fresh paint to the countryside. Sophie hummed softly as she worked, some familiar and nameless tune, and she swayed to her slight song, occasionally adding brush strokes to the mural.

Within a few minutes, Kevin was fighting his heavy eyelids and struggling to focus on Sophie and Andrew. When he was a sliver away from falling asleep, with one foot on the other side of sleep, his eyes started playing tricks on him. The wall of reality crumbled around the lifelike murals. The three of them were no longer in a cramped studio apartment. They were in the countryside, surrounded by rolling hills of wheat heavy with ripe seed. Sophie continued to hum, but she and Andrew set down their paintbrushes. She gave a small curtsey to her husband, and he responded with a deep and respectful bow. They started to dance in a formal manner, all stiff arms and flowing gestures.

A breeze invaded the former apartment and the earthy wheat field smell returned, clouding Kevin's drifting mind. A lone black bird flew overhead, swooping down into the wheat and out of sight. The golden field was at its peak. Sophie and Andrew were happy, enjoying each other's company. And Kevin felt safe. When he finally fully accepted sleep, he didn't need to dream. There were plenty of dreams in the outside world to fill that need.

When Kevin woke with a start, he had a feeling that the day was gone, that night had come and touched the land with its dark hand, and it was now morning. His eyes were gummy and his mouth tasted like a monkey's armpit. He stretched his arms over his head and stood from the cot. To his surprise, his back didn't hurt like it usually did after sleeping on his Uncle David's old mattress. The first thing he did was make sure the dried paint on the walls wasn't moving, and that nothing was about to step from the painted cinder blocks. Then he smelled breakfast food. So, it *was* morning. A half wall blocked off the kitchen area, but he could see the top of Sophie's head from the kitchenette.

He walked over to the kitchenette, his feet feeling cramped and sweaty. Not figuring on staying for more than a couple of hours, he had fallen asleep with his shoes on. He especially didn't expect to sleep through the night and into morning.

"Good morning, Kevin," Andrew said from his seat at a folding chair. Their kitchenette consisted of the kind of card table with legs that could fold under for easy transport, and was accompanied by two mismatched folding chairs. It wasn't much, but Sophie and Andrew didn't appear to need much.

"What time is it?"

"Just shy of 6 a.m., dear." Sophie carried a pan of scrambled eggs over to fill his plate. "Don't worry, I already ate. Have a seat."

He sat down. "Six o'clock. Wow. Didn't know I was that tired." He felt that by staying so long and eating their breakfast, he was taking advantage of his gracious hosts. And also putting them in incalculable danger.

"If you're going to get as far as you say you want, you'll need to fill up."

He was in the process of standing, when Sophie put a hand on his shoulder.

"Nothing is so pressing that you should leave without eating. Dig in," Andrew insisted.

It sounded like an order, and he did what he was told. If Mr. Freakshow hadn't found him yet, maybe he'd lost him. Somehow, he doubted that. He let his hunger silence his better judgment.

"That's some painting," Kevin said, cutting into the steaming eggs with a fork. They were fluffy, coated in salt, and delicious.

"Thanks. We've been working on it for a few weeks now. Someday we'll move back to Bakersfield. It's home to us. We might have moved away, but it's always been in our hearts," Andrew said, his eyes being drawn to the mural.

"It's pretty cool that you work together."

"It's funny, we've always been artists, but had never collaborated on anything until recently. Now it seems as natural as breathing." Sophie cleared the plate from in front of Andrew and came back with a steaming pot of coffee. She poured until Andrew waved his hand for her to stop. He dropped in two cubes of sugar and stirred it with a teaspoon.

"Well, I think you should keep it going. It's a shame no one can see it," Kevin said.

"Art is successful as long as at least one person can enjoy it," Andrew said philosophically.

Kevin didn't know if he understood his meaning, but he nodded in agreement. He finished his eggs and sopped up every last drop of maple syrup with the homemade waffles before he pushed the plate away. "I'm so full. I couldn't eat another bite."

"You're a good eater," Sophie said. Kevin didn't think someone could be talented at something as trivial as eating. He liked the compliment anyway.

"I should get going. It's probably six thirty already."

"Just be careful," Andrew said. There seemed to be more depth in his words than there should be. They couldn't have known about Mr. Freakshow, or that he was after Kevin. They might just be wary in general. That had to be it. Anyone with a conscience would be concerned about a ten-year-old kid walking the streets alone.

Andrew rose from his folding chair, pushed it under the card table and went out to the main area of the apartment. He picked up a brush and bit the end of it as he considered the wall.

Sophie was rummaging through a drawer by the sink, taking out a plastic baggie.

"Before you go, let me pack some of those cookies for you. They won't be warm like yesterday, but I think they're still pretty good cold."

"If you insist," Kevin said cheerfully.

As she busied herself with the cookies, Kevin noticed her canvas purse on a shelf next to the kitchenette. Crisp green bills stuck out from the wallet in the opening, and he realized just how little money he had. He had his seven dollars from when he ran away, and then the money from the water fountain at the park. But all that wouldn't last more than a day or so.

He watched for Andrew, but he was engrossed with his painting. Sophie had her back to him and was filling baggies full of cookies into a brown lunch bag. He felt terrible for doing it, but he snatched the money before their attentions returned to him. He took the money, a bunch of twenties from a quick glance, and shoved them in his pocket. Next to the purse was a pad of paper and pen. The pad had a list for the grocery store, and doodles of three dimensional boxes and abstract faces. He wrote a simple note, tore it from the pad, and shoved it in the open purse.

"Here we are. With your appetite, I bet these are gone by dinnertime." Sophie handed him the bag. It was heavy, and the guilt he felt from his spontaneous theft felt even heavier.

"Thanks. Someday I'll repay you."

Sophie walked him to the door, and Kevin thought something else would come up to delay his departure, but nothing did. Before he knew it, she removed the bar from the door, and had all of the locks and chains pulled aside, and the door swung open. The morning sun hurt his eyes, and after saying a quick goodbye, Kevin walked into that sunlight, feeling rested, but unsure about what even the next hour would have in store for him.

Sophie stopped at the bookcase before entering the kitchen to clean up the breakfast dishes. She noted the money was missing from the top of her purse. "He took it, just like you said he would."

"Feel better now?"

"No. If a genuinely good kid like that is so scared that he would steal money from an old lady, then there is something terribly wrong with the world." Sophie started the water to fill the plugged sink. She cleared the table, putting the dishes in to soak.

"I know. But what could we have done? We did our best. We gave him a warm bed. We fed him. We made sure he had money when we knew he wouldn't accept any if we had offered it directly."

"We could have called the police." She rung a dishrag in her hands, and then noticing her mounting tension, threw the rag against the kitchen wall.

"Sophie, I know you mean well, but you know the dreams are running the police around in circles. They wouldn't stop for one lost boy when they have so many other things to worry about."

"I know, I know. We don't exactly want them traipsing through our apartment, either," Sophie said. She turned off the kitchen faucet and went over to Andrew. She put her arms around his waist, and he squeezed her shoulders, kissed the top of her head. "But it feels so wrong, letting him go like that."

They were silent for a long while. They swayed in their embrace, and Sophie closed her eyes, as if shutting out the cruelty of the world.

The silence was broken by a loud crash against the apartment door. "What was that?"

Andrew cautiously stepped toward the door. Another resounding thud rattled the door. It shook in its frame, but the steel bar held it steady. It wasn't going anywhere. "I'm guessing whatever had Kevin so scared."

"Open up! I know the boy was here. I can smell him." The voice was a shambles, rage bending its rhythm to its will.

Sophie went up to Andrew and held him once again. She shook in his arms. "I know what that is." She didn't need to say the name. Andrew had heard all about Mr. Freakshow from Sophie's time painting at Lucidity. She continued to shake, and her legs became weak. Andrew eased her to a sitting position on the floor, and they clutched each other, even as the pounding seemed to shake the whole apartment.

The pounding suddenly stopped, and after awhile, the Freak spoke in a placating voice, his voice tempered of its anger, "I just need to find the boy. He's gone missing. He's so lost. So lonely..." He was quiet again, and enough time lapsed that Sophie began to wonder if the beast had gone away. "Old lady, I know what you've done. I despise you and everything about you. Right after I kill the boy, I'm coming back for you."

Sophie clung to Andrew for a long time. She was almost certain Mr. Freakshow was now gone for good. He was on a hunt, after all, and his prey was gaining distance. She could feel the pulse of Andrew's neck against her cheek, and it was comforting. She didn't want that steady reassurance to ever leave her. She closed her eyes, and Andrew held her, even as the adrenaline rush left her limbs and she felt weak and old, he held her. Her thoughts went out to Kevin. She hoped he was fast enough and clever enough to evade such a horrible fate.

CHAPTER NINETEEN

White noise, disinformation.

The young man sat on a thinly-padded bucket seat aboard the trundling L-train, his brown attaché case balanced against his thigh. Everything about him was bland. Details, once recalled, someone would immediately question for validity.

Everything about him--the embossed initials, K.L., near the handle of the attaché, his slightly tanned skin (courtesy of a bronzing agent he picked up at an out of town drugstore), his preppy, died-brown hair, his khakis and button up brown shirt--everything about him was a fake, a deception.

White noise. Disinformation.

He looked much younger than his forty-two years. He could pass for twenty-four, maybe a year or two younger still. His goal was to appear to be a young man on the make, decked out for a job interview, or perhaps on his way to work an entry-level position in an office setting. People continually asked him for ID when he entered a bar or bought a six pack. He always smiled inside (never outwardly, for risk of losing the upper hand), knowing he'd fooled them. He could legally buy alcohol around the time of the first George Bush's lone acceptance speech.

The car was empty but for him, even with the early morning thrown into chaos by the startling events of the last twenty-four hours. Dreams escaping from a museum? He didn't know if he believed the stories, but he did know he would find his work easier. As soon as he heard the news on his shower radio this morning, he was certain he would find his victims easier to ply away from their relative safety. After all, with all of the hullabaloo, who would question his appearance, find fear or unease in his proximity?

Whatever was happening in the streets and alleyways, he was happy for the extra layer of tumult cast over the city.

White noise, disinformation.

He brushed his hand affectionately over his attaché. He'd had it long enough. After finishing work for the day, he would have to find a new case to carry his tools. No sense in allowing a pattern of details to develop. Ah, his tools. His diamond-tipped augers, his crude sail thread and needles... he had to clear his mind or risk his true intentions to become visible.

But the train is empty, he thought. But all the better for the practice. The facade must be flawless. Who's to say who's secretly watching him?

Besides, the train is slowing.

The L-train bored through the dimly-lit tunnel, bored through it like his tools at work on human flesh. A gentle hiss of the air brakes indicated the train coming to a stop. He leaned against his inertia until the momentum died, until the train exited the tunnel and eased next to the elevated platform. The young man smiled inside as he casually looked out the window.

A lone woman with luminous auburn hair stood on the elevated platform. She hugged her arms in front of her as if she was trying to hold herself together.

The train doors split open, and the woman tentatively stepped aboard. Her indecision and insecurity made her an interesting possibility for his day. He saw much potential in the curve of her hip, the swell of her breast. And her eyes--alive with some unconventional light. He would explore and insinuate his tools into her soft tissues until he discovered its origin. Then once he understood this woman, he would sew her up again. Leave no trace of his violation.

Without looking at him, the woman braced her hand on a metal handrail, then turned down the narrow aisle, quickly taking a seat with seeming randomness. When she glanced about the train compartment, he offered her his most charming smile.

White noise. Disinformation.

The world was too big, too overwhelming. The scope and complexity--the unending gray blanket of sky, the indistinguishable city blocks, the innumerable buildings. The build up of details, the minutia of every single thing...

Juliet's hand began to twitch.

Tears flowed down her cheeks. She didn't know what she was doing or where she was going. Or really, buried in the back of her mind, who she was.

At least no one took notice of her; her disguise was working. No one noticed her for being what she was. At least so far.

She fell in behind a group of people, trying to blend in as she collected her thoughts. The people were in such a hurry, jogging through crosswalks a split second after speeding cars rushed by.

She couldn't hide forever. Eventually, her emotions would give her away. And when the tears started to flow unbidden, when her moods darkened, things would happen. Strange things. The clouds would clear, the sun would shine, a drizzle of warm rain would patter over her skin. And then she would have the insatiable desire to kill herself. She wouldn't be able to think of anything else but ending her own life.

Her hand continued to twitch. Soon she would conjure up the handgun, then place it to her chin or temple. Maybe seeing her braincase exploding into a cloud of brain and blood--seeing her seemingly dead body tumble to the sidewalk, and then her wounds fade to nonexistence and watch her rise again--maybe that would give these strangers a clue as to who exactly they were walking with.

Juliet hugged the twitching limb to her chest, aware now how hard she was breathing. She hadn't a clue as to where to start looking for Maury, or even how to make her way through the city. At a busy intersection, Juliet fell into lockstep with a woman who exuded confidence. She wore a gray wool jacket the color of smoke. Her feet were clad in white walking shoes. The cuffs of her black pleated pants swayed at her ankles as she walked. She seemed to look down on the world from an unturned gaze. Her lips were tight, her eyes alert.

Without the woman noticing, Juliet followed her for a short while, not taking her eyes from the back of her coat. She was able to block out the rest of the world; as long as she followed this woman, she would be able to keep her dark thoughts at bay. The woman turned down a stairway that looked like an entrance to a catacomb. After a moment's hesitation, Juliet followed. At the bottom of the stairs, they reached a turnstiles, over which the woman deftly jumped.

For the first time, the woman acknowledged Juliet.

"Come on over, no one's here. We shouldn't have to miss our train just because they can't keep up on their repairs."

Juliet noticed a handwritten out-of-order sign hanging from the turnstiles. It also indicated they should enter the subway two blocks north.

The confident woman didn't wait for her reaction, and soon, a man in a business suit was impatiently waiting behind Juliet.

She had latched on to this unsuspecting woman as a chick will imprint on its parent after cracking through its eggshell. She felt a surge of panic as the woman walked down yet another set of concrete steps. Juliet hopped over the out-of-order turnstile, hurrying down the steps after the woman.

Before exiting the stairwell, Juliet looked over her shoulder. The view of the sky was shrinking. Seeing this, her heartbeat slowed, and she was regaining her composure somewhat.

She needed Maury. He was the only human she could trust. He was so kind, and she knew, even in her self-aware naiveté, that they shared a flawless love.

The humans were getting restless. She could feel it building; soon blood would be shed. The city was a powder keg. In the few hours since she left the museum, the streets had cleared of most people. They had scurried into buildings, into the security of their homes, hiding from the uncertainty and fear that had so suddenly swept over the city. Somehow she knew those who remained on the streets were either trying desperately to get home, or were predators seeking out easy prey.

At the bottom of the stairwell, train rails ran on either side of the platform. A few people were boarding a train, and as Juliet scanned the crowd, she noticed the confident woman boarding just as the doors were sliding shut. The woman looked ahead of her without flinching or a sign of fear and the train quickly pulled away from the platform, disappearing as it rounded a bend in the tunnel.

Juliet was alone. She sensed rats nearby. The subway's air was heavy, pungent with the odor of urine and something else, something possibly wicked. Her hand began to twitch again, and tears gathered at her lashes, ready to fall.

She pulled her trembling hand tight to her body, and willed the dark thoughts away.

She didn't know what she was going to do. She didn't exactly have a plan beyond following that woman, and it wouldn't have taken long for the woman to grow weary of having someone straggle behind her like a neurotic shadow. And now she was alone in this oppressive, dank place. At least the world felt smaller, more manageable.

White light, shining like starlight, gleamed around the bend of the tunnel. The ground was shaking, and then in short order, a train appeared. At first, Juliet thought the confident woman had come back for her. She felt certain she would step from inside the train, calling out to her. She would invite Juliet to come home with her and welcome her into her confident family. But this train was following the previous one. Her brief hope snuffed out like a blown match.

She didn't know what else to do, or where to go, so she stepped aboard the train when the doors opened. She kept her eyes to the floor, hurrying down the aisle to find a seat before the train took off again. She scanned the car, noticing only one other person.

An odd man with a sneer of a smile pinching his face.

His gray hair was creeping through a dye job the color of drying mud. His skin shone like that of a cooked turkey. He looked old, used up, unhinged.

Juliet had been free of confinement and able to walk the streets for a total of a few hours. Even so, right away she knew this man was trouble.

He stood up, holding his briefcase at his side, and approached her. His stomach was paunchy, straining against a shirt that might have fit him in his youth. He stopped less than a foot away from her, taking hold of the vertical metal handrail. Her eyes leveled on his protruding stomach. She saw crumbs dotting the brown shirt's wash-faded fabric.

She didn't want to look up.

When she did, the man was smiling his ugly smile.

"Hello."

He shifted his weight as the L-train jounced against the rails. The side of his leg came in contact with her knee. He didn't move away when he righted himself.

She didn't respond to him, and after a few tense moments of silence, his leg wedged between her knees, spreading her legs slightly. She still didn't say anything, and could only look ahead, look ahead and hope this nightmare would end.

The tunnel blurred outside the window, becoming a dirty, milk-white sky.

Her hands were now quaking.

She wondered if she would be able to turn the dream-gun on this man to scare him off before she would inevitably blow her brains out.

The train shifted speeds, adjusting to climb a slight incline. The unnatural tunnel light was meshing with the day-lit sky. They were rising from the underground.

The first building she saw was on fire. Flames guttered from broken windows; black smoke billowed into the sky. For an instant, Juliet was distracted from the creepy man. She knew he was still looking down at her, and his leg was still pressed between her knees, but suddenly someone shattered an apartment window with their face. She couldn't tell if it was a man or woman. The flames had done too much damage. Just as soon as the building appeared, the train left it behind. Another building appeared, also on fire. The whole neighborhood seemed to be in flames.

"I like your eyes."

The man's gravelly voice ripped back her attention.

Before she could react, the train slowed as the hiss of air breaks punctured the steady hum of the ride. They were coming to another train stop.

The man quickly sat down next to her, and placed a hand on her thigh. She gasped. His grip hurt, but she didn't want to find out what he would do to her if she tried to move away.

"This was going to be our stop. It's near a secret place I know. Looks like that's out of the question."

As the train slowed, Juliet hoped she could make a break for the open doors. After seeing the burning neighborhood, and the people crowding the train stop, she'd changed her mind.

The doors opened and a handful of people filed onto the train. They looked like they had been through war. Their eyes were vacant, their faces grimed with ash. A man was crying into his hands.

The doors closed, and they were soon away.

"Don't worry." The man's hot breath licked her ear. "I know another place. A better place. Then we'll have time to get to know one another. Just keep on doing what you're doing. Everything'll be just fine."

A girl clung to her mother's arm. The mother was spacing out, her mind off to some saner place. But the girl was staring down at Juliet, staring at her, then to the crazed man. She looked worried.

The man noticed the girl watching them. He leaned over to Juliet, whispering, "Smile for the little girl. You're scaring her."

She did her best to comply. The girl looked away, not really satisfied by the gesture.

The man squeezed her thigh again, painfully, and said, "Good job, honey."

The young man imagined how he looked with his new lady. They probably looked like a young couple on a date. His hand squeezing her thigh, just one of those impetuous gestures of youth.

White noise, disinformation.

He smelled her auburn curls, trying to pin down its light scent. Couldn't place it. Puzzling--he normally could name the scents of shampoos, perfume, feminine hygiene sprays. His new lady was a mystery.

He had planned to get the girl off the train when it stopped, but there was no way he could wend his way with her through all that smoke. His secret room at the factory would most likely be in flames. The place manufactured electronic components. If looters hit any place, it would be that factory. In a way, he hoped they torched the place, sent it to the ground in gouts of fire and ash. He needed to find a new place; four months was probably too long as it was. The flames would clean the abandoned storage room of any trace evidence of his work. Would incinerate the blood-stained mattress, the tapestry of skins he'd left to dry on clotheslines.

The little girl glanced at his new woman, her face pulled taut with concern. She looked up to her mother, but sensed it was useless asking her for help.

His new woman's hands were shaking in her lap; he could feel it through the flesh of her thigh. He found her mounting fear arousing.

She turned to him, whispering through gritted teeth, "Don't hurt anyone. Please."

He purposefully laughed loud enough so everyone in the train car could hear. He leaned over to his new woman and kissed her on the cheek, again squeezing her thigh, this time playfully.

White noise. Disinformation.

A couple of mousy women looked their way, then quickly turned back to face the chaos sweeping the city. They were quite obviously seething with jealousy.

The two women looked at Juliet with sympathy; a sad look that reminded her of Sophie Marigold's expression when she would come to visit her in her enclosure at the museum. They sensed something was wrong, Juliet could see it in their eyes, but there was little they could do.

The L-train left the warehouse district to cut through a neighborhood of old brick apartments. It looked like the buildings would have been in sad shape even before the tenants had taken up arms against one another. As the train blurred by, Juliet caught a glimpse of a handgun held pointblank in someone's face. Then, somewhere at street level, gunshots resounded like scattered firecrackers, punctuated by occasional explosions of automatic weapons' fire.

The other passengers instinctively ducked down, and she imitated them. The man took this time of confusion to grope her breast.

Juliet slapped his hand away, and he exploded with oily-slick laughter.

"You're right, honey. Such displays are impolite in public. I can wait until we get home."

The train quickly left behind the battle zone neighborhood, and for the time being, it was quiet.

When Juliet sat back in her seat, her hand was trembling. It was going to be soon. In an instant, a gun would appear, and then she would add one more fright to the day of these strangers.

She overheard bits of a conversation between the women who had earlier looked to her with concern, "I heard she's covered in rats."

"Me too! They cover her like a winter coat."

"And she doesn't seem to be bothered at all by them."

"Can you imagine?"

"I think I would die."

"So would I. I just can't believe what the world is coming to."

"Don't worry. The mayor will call the president. The military will swoop in. Everything will be back to normal in a week."

"I hope you're right."

"I know I'm right. Dream creatures running wild through the city? Who would've ever thought..."

Juliet looked to her clasped hands resting in her lap. It was time. In the blink of an eye, the heavy steel appeared in her sweaty palm. She felt her arm begin to raise the gun.

The sunlight outside brightened, the gray cloud cover instantly burned away. Clear, warm rain peppered the train's windows.

"Well, would you look at that?" one woman turned to the other. "The sun's out, and it's raining. Some day this is turning out to be."

The man noticed the gun. His brow tightened, perplexed.

"What the hell?" he blurted, pulling his hand from her thigh and sliding away.

The air brakes hissed as the train slowed. The passengers didn't notice the gun. They all seemed intent on leaving the train. They gathered at the closed doors, waiting for the instant they could leave the train and then do whatever they could to make sense of what was happening to a once sane world.

"Don't touch me. Ever again."

The doors split open a second after the train stopped, and the people spilled through the opening. Juliet's rain clouds pushed under the corrugated metal ceiling of the train stop, pushed clear through the doors and into the train car. The man watched all of this happening, then turned his gaze to Juliet.

She was struggling against the suicidal impulses guiding her hand. The gun was at shoulder height, cocked toward her head, moving jerkily toward her temple. She was fighting it, fighting it and losing. The car was once again empty but for the two of them.

Understanding swept over the man's features. His crow's feet deepened, and his hair seemed somehow grayer than just moments before.

"You... you're one of them! You're a dream-woman!" he shouted accusingly at her.

Juliet stood and backed away from the man. Back all the way to the still-open doors. She exited the train, but held her arm inside the doorway. The doors slammed shut on her wrist, and just as she hoped, the dream-gun fired directly at him.

Of course, he was unharmed--her dream-gun could hurt no one other than herself--but his hands flew up to his chest anyway. His horrified expression shifted to one of defeat. The train pulled away, stripping the gun from her grip.

Juliet saw a group of policemen disembark from the train a few cars ahead. They wore riot gear--helmets with visors protecting their faces, shields held out as if they were medieval knights--and they were heading in her direction. One man broke ranks from the rest, approaching her.

She was on the verge of running when the man spoke to her, his brown eyes like pits of chocolate buried behind the visor, "Are you okay, ma'am?"

The dozen or so riot-ready police officers continued walking by before turning up a set of stairs, ready to face whatever craziness they would find above.

"Ma'am?"

"Yes... fine. I'm fine. Thanks."

"You should get to safety. There's a curfew, you know. Eight o'clock. I'd escort you myself, but things are starting to get out of hand."

"Thanks. I'll be fine. Really."

The policeman nodded, then left, hurrying to catch up with the others.

Juliet was reenergized by the exchange. She felt confident. Maybe not nearly to the level of the woman who had led her to the subway, but perhaps enough to allow her to get by in this world. Hopefully long enough for her to track down the only man she could ever love.

CHAPTER TWENTY

When Kevin left Sophie's apartment, he had no clue about where he would go. Fear gnawed at him again, the security of his new friends left behind. He just kept moving--down Sophie's street, turning at random, zigzagging through blocks of residential homes and mom and pop businesses. He still couldn't get the image of Andrew's mural out of his head. The image of the tranquil fields was appealing. He had to get away from the city. There were too many hiding spots from which Mr. Freakshow could swoop down on him. He thought about the painting, and he suddenly knew where he should go. Instantly he understood, yet it was so obvious he felt like kicking himself for not thinking of it sooner.

Kevin was going to go home. All the way to Warren Cove, Kevin was going home.

But the logistics of it seemed far too daunting. First, he had to accomplish the simple act of finding the bus station. And then he would need to buy a ticket and ride for hours on end without blowing his cover. How he would pull off every step of the journey without Mr. Freakshow finding him, he hadn't a clue. He felt like running, but he didn't know which way to find the bus station.

He watched the early morning people as they walked by. A man shambled in rags for clothes, his scraggly beard hiding the details of his face. All Kevin saw were his dark eyes, and the uneasiness they caused made Kevin offer a wide berth. People enclosed in their own little worlds hurried down the sidewalk, on their way to work despite the curfew and increased police vigilance to track down the dreams. A mixture of spray starch, hair spray and toxic amounts of cologne trailed them like Pigpen's dirt cloud. He avoided all of these morning people. Either they were too busy to be bothered, or not busy enough. He didn't feel comfortable in either case.

At the next intersection, with the rambling L-tracks overhead, the pillars and rails blocking the sun, he came across a newsstand. Inside the wooden shed was a short man, nearly as short as Kevin, his bushy gray eyebrows like ancient caterpillars resting on his forehead. His expression was not too busy or not busy enough at all. Somewhere in between. Kevin reached into his pocket and handed over some coins for a Sun Times. Stolen water fountain coins.

"Where's the bus station?"

"Which one?" the newsstand guy barked.

"I don't know... the closest one?"

"End of block, first left, another block, turn right, four blocks down." The man sounded like he had recited this bit a thousand times.

"Okay, thanks."

The newsstand guy helped the next customer, someone buying a Crane's Business and a sickly brown banana from a wooden bowl sitting next to the cash register.

As Kevin walked away, he ran through the directions in his head and realized he had forgotten most of them. It probably didn't matter. The station was somewhere *over there*. It would be big and loud, hard to miss. If those office buildings weren't in the way, he would probably see it from here.

He lost his bearings more than once, doubling back several blocks in the process, but eventually made it to the bus station. It was a steel and glass structure with long corridors with Plexiglas cases on the walls with ads for the U.S. Army, and the National Bank of LaGrange. The morning sun shone through the girder and glass roof, throwing a web-like shadow across the floor. These station people seemed to be in more of a hurry than the pedestrians just down the block. A dozen people bumped him, pushed him, and griped at him by the time he reached the enormous waiting area. Row upon row of wooden benches lined the white tiled floor. Caged-in ticket windows dotted the waiting area at odd intervals. The place teemed with people, like ants scurrying over garden soil.

A policeman walked slowly through the crowd, giving people the eye. No one bumped into him, or griped at him about how slowly he walked. He moved at his own pace, scrutinizing everyone in his path. Kevin imagined the police department having a sketch of him, that they had put out an APB on him, whatever that was, all because he stomped on that policeman's foot yesterday. He spied an open spot at a wooden bench and sat down quickly. He opened his newly bought Chicago Sun Times, and waited for the heat to blow over.

He figured it would be no time at all before the cop ripped the newspaper from his hands and cuffed him. But nothing happened. The young couple next to him stood up to leave and a woman with three kids filled the empty spot on the bench. She swayed a bundled boy in her arms, trying to calm his cries. Kevin tried to ignore his new bench neighbors. The headline from the newspaper caught his attention. Actually, he was surprised he hadn't noticed the huge block letters before now.

A CITY TERRORIZED!

He didn't read beyond the headline. Didn't want to. Lucidity was on the other side of the city, yet he could still sense the tension in just about everyone he came across. Since he left Sophie's apartment, he'd overheard people mumbling about riots and random violence, of dream-creatures attacking people, and people banding together to fight back since it seemed like the police didn't know what they were doing.

All because of him.

He folded over the paper quickly, as if trying to capture a cockroach, and the woman next to him gave him a dirty look for further upsetting her crying child with his noise. Kevin gave up his spot and went to the nearest ticket window.

"One one-way ticket for Warren Cove."

A sleepy-eyed ticket agent looked down at him. "I.D. please."

"What for?"

"Security. You're too young to buy your own ticket."

"I don't have I.D."

"No I.D., no ticket."

Kevin could see his plan crumbling before his eyes. If he couldn't take the bus to Warren Cove, how was he going to get home? An idea popped into his head.

"Mom sent me to buy the ticket because she's kinda got her hands full." Kevin pointed behind him, indicating the woman with the crying child. "Believe me," Kevin's eyes went wide and he lowered his voice, "You don't want to mess with my mom. She's got PMS." He hoped he had his terminology right. From what he saw on T.V., women just get angry sometimes, terribly angry, for no other reason than PMS. Whatever that was.

The sleepiness lifted from the ticket agent's eyes. He leaned forward, giving Kevin a knowing look. He watched the woman holding the child, and he shook his head. She was bouncing the baby in her arms, a little too roughly, while staring daggers at Kevin. Obviously, he ruined her day by ruffling his newspaper. The other two children, boys or girls, Kevin couldn't tell by their neutral clothes and blunt haircuts, were dancing in a small circle, one of those square dance routines Kevin remembered having to do in gym class.

"Should I get her to pay for the ticket?"

"No, I guess if she's right there. We don't want to bother her. Warren Cove, right? That'll be $23. Bus boards in... let's see, twenty minutes."

Kevin pulled one of Sophie's crisp twenties from his pocket, along with three dollars in quarters from his water fountain treasure.

The ticket agent gave him a too friendly smile and slid him the ticket.

Kevin felt empowered holding the ticket. He didn't know he could think on his feet so quickly. He held the ticket in his hand, not trusting it out of sight, and walked back toward the woman. He stood just behind her, close enough to appear to be her son, far enough away that she couldn't swat him with an angry paw. The ticket agent watched him before helping his next customer. The man still shook his head sympathetically, and then the shifting crowd swallowed him from sight.

Kevin scanned the ticket for his departure gate. He left his bogus family and sat on a wooden bench closer to where he would board the bus.

He ate five of Sophie's cookies while waiting for the departure time. As people began to board, he dusted the crumbs from his lap, lifted his backpack to his shoulder, and waited for the line to thicken. He thought the bus driver would challenge him as he came aboard, but she didn't even give him a second glance. The driver was middle aged with greasy blond hair plastered to her head. From the narrowness of her head, she widened all the way to her waist, until her ample thighs overhung the plush captain's chair. She smelled like fast food chicken, and Kevin was glad when she handed him his ticket back. Another step taken. A few more steps, and he would be home.

The people boarding were anxious, eager to be away from the city. Just to complete his playacting, he stopped and waved to a couple sitting on one of the wooden benches. They looked to be about his parents' age and they gave an indifferent wave in return. He turned and made his way to the back of the bus before he drew any attention.

The bus jumped as it started and kicked into gear. The people crowding around him took out headphones or crosswords or paperbacks to wile away the time. Kevin was antsy. He had nothing to do to ward off boredom. Or fear. He was buzzing off the sugary cookies he'd just eaten, and needed to take a leak. The door for the restroom was nearby. He stood, taking his backpack with him.

He realized he was going to finally take a leak on a bus. Just what his dad wanted him to do in the first place. If only... if only.

Kevin stayed in the cramped restroom long after he had flushed the stainless steel bowl, his urine mixing with the mysterious blue fluid, dropping into some holding pod. To help dry up the tears that flowed as soon as he entered the restroom, he thought of aimless stuff--T.V. shows and comic books and his new school. But what lingered after everything else drifted away was the feeling of responsibility for the death of his dad, that he had somehow killed him. He knew he would never be free of the thought. He wiped the few tears from his eyes with a gritty paper towel before returning to his seat.

The engine roared beneath him, and it was easy to let it lull him to sleep. As he closed his eyes, he hoped the next time he opened them he would find himself looking at the arching sign of his hometown bus station. Warren Cove: pop. 7220.

When he woke groggily, he looked out the window. The driver had stopped the bus, and the folding doors at the entrance were open to the chilly dusk air. He saw the bus driver wobbling back to the bus after purchasing a fill up of gasoline. Held in her meaty arm were at least three packs of Zingers and a two-liter of cola. A couple of passengers came aboard after finishing off hastily smoked cigarettes. In no time, the bus was moving again with night rapidly descending. Kevin had no idea where they were or how soon he would be home. He was chilled from the cold air coming through the open folding doors. He unzipped his backpack to take out his windbreaker, but it wasn't there. He could have sworn it was in the main pocket. It wasn't in the medium sized pocket, either. He must have lost it.

He thought back on where he could have left the windbreaker, tried thinking of the last time he had it. The last day or so had been relatively warm, so shirtsleeves had suited him fine.

The water fountain. It was the last place he could remember having it. He had taken it off so he could fish out the change. His mom would be so pissed if she found out he'd lost it. The bus rambled on, and Kevin tried to block out the thought of his mom. He no longer had a mom. If he had a mom then she would be in danger by association. Goosebumps danced up his arms, over his shoulders and across his back. He pulled the fabric of his gym shirt tighter, knowing that as he

177

got closer to home, he still didn't know what he expected to find there.

When he opened his eyes, it wasn't to the familiar Warren Cove sign or the bus driver stopping off for more gas and junk food. A terror-filled shriek tore at his eardrums. He snapped awake, as did everyone else aboard the bus. The driver slammed on the breaks, the wheels skidding along the gravel-littered blacktop. As the bus came to a stop, the shrieking also stopped abruptly. An eerie silence filled the bus.

A man seated halfway to the front called out, "Did you hit someone? Maybe we should check..."

"I didn't hit nobody. I never hit nobody in my life," the driver shouted back.

Passengers peered out windows, everyone keeping their ears perked for that stomach-turning shriek. Sure enough, it started again, crying out in fear, pained to the point of near-rapture, and the shrieking became louder with each passing second. Kevin gathered his backpack and readied himself for the unexpected.

Quite suddenly, the roof of the bus came crashing in, bringing the shrieking in with it in the form of a woman. The passengers pushed away from the crumpled body. Shattered bones stuck through skin, and the body was doubled over at a weird angle as if it had no spine. Kevin pushed along with everyone else as the bus emptied. He had to duck under the caved-in section of the bus roof, and as he lowered his head he saw her smashed face and that she was still alive. She was, in fact, smiling. As he tried to walk by, she reached out for him with an arm that had far too many joints. Her blood-thick laughter carried with him as he exited the bus, the cold wind ruffling the thin cotton of his shirt.

"Dear mother'n Jesus. JesusJesus," the driver spouted at Kevin as he walked past her. The passengers formed a small circle outside the bus, rubbing their arms for warmth, hugging one another, scared out of their minds.

"What the hell is that?" one passenger asked.

"What do you think? It's a dream you dumb ass. You think a woman falls through the sky, comes crashing through the roof of a bus moving through corn fields could be anything else?"

"Well, maybe..."

"Haven't you read the news or seen the T.V.? Have you had your head stuck up your ass the last three days?" The man was livid. His wife took hold of him, burying her face in his chest. "God damn it! What a fucking world we live in."

"What do we do now?" a timid-looking woman asked.

"I don't know, but my cell phone doesn't work out here."

"I'm not getting back on that bus, not with that... that thing in there."

Kevin folded his arms across his chest, not sure what was going on.

The falling dream's laughter became louder, a wheezing liquid-sick noise. Something crashed within the bus, and looking through the windows, Kevin saw the dream-woman walking down the aisle, toward the front of the bus.

"Hell with that. Damn bus company can get their damn bus," the bus driver said. "Next town's just up the road. I'm gonna huff it, find a motel." She was opening a pack of raspberry Zingers as she walked away toward a low halo of light just over the horizon.

"Hey, what's the next town?" Kevin shouted.

"Podunk piece of shit. Warren Cove," the bus driver called out over her shoulder.

The falling dream tumbled down the bus steps, her shattered limbs unable to carry her weight. She was a broken bundle of twigs, blood dripping over her denim clothes looking like black syrup under the light of the weak moon.

The crowd of passengers scattered. Kevin didn't need to be told twice. His hometown was just over the hill. He started sprinting, quickly leaving behind the other passengers, passing the bus driver as she bit into a Zinger, an indulgent look on her face. He took a quick look over his shoulder before he lost sight of the stopped bus. The falling dream writhed on the gravel shoulder, writhed under the pain of her wounds. Somehow she still laughed, coughing up convulsive mouthfuls of blood. But she started to fade and soon disappeared altogether. As Kevin crested the hill, he saw the outskirts of Warren Cove, saw the abandoned and familiar Michael & Son's Service station (where he used to buy his baseball cards before it closed a year ago).

Kevin heard the falling dream's shriek. Somewhere high up, far away, falling through the air, enraptured by the thrill of falling, frightened by her impending impact, the falling dream carried on her cycle of life and death.

Kevin slowed as he reached the service station. It looked run down, more so than when he left Warren Cove at the beginning of the summer. Plywood boards covered the windows now, and they had graffiti decorations. *Drew luvs Emily*, one read, with a big black X through the Emily. Below it, another name, *Taylor Swift*. Kevin didn't need to think about it. Right away, he knew who Drew was. Drew Johanson had bullied him last year, had punched him in the face at the bus stop the day Kevin wore a new pair of Nike's. Emily what's her name--she was some cheerleader from Harrison Academy in Claremont, the next town over. After coming home with a fat lip, Kevin's dad had a little talk with Drew after school the next day. He had taken off early from work, had stopped Drew outside the school, and pulled him aside to where no one could hear or see them. By the end of the conversation, his dad had Drew crying. The big bully was crying. To top it all off, his dad drove the bully home.

That night over dinner, his dad told him that Drew Johanson was someone to feel sorry for, not fear. While blubbering to his dad, Drew mentioned his clothes were from the Salvation Army because his family had no money. His dad drank his paychecks and his mom worked all the time. While telling Kevin this, he put his strong hand on his shoulder, gaining his full attention. He told him that humiliating Drew by letting him ride the bus with his eyes all puffy from crying would only make him strike out at some smaller kid again. That's why he drove Drew home while Kevin had ridden the bus that day.

At first, he was mad at his dad. Kevin had wanted him to punch Drew's lights out. But as time went on, Kevin had gained a deeper appreciation for his dad. Not only that, but Drew Johanson had left him alone.

Kevin thought of all this when he saw that one spray-painted plywood board at Michael and Son's service station. His memories of his hometown came flooding back, seemingly with every step he took closer to his home.

Kevin walked by the baseball field where he hit his first home run. Actually, it wasn't much of a hit. It was a looper over the first baseman's head. The ball trickled down to the right field corner. When the fielder threw the ball back to the infield, it squirted through the infield, all the way in to foul territory. All the while, Kevin was tearing tail around the bases. The opponent's pitcher scooped up the ball and threw home, but Kevin was already popping up from his slide, a cloud of dirt flying everywhere. He smiled at the memory. Smiled even more when he remembered how his family had gone to Renaldi's on Main Street for a celebratory pizza.

Since passing Michael & Son's, a noticeable amount of ease came to his limbs. His shoulders were no longer tense, and his pace slowed. He tight-roped the concrete curb down Chase Avenue. When he reached Winfield Road, the road where he grew up, his heartbeat picked up again. He could see the Stover Realty sign still in the front yard, a white beacon a block away. The houses were quiet and dark as he walked by. The Ruby's, the Hanover's, Scotty Beckman's. All asleep, all unaware that Kevin had come home.

When he finally reached his house, it looked so much smaller than his memory. A dollhouse version of what was in his head. The lawn was mowed, but looked jagged, as if cut with a pair of pruning scissors freehand. The bushes lining the front walk had over-grown their manicured shape--some kind of plantlife on steroids. It seemed like a stranger's house.

Did I ever live here?

The eaves needed a coat of paint. Funny how he never noticed the eaves when he lived here. The kidney-shaped rock was still where he remembered it, under the bush near the front door. He turned it over and picked up his spare key. They had been in such a rush to move to his grandma's house and so blinded by the loss of his dad they had forgotten about little things. He wondered what else he would find once inside.

He pushed aside the realtor's lock box and unlocked the door. When he pushed it open, the door's weather strip gave him a swooshing hello. Once he closed the door and had the key in his pocket, tears again formed in his eyes. The smell of the house did it. It smelled warm and soothing. It smelled like family. He blinked away the tears and walked to the empty fireplace. He lowered his backpack to the floor, only now realizing how sore he felt. He nearly collapsed to the floor of the empty living room. Using his backpack as a crude pillow, Kevin settled in, closed his eyes. In seconds, he was asleep, sleeping the deep and easy sleep of someone who is finally home.

The stars over Warren Cove cut through the sky as thin clouds peeled away. The moon was a dewy apparition haunting the darkness for the short while before it fell to the horizon. The still and somber night soon became unsettled. Dogs barked at shifting shadows. Cats clawed at doors for their owners to let them inside. Children wept, their eyelids tightly bunched as they slept, fearful of the nightmares stalking about their minds. The night had been set on edge, and there was a clear and simple reason. Mr. Freakshow was on his way.

CHAPTER TWENTY-ONE

A policeman was kind enough to drive Carin and Maury back to her mother's house. The early evening sky looked like a new bruise. Dark purple and sore. High winds off Lake Michigan roiled the clouds, bullying them into dropping their fat raindrops. As the squad car pulled up to the curb, the cold late summer rain pummeled the windshield. The street was lined with a few unmarked cars and hastily parked squad cars. An ambulance drove by, leaving the scene without lights flashing or siren blaring. They exited the dry interior of the squad car and hurried through the growing puddles to the front of the house. Just outside the door, a group of policemen milled about the front yard, their clothes heavy with rain. They all seemed to be smoking, all of them inhaling deeply, inhaling like the smoke would purify them of what they had seen inside.

"I don't want any part of this. Even if they took her away, I don't want to see where they found her," Carin said to Maury.

"Don't worry. Just stay by my side." Since he approached her at the police station, she had given in to his influence. He was the one who suggested coming back to the house. She had vehemently opposed the idea, but he reassured her it would only be for a few minutes.

"We'll get the photos of Kevin for the policemen, then we can start our own search." He was also hoping to get some idea of where the boy had gone. Something at the house could jog Carin's memory.

The policeman who drove them stopped before they entered the house. "Folks, you don't have to worry about getting near the crime scene. The immediate area, the living room, the hallway leading to the kitchen, we have that blocked off for the investigation. We've cleared the west side of the house--the bedrooms, bathroom, and so forth. You can go there as long as an officer tags along."

"I have the photos in my room. I'm also going to get a few things. I don't think I could stay here. Ever."

One of the milling policemen dropped his cigarette to the wet grass and stomped it out with his foot.

Quite suddenly, anger surged through Maury. "Pick that up," he said, an unfamiliar strength to his voice.

"What?" The policeman was young, brash. He would look as big as a football player even without his Kevlar vest.

Carin stopped just shy of the door. As far as Maury could tell, she hadn't noticed the group of officers, and hadn't been able to focus on anything for more than a few seconds.

"The cigarette. Pick it up. Show some respect." Maury said, his voice stern. He didn't know what had come over him. He was never demonstrative, and would never envision speaking up to a policeman. He glared at the policeman, and he felt like he would vomit if he said anything more. If this young bag of muscles wasn't going to pound him, he was at least going to ask for his driver's license, and run his info through whatever supercomputer the police used to dredge up dirt on people. If they had a file on Maury that contained only suspicion and insinuation, it would fill a file cabinet.

The policeman picked up the butt and dropped it in an empty Coke can he was carrying. "Sorry." He looked like a beaten dog. Maybe he saw the strain on Maury's face. A buzz seemed to travel through the other officers, but no other interaction took place. Maury heard a muffled chuckle from the group as he turned away and entered the house.

"Thanks. Mom always took care of the yard herself. She worked hard. I appreciate it."

"No problem. Let's get the pictures so we can get you out of here."

Maury didn't want to see her mother's blood any more than Carin did. He couldn't tolerate the sight of blood, and he had already seen enough today to last a lifetime. Lucidity was in ruins. At least three people were dead. Nolan Gage, his daughter, Nicole, Peter What's-his-name. Four. Four people dead if you count Carin's mother. How high would the death toll soar? If they could find Kevin quickly, Maury could limit the damage. If Maury killed the boy, Mr. Freakshow would be no more. He would take his killing ways with him. And Juliet would no longer be in danger. At least from the boy's nightmare.

The police officer shielded Carin from the view of the living room as they walked toward the bedrooms. Maury did his best to avoid seeing the bloodstains, the bits of flesh undoubtedly smashed into the carpet after they took away the ravaged body of her mother. But the smell. It reminded him of when he was a kid, long before the apartment fire, when his family had picnicked at a roadside park. The sun was shining, a breeze whipped through the trees. Dale was horsing around with the souvenir black bear statue from Machesney State Park, where they had just camped for a week. Dale roared like a bear in his little kid voice as their mom spread the blanket and their dad readied the food. But the wind picked up, changing directions, ruining the picturesque end to an enjoyable vacation. The stench hit them like a physical blow. Like roadkill--flattened meat, seeping internal fluids seeking lower ground-- this odor magnified ten fold. Their father didn't know he'd chosen to picnic a quarter mile from the Fredrickson Meat Co., a meat packing plant in the middle of nowhere, a place where two hundred people slaughtered animals and processed meat for a living. A plant surrounded by miles of postcard scenery.

The rotting flesh stench of the meat packing plant was in Carin's childhood home. The stench of thousands of slaughtered animals at a quarter mile away.

Maury didn't realize Carin had left him and was down the hall, in one of the bedrooms. While she was gathering a few belongings, he had subconsciously turned to face the living room, with its framed family photos, dated furniture and small T.V. He was looking in on a slaughter, seeing the stains that would never leave this place, a man wearing a brown tweed jacket, a loosened and wrinkled tie, checking the murder scene for any left behind clues. Maury's head was swimming. The bluntness of this. The crudeness. Stumbling away from the living room, he made it down the short hallway to the bathroom and closed the door. He turned on the faucet and waited to heave up whatever was in his stomach.

A knock came to the door. He thought it might be the officer telling him that the bathroom was off limits to him unless accompanied by a chaperone. Someone to hold back his hair as he vomited, making sure he didn't touch anything that might be evidence.

"Maury, I found something. Possibly a clue. Maury, are you okay?"

Carin didn't know what to think of it. It wasn't exactly evidence, she supposed. Could something be evidence if it was missing? Maybe the fact she didn't find Kevin's windbreaker only meant something to her. A mother-thing, a mother-clue. It wasn't on the back of his desk chair or in his closet. He had taken it with him. It could only mean that he had prepared his escape into the night and hadn't been stolen away by some vile beast.

"Maury?"

She waited at the bathroom door, her attending officer never more than a couple steps away.

"Ma'am, if you have any information, you should tell the investigators."

"It's nothing. I just didn't see my son's jacket. It's a red windbreaker."

The officer took a nub of pencil from his pocket and jotted something in a small black notebook. He didn't press her for anything more. He put away his notebook and looked quite bored. "I'll pass it on."

The door opened, and Maury stepped out. His face was blanched, his eyes watery. "Sorry. I... I don't know, I just didn't feel well."

"Kevin's windbreaker is gone."

"So? Perhaps it's in the living room." Maury immediately regretted the words. He didn't want to go back to search for the jacket. He wanted to go outside, even with the rain-soaked skies making it seem more like the middle of the night than dusk, he wanted to go outside and get some fresh air.

Carin spoke quietly, but excitedly, "Kevin knew. Somehow, he knew Mr. Freakshow would come for him."

"He could have seen something on T.V. about what happened at Lucidity."

"What exactly happened at the museum?"

Maury wasn't about to tell Carin that his mind was foggy and not so sharp because he had just lost his virginity at thirty-five years to a dream-woman.

Oh yeah, Mr. Freakshow, your son's nightmare, tricked me into opening his enclosure. Now your son will most likely die a horrible death.

"Some kind of containment failure. Not sure yet. But that's not important right now. We need to find Kevin."

"If that's the case and it was on T.V., he didn't see it. We rented a movie. He went to bed right after." She approached an officer. "Can I pack a bag? I don't want to stay here. If anything, I'm getting a hotel room." The idea that her son was out there somewhere, aware enough to run from Mr. Freakshow, aware enough that he should fight for his life, brought her a strange sense of calm. For the time being, she buried any thoughts of her mother. It was cold of her to do, but Kevin still needed her. She couldn't be weak now.

"Just don't disturb anything. It looks cut and dry. Everything took place out in the living room. Nothing appears to be stolen..." the officer trailed off. He was going to carry on, Carin realized. Without thinking, the officer was going to say her mother's murder was routine. The look on his face said it all. The officers, all the investigators, they could all see the blood and gore spread throughout the living room and divine the killer's intentions, his motives. Just that quickly. They didn't know what they were getting themselves into. They weren't dealing with an ordinary sadistic killer. They were dealing with a nightmare.

Carin shook her head at the officer as she went to her room to gather a change of clothes. She had to be honest with herself. She wasn't going to rest until she found her son, and she was never coming back here again. This was the beginning of some kind of end game. A game in which she didn't know the rules.

She took her credit cards from the top drawer of her dresser and put them in her wallet. She saw Kevin's smiling face inside the bifold. His class picture from last year. It was the best picture she had of him. It showed his innocent eyes. His warm smile. As she slipped the picture from her wallet, she noticed her hands were shaking. She grabbed clothes at random from her dresser and tossed them into a gym bag. She took one last look at the room. Her cheerleading trophies were on a nearby shelf and she felt like she was robbing some girl's bedroom.

Maury leaned against the doorframe, watching her as she gathered her belongings. "Can you think of where he might be? A safe place he might go?" His cheeks had returned to their normal color, but he still looked nauseated.

"No. I don't. Kevin doesn't know the city. Well... maybe the park. He's played baseball a couple of blocks from here." She carried the gym bag as she walked by Maury. "This is the best picture of my son. I trust you can make copies?" She handed the picture to the officer who had given them the ride to her mother's house. He nodded grimly.

Carin continued down the hall, and using the gym bag to block her view of the living room, she left the house. She didn't wait for Maury. She ran through the rain and was inside her Explorer before Maury had even reached the front door. She turned on the engine and put the heat on high.

While she waited for Maury, she wondered why she was with him.

Why would he want to help Carin? He had always struck her as odd. It wasn't just his appearance, his scars, his worn baseball cap. Maury seemed twitchy, like something was wriggling inside of him, trying to get loose, and he had to use all of his will just to suppress whatever it was.

She thought of the night she found Kevin outside the garage, in the throes of a terrifying dream. As she and her mother tried to calm him, Carin had noted the clutter on her father's workbench. Kevin had nailed wooden blocks together in peculiar formations. She first thought someone had desecrated her father's favorite place. The place where he had made toys and dollhouses for Carin and the bookshelves lining her bedroom walls. With Kevin's cries weakening, Carin had realized what he had been building in the middle of the night. The odd formations of wood blocks, in a crude way, reminded her of their old house.

If there was one place where Kevin would feel safe, it was their old house in Warren Cove. She felt an urgency to drive there as soon as possible. But Maury Bennett. Something just wasn't right with him.

Maury ran to the Explorer and waited outside the locked passenger door, getting wetter by the second, before Carin decided to unlock it.

"Sorry about that. My mind's elsewhere."

"Should we go to the park first?" Water dripped from his face.

"I have a better idea."

Their breath quickly clouded the windshield. She didn't know what bothered her about Maury, but if he could in some way help with Mr. Freakshow, she realized it didn't matter. The only thing that mattered to her anymore was the safety of her son.

"We're going to Warren Cove." She backed the Explorer onto the street, pausing after she shifted into drive. She looked at her childhood home, with the officers standing in her mother's front lawn, cupping their cigarettes from the rain, the investigators inside searching the living room's bloody carpet fibers for extraneous information. It was as if she was staring at a stranger's house.

They're having a block party.

The mingling policemen were partygoers and the investigators were the overworked hosts of the party, so busy that they didn't know what was going on. She drove away, certain she would never see her childhood home again.

That bitch-whore. Barring the door. Keeping him from entering her home. Mr. Freakshow was livid over what happened at Sophie

Marigold's apartment. And the sheer amount of dream energy the place contained. It had confused him, temporarily making him lose contact with the boy. He would definitely pay another visit to that bitch-whore's apartment.

Just as soon as--

Tires squealed from the street as a driver tried to control his fishtailing car in the rain. The car jumped the curb and was barreling down on Mr. Freakshow. The rain had chased away most of the pedestrians. He was alone on the sidewalk.

Leaping into the air, he ripped off his tan overcoat, exposing his limp wings. The car hurtled by below him, crashing into the brick wall of a bakery. Blood filled his wings, and he swept through the air, cutting through the rain, feeling alive, alert, and oh so ready to kill.

He flew in a small arc, getting used to his wings in the human world. He landed on the hood of the car that had nearly splattered him. The car horn blared, and people from inside the bakery spilled out into the rain. One man held a cell phone to his ear. Another used his phone to snap photos of the wreck. As soon as they saw the Freak without pretense of disguise, with his clawed feet piercing the hood of the car, his wings fluttering behind him, they ran back into the building.

Mr. Freakshow jumped down to the sidewalk. The driver was bleeding from several wounds--his forehead, nose, mouth--and was holding a newspaper in his lap, trying to catch the blood before it could stain the car's interior.

The driver gave Mr. Freakshow a defensive smile. "It's a rental. I... I just want... I have to get my deposit back..." he said with a short laugh. A gob of blood burst from his ruined nose as he coughed, a blackish splatter hitting the steering wheel. Still, the horn blared.

"Don't worry about that deposit. I'm afraid it's lost already." Mr. Freakshow took hold of the driver's head, slamming it into the steering column. With the force of the blow, the man's face compressed the steering column and silenced the annoying horn.

The car's engine continued to sputter, stuck in idle, smashed against the brick wall of the bakery. Otherwise, the rainy dusk was peaceful. Blissfully quiet. The Freak leapt into the air, glancing over his shoulder at his glorious wings. He flexed the muscles in his back, pumping his wings, and gained distance from the ground, the rain beating down on his face, feeling cold against his deadman-blue skin. He flew higher, passing the roofs of buildings, passing the antennae towers and ventilation grates spilling plumes of white smoke to the sky.

Mr. Freakshow glided on the thermals given off by the humans.

Their heat cast off like waste, like some kind of fecal matter. The limitless sky spread before him, an uncharted map for him to explore.

But the boy... How could he have forgotten the boy?

As he flew higher into the heavens, the rain freezing pinpricks into his skin, Mr. Freakshow reached out to Kevin. With the tenuous strand of energy connecting them, he reached out, finding a confused and addled mass of raw misery. Kevin was on the move again. He had been with Sophie, there was no doubt. But afterward, when he left the old bitch-whore's welcoming embrace... ah, Mr. Freakshow knew the answer, his destination.

He changed directions, finding joy in every motion of his flight. He pumped his wings, launching toward the horizon, a pale blue streak. He knew where Kevin wanted to hide out, and he would make sure he was there when Kevin arrived.

CHAPTER TWENTY-TWO

While Kevin was riding the Greyhound to Warren Cove, and while his mother and Maury were driving to intercept him, the city of Chicago was suffering under the weight of uncertainty and fear.

A fender bender brought a section of midafternoon traffic to a standstill as drivers gawked at a group of four dream-children flying through the concrete and steel skyscraper valleys, chasing one another in a spirited game of tag. Most people stared, some shouted. Even the policewoman directing traffic had to stop and stare at the sight. Drivers climbed from cars, shouting, taunting, soon punching and gouging. Anger welled to the brink of anarchy, then quickly flooded its banks...

A small percentage of the citizenry, bound to slip a bearing at the slightest provocation, took up arms against their fellow man. Shameful displays of violence and exploitation spread throughout the city. Humans attacking humans, using the dreams running amuck to leverage their own advantage. They raided, pilfered, smashed to bits convenience stores, pawn shops, delicatessens. Thieves were filmed in broad daylight by security and tourist cameras alike, carrying armloads of snack food, old worn guitars, foot-long hoagies, anything worth a penny's worth of their spite. These thieves, rioters, no-good, take-it-when-you-can-get-it parasites wore smiles, snubbed their noses at the confused and overworked police force.

The mayor--his beady eyes stinging with sweat, and sporting the expression of a querulous brat--read from a prepared statement during a press conference:

"As you already know, the city of Chicago has instituted a citywide 8 p.m. curfew. All businesses will be closed by the indicated time, including restaurants and taverns, and the streets will remain vacated until 4 a.m." The mayor stopped reading from the slip of paper and spoke directly to the camera, "Let me stress, this is a short term thing. Until we can assess the nature of this situation, until we can mobilize and stabilize this situation, it is in the best interest of the city to move forward in this fashion..."

The mayor mopped his brow with his omnipresent kerchief, and spoke to an advisor off to the side. He addressed the crowd of reporters again, the small conference room awash in cascading camera flashes, "Now, we have a job to do. I will speak again when we learn anything more." He bunched his lips in a way the seasoned reporters knew to be his punctuation at the end of a press conference. It meant, *don't mess with me. You all love me because you know my name, you vote for me, even though I'm as charismatic as a weeklong flu.*

He might have underestimated the reporters' vehemence on the subject. It's not every day a major city has dozens of embodied dreams wreaking havoc. They clamored after the mayor, even as he mopped his brow with his kerchief, sighing the sigh of relief of a man who doesn't feel comfortable speaking in public. Before he could reach the door of the conference room and the security blanket of his awaiting staff of advisors, one reporter's pleading questions rang truer and louder than all the others:

"Mr. Mayor, Mr. Mayor! Will this change how we live, as Chicagoans, can we expect this to change how others think of us?"

The mayor stopped in his tracks, without turning around, thinking about what the young reporter said. He turned and received a face full of flash bulbs. He waited for the room to quiet down. "What's your name, son?"

"Quentin de la Santa, sir."

"Mr. Santo... say, are you related to Ron? No? Well anyway, all I can say is we're working on it. We're setting up a communications network throughout the city... it'll be like a web. We'll have full-blown communications... I'm talking the police and fire departments, local F.B.I., neighborhood watch programs, everything, and we won't stop until this thing is contained. You want to know how this effects how others see us? I can't say for certain Mr. Santo, but I know Chicagoans. We work hard. We're blue collar people, and we do whatever it takes."

The mayor turned and exited into the arms of his advisors. The conference room erupted in shouts and flashbulbs. The room quickly cleared, and the reporters took to the street, intent on making or maintaining their status in the local and national media. They took to the streets ready to cover one of the most unimaginable and perplexing stories anyone could ever remember.

The mayor called upon the chief of police who called upon all of his reserve officers… no one was permitted even an hour off from work. The overtime budget was thrown out the window. Shortly after the press conference, the mayor received a phone call on a secure line. The president's dry tone was a welcome sound. The mayor was assured of national resources to help clear up the mayor's little local problem.

The hub of the communication network was a hastily thrown together office in a closed down cooling shelter. During the wicked heat of summer, the large, open ground floor of the centrally located office building had been a place for people to recoup from the draining summer sun. The ground floor was vacated a week prior, the worst of the heat gone for the year. In no time at all, the dimly lit vastness of the space was buzzing with people trying to figure out this little *local problem*.

All they had to do was figure out how the dreams could have escaped in the first place, and figure out who was responsible. A couple of names surfaced in their initial investigations as possible people of interest: a local businessman named Nolan Gage, and a psychiatrist named Maury Bennett. An extensively detailed list of the dreams, including their descriptions and tendencies, was circulating throughout the police force and other law enforcement assets.

A handful of dream-creatures had already been rounded up, and were being held in secure cells under armed guard. No one knew what they would do with the dream-creatures once they had them all in custody, but they agreed they could worry about that later.

One of the mayor's first actions was to set up an information hotline. The city officials permitted anonymity, but that didn't prevent them from secretly logging and tracing the calls. Two long conference tables were set up with a bank of phones to sift through the distressed calls. As far as anyone knew, the situation was limited to the heart of the city. Public service announcements had gone out almost immediately to the television stations, newspapers and any other news outlet.

Initially, it seemed like everything was under control. There were FBI representatives, the highest police officials, and the mayor himself had a cubicle off to one side. The spindly threads of order were torn apart within a few hours. A bright flash illuminated the street side of the office as a Molotov cocktail smashed just above the window frame.

"What in the world?" The police chief, a man who regularly wondered why he took the position when it was offered to him earlier in the year (his gout was no good, and his feet swelled, and God damn it, he wanted to see Disney World before he died, for Christ's sake), the police chief could only stare out the window at the mounting chaos outside.

"Maybe... how do we get the national guard in here?" a slightly less gray-haired policeman asked, a man waiting in line for the top spot.

A rock crashed into the window, splintering the glass, making the scurrying office workers flinch away. Flames guttered from a car's open doors. Papers spiraled from an overhead office window. Crazed people formed a spontaneous line as they marched down the street. It all looked like some kind of insane tickertape parade.

"Mr. Mayor, sir, you should see this." The police chief once again wondered why he took this stupid position in the first place. He should be retired, sipping fruity drinks somewhere tropical.

The police chief saw what had focused the attention of the people outside. They were striking back, cornering a couple of dream-people in the small wedge of space formed by the building's brick wall and the burning car.

The couple spilled into the office, a bare-chested dream-man, with a hole in his chest the size of a basketball, carrying an injured dream-woman in his arms. The dream-woman had mottled, feather-like wisps for hair, an aquiline nose, long and banana yellow like a macaw's. Blood flowed from a gash on her temple, and she tried to focus her eyes, but didn't quite succeed.

"Help! They attacked us." The man seemed unfazed by the hole in his chest--he was a dream-man after all. "They saw Rahkel's appearance, and they... oh dear, she's not breathing. Someone do something."

A circle formed around the pair of dreams, but no one offered assistance as a collective gasp spread through the room. They watched the dream-woman's wounds spontaneously heal. The gash at her temple knitted itself closed, and her skin seemed to reabsorb her shed blood. Her eyes fluttered as if she were merely waking.

Smoke trailed in through the open door, a corrosive mélange of burnt gasoline and melted plastic.

The mayor, with his sausage fingers flitting about his face with his kerchief, stepped through the crowd. He arrived just in time to see a mob of people forcing their way through the door, swinging metal pipes above their head, rolls of coins in clenched fists, spittle dripping from their chins. It was a collective insanity, this backlash against the dreams. Once their blood-crazed desire to destroy was sated, people would deny partaking in such violence. People would claim to have been at home, with the shades pulled, waiting out the storm, waiting for the calm of everyday to return.

Within minutes, the people calling the hotline only heard the humming of a dead line.

CHAPTER TWENTY-THREE

Kevin woke slowly, afraid to open his eyes. He could feel the morning sun warming his eyelids, a red, welcoming warmth. Stretching his arms behind his head, gripping his feather pillow in his hands, he felt the familiar comfort of his mattress. When he did open his eyes, something was wrong. Totally wrong. He was in his bed, having slept on his mattress. Not his Uncle David's lumpy mattress, not in the cramped bedroom at his grandma's house all the way in Chicago.

He swung his legs off the bed, taking stock of the bedroom. Albert Pujols stared down on him from his life-size poster. Then there was his 50th anniversary corvette poster with models from every year, his favorite being the 1962 classic convertible. His dresser, nightstand, and desk--all in order. All of this was right, and somehow, none of it was right at all. When he stood up, the hardwood floor creaked its familiar creak.

A voice called out from downstairs, breaking the morning silence and multiplying his confusion. "Kevin, come on. You gotta eat something before we leave." It was his dad's voice, sharp and authoritative, but from the tone, he could tell he was in a good mood. Then the voice joined his mom's in conversation. Comforting and reassuring, muffled by the distance to the kitchen, but still closer than he ever thought the two of them would be again. His mind started whirling, creating a list of questions and grappling with their answers.

What's going on?

Like a sheet of paper from a notebook, he took hold of the list of questions in his head and tore it out, crumpled it into a ball and threw it over his shoulder. He didn't want to consider anything. All he wanted was to go to those voices and feel the affectionate embrace of his family.

He padded down the stairs, whipped around the corner, and stopped so suddenly his feet skidded on the wood floor. It really was his dad. With his shirtsleeves unrolled and his tie loose, he offered Kevin a wry smile, and then brought a plate of French toast over to the kitchen table. His mom had her back to him at the stove, turning bacon with metal tongs. The bacon sizzled and splattered, and it smelled like heaven. Seeing his parents midway through their morning rituals, Kevin had an uneasy sense of familiarity. Sure, he had seen his mom make bacon a hundred times. And his dad always set the table. It was something else. Something outré-familiar.

"Nice of you to join us. I'm afraid the French toast isn't as warm as it was five minutes ago, but then again, if you were hungry enough, you would've been down earlier," his dad said as Kevin took his seat on the far left of the table. French toast was his favorite. He could eat it three times a day and never get sick of it. His dad heaped some onto his plate, and then patted his shoulder to let him know he was just kidding. His dad didn't think much of breakfast, and usually only had a cup of coffee before leaving for the office.

His dad had touched him.

Kevin looked at his arm, stunned. Even through the fabric of his t-shirt, he could still feel the rough touch of his calloused hand. All of this was wrong. All of this could never happen again. Because... because he had left his mom at his grandma's house, and his dad... his dad was never coming home again.

"Kevin, what's wrong, honey?" his mom said when she turned from the stove. She was wearing the rainbow brooch he had made for her from plastic beads and pipe cleaners the year before for Mother's Day. She wore it high up on the lapel of her blouse where everyone would see it. When he had given it to her, he had waited for her to wear it. Every time the family would go out for some special night, he would scan her lapels for the rainbow brooch. She had never worn it. After enough parties and get-togethers went by, and he ran out of excuses why she hadn't worn it, Kevin had given up on her wearing it at all. He figured she had not liked it. In fact, she hated it. He had been secretly heartbroken. Now, on this morning, this morning of all mornings, she wore it prominently.

"Really, Kevin, what's wrong? You're crying." She put the bacon on the table and sat down next to him, scooting over and lowering to his eyelevel. His dad was stirring his coffee, that familiar clinking of the teaspoon inside the cup like a rhythmic morning song he'd forgotten until just now. He wanted to cry even harder. But he didn't.

"Nothing's wrong," he said. Her eyes were glassy and distant, without the intensity he had become accustomed to. She looked much younger without it.

"You're not upset about going to your grandma's house are you?" his dad asked and sipped his coffee.

"Grandma?"

"You know, your mom's mom. The nice lady who bought you that baseball glove that's been like an extra appendage hanging from your arm?"

"Grandma," Kevin said again. "No, I'm fine. Just got some sleep in my eye." He rubbed his eye, rubbing away the crust that was not there.

"You sure?" his mom asked.

It was his last chance to explain how he really felt--jerked around, discombobulated. But instead, he only nodded.

"Orange juice?" his dad asked.

"Sure. Grande o.j. on the rocks," Kevin said without thinking, reading off his order as if they were at a Starbuck's. It was another morning ritual, and his alone to perform. His mom smiled before returning to the stove.

His grandma's house. Now he understood.

The familiarity. He understood it completely, but he didn't want to recognize this day for what it was. Didn't want to give it a name. And yet things weren't exactly like that particular morning. He sensed no tension between his parents, no cold silences; in fact, they seemed overly in love, at least by their standards. If anything, it was as if a thick sheen of fake happiness had glossed over *that* morning. An idealized morning with his favorite breakfast, his mom wearing the rainbow brooch, his dad speaking to him, his parents acting lovingly to one another. It was just so wrong. Holding the juice he poured for Kevin in one hand, his dad wrapped his other around his mom's waist, then kissed her on the cheek.

"Grande o.j. on the rocks. Sorry, we only have cubes. If you wanted shaved ice, you can go to the Ruby's house next door, I'm sure they would accommodate you." He slid the juice across the table, like a barman passing a beer, not spilling a drop.

"Thanks, Dad."

His dad went back to his place at the table. He sipped his coffee and read the morning's sports page. After a couple minutes, his mom joined them at the table, bringing along a bottle of maple syrup.

She cut her French toast, drowned it in syrup, like she always did, and took a bite. She looked at his dad, and he turned his attention away from the cover story about the Bears, and they shared a smile. She took another bite, looked up again, and again, the smile. They were like robots. The more methodical their actions became, the more the questions prodded at Kevin. His family together; all he ever wanted. Ever since *that* morning... *this* morning.

"When does the bus leave?" Kevin asked. He had not touched his food. He had lost his appetite.

"10:35," his dad said, unable to pull his gaze away from his mom. Their behavior was overbearing. Creepy. They were looking into each other's eyes as if they were starving animals finding thick slabs of steak just behind the other's eye sockets.

Thankfully, someone knocked on the front door. If something did not interrupt the creepiness, Kevin thought he would scream.

"Can you get that, Kev?" his dad asked. He did not look away from his mom. And she held his gaze, even as she shoveled forkfuls of French toast into her mouth. He kissed her hand, like couples did in old movies, and then wiped away maple syrup that was dribbling down her chin. He licked his finger clean of the syrup, and at that moment, leaving the kitchen was just about the best thing Kevin felt he could have done.

The knocking at the door became more insistent. The rug by the door absorbed the slap of his bare feet. The family suitcases waited by the door for the trip to the bus station. All of them. Even his dad's. He tried thinking back to *that* morning (*this* morning), to see if he could remember if they had brought his dad's suitcase to the bus station. He couldn't remember. He supposed it didn't matter.

Nearly blinding sunlight shined through the small panes at the top of the storm door. He closed his eyes, and once again saw that red warmth behind his eyelids. It was a welcoming warmth, and he did not want to open his eyes again.

But the knocking. More insistent, rattling the door.

Kevin opened his eyes, and reached for the doorknob. When he opened the door, all he saw was a black void. And the stench of something foul, something abused and rotting.

His eyes adjusted. It wasn't a black void outside. It was nighttime. The pure black of night, when the sun is so far gone you can feel the shadows breathing. Kevin saw the winking lights of his friend Scotty's house across the street, and then the red embers, twin fires burning in a somber blue face. Mr. Freakshow.

The Freak was here, and Kevin had willfully opened the door. Kevin's feet were frozen. He could not even blink.

"Kevin. Hello. I'm so glad you waited for me. Hope you enjoyed your final meal." The beast took a step inside, his engorged wings flapping behind him like snapped bath towels.

Kevin looked over his shoulder. His dad was licking his mom's face, licking an errant runnel of maple syrup from her cheek, her chin, her forehead.

But then they were fading, becoming transparent, translucent. Invisible. The kitchen table and chairs faded and were gone, too. Along with the breakfast smells--fried bacon, the sweet French toast aroma, and melted butter... all gone. The kitchen was empty, the living room was empty, the family suitcases were gone.

"Your killing time is here," the Freak whispered, reaching out for Kevin.

He was able to stumble away from the door, and as he turned to run away--to where, he had no idea--he tripped over his backpack. The only thing in his family home except for dust bunnies and memories. He took hold of the backpack strap as he tumbled, able to sling it over his shoulder. Mr. Freakshow lunged at him, claws spreading like a fistful of spears, and tore a swatch from the fabric of his backpack. Kevin finished his roll and gained his feet. He sprinted down the hallway, his footsteps sounding foreign in the unfamiliar emptiness of the house.

Mr. Freakshow was close on his heels, his curled toenails digging furrows in the hardwood with every stride.

Carin and Maury were making good time. They had taken I88 west, and then 39/51 south, and were leaving miles behind, more than a mile and a half a minute. They left the rain behind in the city, and the roads were dry. They had passed through the LaSalle/Peru spur where the highway system rested like a crucifix across the center of Illinois. Darkness spread over the open plains like a sickness, and still Carin sped down the highway, onward south, to their home in Warren Cove, and hopefully, dear God, hopefully, to Kevin.

"This should have never happened," Carin said her first words since leaving the city.

"I'm afraid Nolan Gage didn't invest as much time or money in the containment system as I thought necessary."

Carin saw his profile as he stared out the side window. She thought back to the day she and Kevin moved to her mother's house, to the lost and insoluble expression her son had carried like the heaviest burden imaginable. Maury looked like this; maybe a look of guilt, maybe feeling responsible for the escaped dreams. Like she knew Kevin felt responsible for his dad's death. She wished she could go back in time, how far... a day, a week? and tell Kevin that none of it had been his fault.

"That's not what I meant. I meant I should have never let Kevin talk me into letting him go into that damn museum. None of this would have happened if I would have told him no."

"Oh..." Maury said, sighing.

The thrumming engine was the only sound for many miles. It was numbing, driving at such speeds. They were only a discarded roofing nail or broken beer bottle shy of bursting a tire, of crashing end over end at ninety odd miles an hour into the grassy berm on the side of the road. Driving blind, trusting the safety of the road, trusting the next twenty feet in front of the car, and the next beyond, for miles and miles.

Carin's thoughts returned to Kevin, and she heard his laughter in her head--a sound so rare for so long--his hitching laugh that climbed in pitch with his every breath until it became one long screech, and then dissolving into uncontrollable giggling. This took away the numbness of the drive. She reached over her shoulder, grabbing the seatbelt. She pulled it over her torso and locked it into place at her side without taking her eyes from the road.

The next twenty feet.

Kevin needed her, and she wasn't about to let him down because some drunk idiot chucked an empty beer bottle out the window and she wasn't paying attention to the next twenty feet. She would worry about other things when they reached Warren Cove.

"So, how did you learn about your... abilities?" Carin asked, breaking the silence.

Maury turned, looked at her, and then returned his gaze to the window. "When I was around Kevin's age, maybe a little younger, our apartment burned down. If you couldn't guess from my appearance, I didn't escape unharmed."

"Oh, thank God," Carin said. Maury shot her a look so cold that she could feel it without looking at him. "I'm sorry. That's not what I meant. I just haven't taken this route in a while. We're two miles away from Warren Cove. We're almost there."

"Outstanding," Maury said quietly.

"I'm sorry, Maury, go on. What happened next?"

After a long pause Maury continued. "To tell you the truth, I don't know if I had my abilities before the fire. Maybe I always had the ability and I just didn't know it. The fire could have opened a doorway that had been there in the first place."

They left the highway on a sharply curving exit ramp, slowing to twenty miles an hour to hold the curve. They passed a gas station and a squat red produce stand that was closed for the season. Otherwise, blocks of homes on tree-lined streets spread out before them like a paper fan.

"The first dream I transmuted was from my brother. It was our family pet, a pound cat we'd named Rocky. That cat was a survivor, just like the boxer in the movies. He was a day short of euthanasia when we adopted him. He burned to charcoal in the apartment fire. Soon after, the dream-Rocky started tormenting my brother, and this dream-cat was always on fire, but would never die. Eventually, the dream-Rocky killed Dale."

"I'm so sorry." Carin took her eyes from the road. When she looked at Maury, she could see the pain in his eyes. She wanted to say more, but she knew from bitter experience she couldn't say anything to make him feel any better. She turned onto Winfield Road, and they were only a block away. She wanted to drive up to the old house and see Kevin climbing the oak tree in the front yard. She wanted to yell at him for climbing too high, and then hug him when he climbed down.

"That's how I know Mr. Freakshow will try to kill your son. Because of my brother, Dale. And when I was twelve, I was taken in by my foster family--"

"What the hell is that?" Carin cut him off, pulling over to the curb. Their house was lit up from the inside. Lit up as if by daylight. Golden light spilled from the first floor windows. And the front door was open. A figure, a large, hulking figure, filled the doorway. Mr. Freakshow. "No no no!" Carin threw the car into park before it was completely stopped, and it jerked forward, as if a giant foot had kicked it in the rear bumper.

She opened the door and ran across the front lawn as the Freak stepped inside her family's home. The interior sunlight of the house dimmed to a cold darkness as the door closed behind him.

"No!"

Maury remained in the car. He casually unbuckled his seat belt, then casually pressed wrinkles from his dress shirt. Before leaving the Explorer, he reached over and hit a button on the driver's side door. The locks on all the doors flipped open. He continued speaking as he left the car, continued speaking as if he was still explaining his life to Carin. "And then I learned that a dream could die. But only if the dreamer died. Poor, simple Gabe. I could have loved him like a brother, I think..." he trailed off, as if pondering it. Musing over his foster brother. He popped open the back tail gate and rummaged through the typical car gear. Jumper cables, snow brush, emergency blanket.

This will do. This will do just fine.

Maury hefted the tire iron in his hand, tapping it against the nerveless pink of his left palm. He didn't feel it, but the boy surely would. "And then I let Gabe die. You see, I had to find out. If the dreamer dies, does the dream also? Gabe was such a sweet kid, but I had to know..." Maury's voice became quieter until his words were only in his head. All he could imagine was the tire iron connecting solidly with Kevin's skull, springing loose his brains upon the floor, freeing the world of Mr. Freakshow.

And in the end, loving Juliet.

At first, Kevin thought Mr. Freakshow had slashed him with his claws, but his backpack took the brunt of the damage. The attack had sent him flying across the floor, sliding on the moonlight-bathed wood. He couldn't help wondering where the sunlight had gone. Of all the details Mr. Freakshow had controlled since Kevin woke up, down to the wrinkles on his parents' faces, all he could wonder about was the daylight. It seemed the most unnatural of all. Daylight to night in the blink of an eye.

He jumped from his belly to his knees and then his feet in one fluid motion, and sprinted down the hall, the beast tearing the air an inch from his ear.

"Kevin, oh Kevin, this is for real, isn't it? No more games, no more dreams. Just you and me, flesh and blood--torn flesh and gushing blood. I couldn't be more proud!" Mr. Freakshow said from behind. The beast watched him run away, watched as he fled to... well, to nowhere. The house was a series of dead ends and Mr. Freakshow would know this. Know this because Kevin did. A hallway led to the kitchen, the stairs led to the bedrooms, the hallway to his dad's home office, a basement... all dead ends.

The basement. It had window wells. A way out; if he could only make it outside, it seemed like his only hope. He threw open the basement door and closed it shut behind him. He flipped the light switch, and the bulb remained unlit. He'd forgotten there wasn't any power. No one lived here. The room was darker than night. And quiet. The whole house was quiet but for his own panting breath.

He reached out so he wouldn't run into anything, and then remembered the house was empty. This house was no longer his, and none of his family's possessions would block his path. The room was chilly and damp and felt a mile long. When his hands reached the far wall, touching the coarse concrete, he strained to hear any noise from upstairs. Still nothing. He ran his hands along the wall until he came across the window well. The concrete alcove in the foundation sat at Kevin's chest level. He flipped the lock and pulled the window in on its stiff hinge. He expected to find Mr. Freakshow waiting inside the concrete alcove, waiting for Kevin to step inside where it would be oh so easy for him to gouge out his heart. Kevin waved his hand through the open space, but only felt the smooth pebbles that lined the well floor.

He eased his backpack to the floor and then strained to lift himself into the well. When he reached over his head, he realized why this was such a stupid idea in the first place. He had forgotten about the steel grate his dad had welded to seal off the top of the well. A number of neighborhood homes had been broken into, and his dad didn't want to take any chances. He equipped the home with steel-reinforced doors, deadbolts and lock bars, as well as capping off the window wells. Kevin pushed against the grate, and he could feel it give a little, but not much at all.

With a little more time, he could bust out the welds holding down the grate. He stood inside the well with his hands braced against the grate above him and forced himself up like a jack lifting a car. He was practically jumping up and down, wiggling the welds until they weakened. Finally, he felt something give above him.

Almost there, come on, come on...

Carin tried the front door, but of course, it was locked. She found the kidney-shaped rock where they kept their spare key. It was freshly overturned, and the key was missing. Kevin must have taken it.

Damn.

"I thought we could use a weapon of some kind." Maury joined her on the front step, holding a tire iron in his hand. From the look on his face, he didn't want to switch out a bad tire. He looked ready to pummel someone.

"Good. Give me that." Carin reached for the tire iron. He almost protested giving up his weapon, but reluctantly handed it over. "If I can only..." Carin wedged a blunt tip into the door seam and yanked against it. It didn't budge. Not one spare millimeter. "Damnstupidfuck!" she yelled at the door, yelled at the tire iron, and at herself. She couldn't get into her own house.

"Is there another entrance?" Maury asked.

"There's a big picture window in the back." She handed Maury the tire iron and then futilely rammed her shoulder into the unforgiving door. The only reaction she got was a dull ache in her shoulder. She was going to start crying at any moment.

Maury tapped the tire iron in his palm as he watched her mad behavior. He seemed unfazed by any of this. Maybe it was because it wasn't his child they were trying to save. "I'll go check out that picture window." He left in a hurry, and was around the corner of the house, taking the only weapon they had with him.

She lowered her eyes and could feel the tears building, ready to fall. Her eyes came to rest on the kidney-shaped rock. When she picked it up, it felt solid in her hand, eight, maybe ten pounds. The tears dried in her eyes before they could fall and she could feel her determination returning. She wasn't about to let a steel-reinforced door stop her from protecting her child. She forced a path through the thick bushes at the front of the house until she was in front of the living room windows. She lifted the rock over her head and threw it at the window.

A second weld gave loose, and then a third ripped away, and Kevin was nearly free when he heard glass shattering upstairs. He struggled harder, sweat spreading over his body, adrenaline rushing through him, when he heard his mom's voice from upstairs. She was screaming, a blistering rage that quickly became a whimper of pain.

"Kevin, Momma's home!" Mr. Freakshow shouted.

The sound of the Freak's voice stole his breath. He jumped down from the moonlit window well and cautiously walked across the concrete floor. His pulse shot through his head, in his ears. The wooden stairs creaked every step he climbed. He unlocked the door. When he opened it, the first thing he saw was his mom sprawled on her back in a pile of broken glass, propped up by her trembling arm. Blood flowed from her cut cheek, dripping into a sticky mass on the floor. She looked angry enough to eat nails without wincing. Her right leg was bent at a weird angle, just below the kneecap. Kevin realized the Freak had broken it. His nightmare had hurt his mom.

Mr. Freakshow stood over her, clenching his fists, his wings swaying gently. His every movement was an expression of pure joy.

"Leave her alone. Take me. Just leave my mom alone." Kevin stepped forward from the shadows.

CHAPTER TWENTY-FOUR

"Kevin, get away from here! Damn it, run!" his mom shrieked, horrified that he would voluntarily approach his nightmare. She grimaced as she crawled the five feet to where Mr. Freakshow stood. She latched onto his ankle, as if to hold him in place.

"Just leave her be."

More glass shattered, this time coming from the rear of the house. Kevin and Mr. Freakshow exchanged a questioning glance, and then Kevin looked at his mom. She was motioning for him to run, to get away as quickly as possible. He waited, listening to glass crunching, to someone clumsily climbing through a window.

"Who might that be? It isn't our boy Kevin, or dear ol' Mom. We know that much. Secretary-fucking Daddy is dead, and let's see... oh yes, I have my grandma souvenir right here..." the Freak said. "I know I put it someplace close..." He reached into a leather pouch strapped to his bare waist and removed something from the voluminous pocket. It looked to be a blood-caked skull.

Kevin stared at the skull in disbelief. Of course, Mr. Freakshow would try to fool him again. His grandma was out of harm's way, tucked away in her quiet neighborhood back in Chicago.

Of course, Grandma was safe, and he would never... the Freak wouldn't harm...

He looked from the skull prized in the Freak's palm, to his mom's face. As soon as he saw her expression, he knew the skull was real, that his grandma was dead, murdered. Murdered in some cruel, senseless way. Just because she was his grandma.

Walking through the dining room, someone ground broken glass underfoot. For a brief moment, the slimmest fraction of a second in which Kevin had forgotten the last two months, he thought he would see his dad walk around the corner with a gun in his hand, ready to save the day. Seeing Maury Bennett enter the kitchen threw him off. Maury's eyes were gleaming with menace as he gripped a tire iron in his right hand. As the man from Lucidity brushed shards of glass from his clothes, he glanced at a laceration on the back of his hand. He sucked on the wound, approaching Kevin.

"Maury... thank God you're here. Mr. Freakshow--" Kevin quickly trailed off as Maury wheeled back the tire iron in a thick arc, ready to strike.

"No!" Carin screamed. She tried to get to her feet, but pain forced her back to the floor. A puzzled look came across Mr. Freakshow's face, and as he watched Maury, he backhanded Kevin's mom into silence.

All Kevin could do was throw his arms up in front of his face before Maury whipped the tire iron down on him. The heavy bar crashed into his forearm, biting clear to the bone like a vicious animal, radiating jolts of pain throughout his body. Kevin didn't hear any bones braking; his scream drowned out all other sound. He fell to his side, cradling his arm, feeling his whole body tensing, awaiting another blow.

A deathly silence filled the room. But then Kevin could hear his mom fighting unconsciousness, fighting the blood flooding her open mouth, choking her. The tire iron whirred, splitting the air as it descended on Kevin's skull.

The Freak's nails scraped across the floor.

Kevin closed his eyes, knowing this was the end, hoping he wouldn't feel his skull shattering.

The whirring noise ended with a dull thud. And no pain. No deathblow. When he opened his eyes, Mr. Freakshow was standing over him, the tire iron caught in one of his enormous hands. He was glaring at Maury.

"Tisk, tisk Mr. French Fry. Trying to kill the boy out from under me, huh? That's my job." He ripped the tire iron from his hand and threw it against the far wall, the point impaling the drywall.

Maury looked at his hands, as if even he doubted what he had attempted. He fell to his knees, trembling, groveling at the feet of the beast. "Please... I was just trying... Dear God, I love her."

"You may have sprung me from the boy's head, but you're no different than all of the others." Mr. Freakshow kicked Maury in the ribs. Maury curled into a ball, cowering, making himself as small a target as possible. Mr. Freakshow pummeled him a few times, dispirited, not really into his assault, before picking him up by a patch of his hair. "You weren't invited to the party, so I suggest you leave before you make me angry."

The Freak held him by his hair and the belt of his pants. He spun in a circle like a discus thrower, and then heaved Maury at the living room window. Through all the pinwheeling arms and legs, Kevin saw Maury's eyes flinch closed the instant before he went flying through the pane. There was a sudden oomph as Maury crashed against the sidewalk. Then it was quiet again. Like any other middle of the night in sleepy Warren Cove.

"Now, on with our show!"

Kevin wanted to go over to his mom, shake her awake, do something, anything to make sure she did not slip away like his dad did. Her eyes were half shut, and what he saw was all whites. Her blood pooled from her many wounds on the hardwood floor, just as his dad's blood painted the bus station tile. She wasn't moving.

Mr. Freakshow sauntered over, his hands outspread, as if he was about to hug Kevin. But he knew the beast would never be kind, that he had nothing but a black pit where his heart should be.

"Enough histrionics, my boy. Time is late. We need to move on with our lives, and I'm afraid that my moving on means the end of yours." Mr. Freakshow swiped a hand through the air, a second too slow. An extra second caused by cockiness.

Kevin dived to the floor, his cheek burning against the wood as he crashed awkwardly. From floor level, his mom's face was partially covered by mats of blood-soaked hair. She still hadn't moved. He didn't see her breathing. She was gone. He really was on his own. His heart trundled along in his chest, and he knew he was reaching his limit. He rolled over, his right forearm, most likely broken and a throbbing mass of agony, trailing slightly behind the rest of his body.

"You cocksucker, get over here," Mr. Freakshow growled, for the first time a tinge of anger to his voice. "Get over here and die."

Kevin braced himself with his left arm and pushed up to his feet. The Freak cut off his escape to the front door. Kevin faked as if he would make a run to the back of the house, but then made a break for the basement again. The welds would pop free with one more swift push. If he could only get downstairs with enough time...

Why bother? he thought. *Just slow down, let Mr. Freakshow catch you. What's the point anymore?*

He grappled with his thoughts, not sure why he was fighting anymore, not sure what he could look forward to if he lived through this. There was nothing left. His family was gone, all murdered. The one thing that was stopping him from giving up was the possibility of pain. Sure, his arm hurt, and even if it wasn't broken, it hurt like hell. But that pain wouldn't amount to much compared to what the Freak had in store for him. That's what subconsciously kept him going, not the fear of dying, but the fear of pain. Immense pain. Unending pain. If the Freak would only agree to kill him without brutalizing him, Kevin would hand himself over. Willingly and without regret hand himself over.

But I'm a chicken. And what do chickens do? Chickens run.

He stopped his momentum by grabbing hold of the basement doorknob with his left hand. His body kept moving on its own, his inertia throwing him down the hall. His arm pulled tight, a rubber band with no more stretch to give. The muscles in his arms strained, feeling like a dozen exploding beestings, but he was able to right himself and swing the door open. He hastily threw the lock after slamming the door shut behind him.

As he jumped down the steps, Mr. Freakshow battered the door, noticeably bending the steel-reinforced structure inward.

"YOU PATHETIC FUCK YOU COWARD YOU PIECE OF SHIT!" the Freak railed, pounding the door with his fists.

Kevin didn't glance back. He charged through the dark basement and climbed into the window well. Most of the grate was loose. Only one weld remained. He pushed up with his good arm and could feel the grate bending. The weld held firm, but if he could only bend the grate a little more…

And once outside, then what? Would Mr. Freakshow relent? Could he just leave the yard, walk down main street Warren Cove? Once outside, he was as surely dead as if he stood here and waited for the end to come to him.

The grate continued to bend, and there was now enough room for him to skinny his way out. The basement door held, but the doorframe was giving way, the Freak rending it from its moorings.

No, he wasn't going to run. He couldn't do it. He hadn't the will to take another step from the house where he grew up, or to endanger his neighbors or anyone else kind enough to help him. His thoughts turned to Sophie and Andrew, and he hoped they were unharmed after giving him aid in his time of need. But what the Freak did to his grandma… he didn't want to think anymore about his nightmare hurting the people he loved and trusted. Hopping down from the window well, he was overcome by a strange sense of relief. He was going to meet his tormentor face to face, stare him down until the end. Perhaps his lack of fear would make it go swiftly.

His legs were shaky and could barely hold his weight. As the Freak continued to destroy the door, an occasional shank of wood flew from the disintegrating doorframe. Kevin went over to the washer and dryer set in the corner. They had left the appliances, all of them, when they had moved away. His mom didn't want anything carrying over to their new life. She didn't know at the time that so much of Kevin's life now would hinge on those things from the past. The memories of his dad, being in the family's old house… He sat on the washer, leaning back against the control panel. He faced the door and waited.

"Cocksucker… when I get my hands… you're going to regret…" the pounding eased as Mr. Freakshow caught his breath. The straining of his lungs sounded foreign coming from the beast. It reminded Kevin of the first time he had to run the mile in gym class last year. A whole mile. Before that it was a half mile, and that had always been a chore. But a mile? He remembered wheezing on the side of the school's dirt track after he finished, feeling like he was going to die. He supposed that's how Mr. Freakshow felt right now. He was running a mile for the first time, and not really liking it.

As Kevin waited, he looked at the ceiling, with its unfinished rafters looking like a network of parallel ribs. He wasn't focusing on anything, finding a certain serenity that he could never remember experiencing. His eyes came to rest on the square blocked-off end of the laundry chute. It had a hinged door, shutting off a tunnel leading to the two floors above him. Like a sealed mineshaft, the wooden tunnel lined the foundation wall and disappeared into the unknown. The serenity and calm shirked his limbs. He once again tensed, and as if sensing this, Mr. Freakshow attacked the basement door with renewed vigor. The terrible cry of bending wooden beams filled the basement. Snatches of the comparably brighter upstairs light were visible as the Freak worked the door in its frame. It was only a matter of seconds now. The Freak would be on him in seconds, doubly angry for having to go through the door.

Kevin stood on top of the dryer and reached up to the laundry chute door. He had never opened it before, since his family never used the chute when they lived here. His mom had been afraid that their clothes would travel through a tunnel of spider webs and end up even dirtier than before.

210

In the darkness, he fumbled his hand around the edges of the chute. He came across a latch, and opened it. The door fell open on its hinge toward him. The open mouth of the chute sat at armpit level, making Kevin wonder if it was a fool's dream to even try climbing in there with his bad arm. But he had to. He had to try.

He reached inside the chute and felt a wooden frame jutting out. He dug in with his fingers, stabbing them at the framing as if intent on driving them into the wood. Tiptoeing on the top of the dryer's control panel, he did a little hop. He pushed up with his good arm, throwing his broken limb in front of him. The arm was still good from the elbow in, and he was able to use the joint against the framing like a lever. He was waist-high in the dark tunnel. It was just a matter of pulling his legs up behind him, grabbing hold of the door, and holding it in place.

The basement door came crashing in, a cumbersome and deadly bulwark skidding down the stairs. His dad's paranoia of some punk kids breaking into their house had bought Kevin enough time to hide. Maybe enough to get away somehow. He held the laundry chute door closed, listening.

The Freak took the steps two at a time. His ragged breaths hissed through the basement, sending shivers down Kevin's spine. *What am I doing? I'm a trapped rat.* All the Freak had to do was find him holed up in there, and lash out with one fist, and...

The Freak ran across the concrete floor, immediately coming to the window well with the bent metal grate.

"Fuckingshit-human!"

Kevin listened for any sign the Freak would fall for it, if he would go through the window well and outside, into the wide, opening night. All he could hear was his ragged breaths. And he was inhaling deeply, filling his lungs, sniffing the air.

He's tracking me like a bloodhound.

Panic surged through Kevin. Regardless of the noise he was making, he started shimmying up the chute. He braced his feet against the sides, clamoring above with his hands, searching for handholds.

"Found you, little boy. I thought you had gotten away. But here you stay, a holed up larva, waiting to be set free," the Freak said, backtracking to the washer dryer set.

His mom was right--the chute was full of cobwebs. They covered his face, ripping apart near his ears with the sound of tearing cotton candy. Something crawled across his naked arm. Straining to climb up the chute, he couldn't spare any energy to shoo away whatever it was. A small opening branched off to his right, and from the size of the door, he knew it was the chute door leading to the kitchen. Too small to escape through. He continued on, sweat drenching his skin, crawling higher into the darkness. The pain in his arm eased a bit. Either his arm was unbroken, or his adrenaline dulled the pain. He no longer cared. He reached above, grabbed a handhold, and pulled.

The trap door leading to the laundry room flew open, and a cool blue light illuminated the tunnel. Kevin glanced over his shoulder, and looked into the beast's red flame eyes. As Mr. Freakshow held onto the lip of the chute, his body appeared to shrink. His nightmare broke his own bones--clavicles, ribs, scapulas--audibly snapping like twigs. He dislocated his joints, tore and refitted sinews and cartilage. Shrinking to fit inside the cramped chute.

But the light. Emanating from his skin. Like a hidden light. *Mr. Freakshow's hidden color.*

The Freak's hidden color illuminated the shaft enough that Kevin had an easier go of it. He reached ahead, grabbing hold, climbing higher. But the Freak was in the chute, writhing, digging into the wooden walls, propelling himself higher. Gaining on him.

"Why Kevin? Why must you torment me like this? I should be done with you and on to better things. Collecting skulls, eviscerating humans, destroying petulant dreams."

"Your color..." Kevin watched his own arm reaching over his head, watched the skin of his arm glowing with the same cool blue glow as Mr. Freakshow. "You're just like me."

"You're right, I am just like you. You want to live. Just like I want to live. You fight to get away to extend your life, while I will do anything in my power to end *your* life to extend *mine*. Forever."

Kevin reached the summit of the chute, and reached out for the door to the linen closet in the second floor hallway. So it was hopeless. Mr. Freakshow would never stop chasing him. He would never get away.

Mr. Freakshow slashed with his fist, ripping through Kevin's calf. The beast chuckled. Blood gushed from the wound, and Kevin heard Mr. Freakshow lapping up the hot droplets of blood as they fell.

Kevin opened the chute door and saw clean moonlight shining through his old bedroom window. He kicked back with his heel, catching the Freak in the bridge of his nose, and used him for leverage as he kicked clear of the chute. He flopped from the opening like some kind of animal borne of the wild, gaining his feet and running within seconds of hitting the ground.

Mr. Freakshow's face appeared in the narrow opening as Kevin backed into his old bedroom. "Ah, how you tease me, Kevin. You give me a taste of your blood, and I think your will is broken. But then you continue your fight."

The angles of the room looked sharper, the length and width elongated with its emptiness. The Freak extricated himself from the chute, a smashed version of himself. He bowed his head, clenched his fists, and forced his body to his full form. Sinews and muscles became taut under his deadman skin. His bones reformed, snapping back into place. The wood slivers piercing his nipples rose and fell with the rhythm of his breathing as his chest expanded to full size.

Kevin raced to the window and threw it open. He peered down and his eyes boggled at the height. Had he climbed that entire shaft from the basement?

"Kevin. Be careful. You don't want to misstep out there. The ground can be even less forgiving than I."

To the far left, over a two foot chasm of emptiness to the ground, was the upward slant of the roof. When he lived in Warren Cove and looked out the window, Kevin had never imagined trying to reach for it, but now he had no other choice. As the Freak easily closed the distance behind him, he leaned out with his stomach braced against the windowsill, measuring the distance with his arm. At the far reach of his fingertips, he was able to brush the lip of the overhanging gutter. Too far away, just too far...

Kevin looked down, and his stomach flipped. He could sense Mr. Freakshow waiting behind him, waiting to see what move he would make. Waiting nervously. It dawned on Kevin. The Freak had said the ground was unforgiving. He wondered what would happen if he let himself fall to the ground, let the ground take his life instead of handing it over to his nightmare. They shared the same color. They were one and the same.

"Kevin... you don't want to do that. It's dangerous."

Dangerous for you, Kevin thought. "Just leave me alone."

"I'm afraid I can't do that."

Kevin took this as his cue. Bringing his right knee up to the windowsill, he pushed off, lunging for the overhang. In his adrenaline-drunk mind, he thought he would land feet first on the roof. Instead, his palms slapped against the shingles, taking a precarious hold, his legs kicking out beneath him into nothingness. Pain shot through his right arm, and his hand quickly fell away. The fingers of his left hand began to slip, and Kevin felt the sudden fullness of his bladder, the pulse in his temples, felt the grit of the shingles grating his skin. He was too weak, too injured. He held fast to the edge of the canting roof, but couldn't kick his legs high enough to take hold of the gutter. His grip was slipping away, the sweat of his palms slicking the surface of the shingles.

The moment his hand broke contact with the roof, the Freak reached out with blurring speed, digging his claws bone-deep into the meat of his shoulder, holding him dangling in midair. His tormentor, this nightmare created from his own mind, had for the second time tonight saved his life. Mr. Freakshow whipped Kevin up onto the roof, well away from the edge and a certain death from falling.

Kevin's shoulder felt like a mound of raw hamburger. He was tired, so incredibly tired. He was also mad, not realizing just how mad until he rose from his haunches to see Mr. Freakshow emerging from his bedroom window. With agile ease Mr. Freakshow leaped from the window sill to the edge of the gutter.

"I can't do this." Blood flowed from his wounds to the shingles at his feet.

"I was hoping you would come to that conclusion. My only hope was that it wouldn't take you this long." Mr. Freakshow spread his wings behind him, flapping them gently. The blue glow of his skin, his hidden color, glimmered with his wings' movement.

"I can't let you kill me. I can't go on, but I can't let you kill me."

Mr. Freakshow's expression drained as he noted the strength of both Kevin's intentions and his resolve to follow through.

Kevin took a deep breath and then ran, picking up speed on the downward slant of the roof, kicking up grit from the shingles as he sprinted toward the edge and the open sky. Gravity took him in its welcoming arms and pulled him in. The freefall blew the sweat from his brow, and the ground approached with maddening speed.

"No!" Mr. Freakshow cried, taking flight, following the trajectory of Kevin's death spiral.

Kevin closed his eyes, but could feel the closeness of the ground, could feel its ascending finality.

His body raced Mr. Freakshow to the waiting earth, and finally, his mind cherishing this moment like a hard fought victory, he impacted the ground, crushing the soil beneath him with nothing more than his bones and blood.

It didn't hurt. He didn't know what position his body had taken as he landed, but it didn't matter. Nothing mattered any longer. Kevin could feel his life draining away. When his eyes fluttered open, all he saw were the twin embers of Mr. Freakshow's eyes hovering over him in a flagging blue background. Such torment in those eyes; projecting fear, hatred, and nothing resembling remorse. The embers cooled, turned to soot, and then they disappeared, taken away from this place. Forever. Kevin was dead.

"Kevin... my baby... please..." Carin sobbed, dragging her twisted leg behind her as she crawled out the front door. His body was a sprawled mess, his eyes open to the final minutes of night. The sun was at the horizon, pushing away fears of the dark, pushing away the dreams and nightmares until tomorrow.

The pain had woken her rudely. Her face felt like a monster mask of swollen bruises and bleeding lacerations. Her leg was useless and she didn't want to look at it until she found her son. She would never make it up the stairs or into the basement. When she left through the front door, she would crawl to the nearest neighbor's house. Plead for them to call the police.

But when she looked around when she left the house she saw Kevin's body pressed into the ground like a squashed bug. And his eyes were empty.

She hobbled to his side, her trembling hands searching his wrist for a pulse. Nothing. She pressed her fingers against his neck, and still found no sign of life. Touching his cheek, she wiped a bloody streak away.

She sobbed, her tears falling onto Kevin's face. The fact that he didn't react to their wetness made her cry even more.

"I can't do this... You can't die! Baby..." she screamed, feeling as helpless as she had ever felt.

Carin didn't hear the sirens of the ambulance or the squad cars as they pulled up in the empty driveway and along the street. She did not recognize Officer Mullens, a man who was not only a Warren Cove police officer, but also a former tax client of Carin's, as he took hold of her shoulders and tried to look into her eyes. The paramedics slid a gurney from the ambulance and joined them in the grass.

"Mrs. Dvorak? What happened here? Can you tell me what happened? Who called 911?" Carin watched as a paramedic examined her son's body, hearing the officer, but not understanding. Not caring to. "Mrs. Dvorak? Carin? Is this your son? Are you hurt? Oh God. Look at her leg. Guys, get her some attention. The bone's sticking clear through the skin. She's in shock."

Soon after the paramedics valiantly went to work on a body no one thought would survive, Kevin's heart caught the fleeting spark of life. He took hold of that spark, and held it until he was breathing, shallowly at first but with ever-increasing strength.

As Kevin took his first breaths, Carin was in an ambulance, getting attention for her own wounds. Being sedated. She didn't know that her son was alive. As the police officers canvassed the house for clues as to what had happened, and wondering who had called 911 from the payphone at the abandoned Michael & Son's service station, no one wondered who Mr. Freakshow was. There was no body to find, no trace that he even existed, but for the battered basement door and scrapes in the floor from his tearing claws. The Freak was gone, vanquished by Kevin's ephemeral death.

CHAPTER TWENTY-FIVE

The last Indian Summer ended, followed soon after by bitter winds blowing in off Lake Michigan, an angry marauder let loose on the city. Ever since their standoff with Mr. Freakshow, Sophie hadn't felt quite right. She felt drained, utterly exhausted. She spent days on end in bed, watching as Andrew painted a new mural over the old. He painted a red sun low at the horizon, a wisp of cloud skirting the diffuse sunlight, the rolling wheat fields reaped of their summer seed.

She watched his hands flex as he moved through a brushstroke, his artist's hands--long, agile fingers, the ridged tendons close to the surface. His blood flowing through his veins. Her thin lips spread in a gray-lipped smile.

"Andrew?"

"Yeah, hon?"

"Come to bed. I'm cold."

"Should I turn up the thermostat?"

"No, it's fine. Come here."

Andrew was about to set down the brush, but made one last dabbing stroke. "I was just finishing anyway." He wiped his hands dry on a paint-caked rag and then came over to the bed. "It's done."

Sophie pulled aside the blankets, and her husband joined her. Andrew fit one arm in the crook of her neck, the other arm on her side. His rough hand rested on the small of her back. She sighed deeply, her eyes closing in contentment.

Sophie's breaths became shallower, more erratic. She stirred as if dreaming and Andrew held her gently, lovingly.

At some point, Sophie stopped moving, her lungs at rest for the first time since before they formed while she was still inside her mother. Her breath expired. Such a subtle transfer of energy, of life. So subtle as to be almost unnoticeable.

But for Andrew. Her husband of so many years, waiting for her in the afterlife for these last twenty years. Finally, they would reunite.

The Andrew dream faded away, the blankets falling where he once rested next to his dreamer. The beautiful murals, the thousands of brushstrokes covering Sophie's walls, her ceilings, they too faded.

Carin had three surgeries to fix her leg. After two months, she had graduated from her walker to a cane. Kevin playfully teased her and called her an old lady, but Carin did not care. She had her son again. He had come back to life, by some miracle, he had come back to her.

Until the end of winter, Kevin had to wear a fitted helmet to guard his broken skull. On impact, he also suffered a broken pelvis, a bruised liver, and a shattered ankle. Pressure had built up in his brain, and shortly after they removed him from the lawn of his old house, he was in surgery at Warren Cove Community Hospital. When he woke, the doctors told him he was lucky to be alive. If he had landed at a slightly different angle, he would have died from any number of his injuries.

While he called his mom an old lady for walking with a cane, she quickly forgot he was even wearing the helmet. The public was less forgiving. People would stare at him, curious. Some children pointed at him as if he was some kind of freak. Their parents would have to force away the pointing fingers and gawking expressions. It was one of the happiest days of his life when he was able to leave the helmet for good.

In the springtime, Carin was getting around well enough without her cane, except for particularly damp days, and then she would only use it if she were on her feet for extended periods. Kevin, being so young, had healed almost completely. He still walked with a slight limp as his healing ankle regained strength to match its twin.

They never returned to live in Agnes's house. They could no more live there than in their old house, or anywhere else in Warren Cove. They needed to find a place to start fresh, where they had no ties, but where they would be happy to start new ones.

On an early Sunday afternoon, they shared a plateful of warm doughnuts at a coffeehouse near Carin's childhood home. The house had recently sold, well under market value because of the stigma of what had happened inside, and they were staying at a nearby hotel. Kevin was gulping down an orange juice chilled with ice cubes. Carin's coffee was getting cold as she searched a stack of newspapers for inspiration for their next move. Should they stay in Chicago? Neither one of them wanted to deal with the traffic or craziness right now. They wanted to live somewhere peaceful. Quiet. Peoria? Too far in the sticks. Out of state--where? Seattle, San Antonio, Philadelphia? She was searching for a clue, a hint that would lead them to the end of this frustrating quest.

Kevin set down his empty glass, smacked his lips, enjoying his juice. "How about Bakersfield?"

"You want to move to California?" Carin asked, a grin on her face. "I haven't heard the best of things about that area."

"Not Bakersfield *California*, Bakersfield *Illinois*," he said with exaggeration, as if it were the most obvious place imaginable.

"There's a Bakersfield in Illinois? I've never heard of it."

"A friend of mine used to live there. So did her husband."

Carin gave him a skeptical look. "I'll look into it," Carin said, returning her attention to the newspaper.

"Mom, can I ask you something?"

"Sure."

"I feel bad."

"About what, dear?"

"When I was running away from... when I was running, I took money from that friend I was telling you about. The one from Bakersfield. I left a note saying I would pay her back. Now I feel bad."

"Would you like to pay it back now? We aren't really doing anything today."

"Really? We can go now?"

"I don't see why not. It's not far is it?" Carin packed up her newspapers. She gathered up the bill and her purse, ready to leave. "This old lady can't get around like you kids."

"Only blocks away, I'm pretty sure."

"Let's go. Lead the way, young man."

They could have driven, but Kevin insisted on walking. Carin dropped the newspapers off at the Explorer parked on the street, dropped another quarter in the meter, and followed her son. As they walked, he explained who Sophie and Andrew were, and how they had taken him in. He did not mention that the real reason he wanted to seek them out was to make sure they were okay, to make sure Mr. Freakshow had not harmed them like everyone else Kevin had trusted.

"Are you sure you know where you're going?"

"Yeah, it's... here we are. I remember now. It's a couple blocks up at the next intersection. It snuck up on me last time because I was talking with Sophie as we walked."

Kevin knocked on the heavy door. The metal had gouges, as if attacked by an animal. Or something worse. Kevin's stomach did a little lurch, afraid for what had happened to his friends. After a growing silence, he was about to knock again, but then the locks started unlocking from the other side. Chains were pulled aside. The door opened to the length of the remaining chain.

"Yes?" It was a woman with green eyes. Kevin could not see much more of her.

"We... I mean, I wanted to see Sophie."

"I'm afraid that's not possible."

In that instant, Kevin knew that the Freak had hurt his friends. No one had been safe.

"She died in her sleep a couple weeks ago."

"Oh," Kevin said, somehow relieved. "She helped me out. She lent me money. I wanted to pay her back."

The woman with the green eyes said nothing.

"Is Andrew home?"

"Andrew?"

"Sophie's husband."

"My grandfather died in 1983."

"Okay." Hearing that a man that Kevin had believed to be a real person had died more than twenty years ago did not faze him. The world was a different place. He remembered when he was exhausted, reclining on Sophie's pull-out cot, a homemade quilt covering him with warmth. As he was drifting off to sleep, the room swirled with dream-like qualities. Sophie and Andrew danced an old fashioned dance, and the farm fields from the murals stretched out from the ground on which they stood. The air smelled earthy, freshly turned. It all made sense, and he had no doubt now. Andrew really had been a dream.

He turned and looked at his mom. "Can we still give her the money, then?" he asked in a quiet voice.

She nodded.

Kevin pulled the five twenty dollar bills from his pocket that his mom had given him. "Since you're Sophie's family, I want to give you this."

The door closed and the last remaining chain scratched aside. The door opened, and Kevin was greeted by a woman who looked remarkably like Sophie, but much, much younger. She was probably about thirty.

"Is your name Kevin?"

"Yes."

"I was instructed to give you something. Come with me."

Kevin followed immediately, Carin with more hesitation, but the hallway was short. Within a few steps, they were inside the small studio apartment. All of the furnishings were gone. A few moving boxes were stacked by the door; otherwise the apartment was bare walls and clean floors. The white cinderblock walls made the room seem smaller than it actually was.

"Ma'am?"

"Oh, I'm sorry. My name's Gretchen," the woman said. She was digging through a moving box, and then pulled it off the stack and opened the one beneath. "It's around here somewhere. Were you going to ask something?"

Kevin wondered where the murals went, wondered if someone had painted over them, but as soon as he had the urge to ask, he knew the answer. Sophie had taken her memories with her.

"Oh, nothing. Never mind."

"Here it is." Gretchen removed a yellowed envelope from the box. She handed it to him. He read his name, written with a frail hand, across the front.

"A letter?" his mom asked. Kevin shrugged and tore it open.

He unfolded the letter and read silently:

Dear Kevin,

I knew you would come to see me. I could tell the moment I set eyes on you that you have a kind soul. I know you're here to pay back the money you borrowed from us. Trust me, if you receive this note, it's because we no longer need that money. But let me just say, that since you are an honorable person and I know you would feel guilty about not paying back your debt, Andrew and I will consider the debt paid off if you do one thing for us: Help a friend in need. It is the most generous thing you can do. Andrew and I helped you in your time of need. You do the same and we'll be square. Take care, young one.

Sophie

"Kevin what is it?"

"I need to help someone. Sophie wanted me to help a friend."

"Okay... who might that be?"

The name came to him, suddenly, and it made perfect sense. "Reid. I can't think of anyone who needs more help."

Maury Bennett walked through a flowerbed, the trampled, dried husks sounding like breaking bones in the frigid air. His body was healing from his wounds inflicted by Mr. Freakshow. A star-shaped scar bloomed across his cheek, the result of his face crashing through the picture window. When he hit the sidewalk in front of the Dvorak house, he separated his shoulder. Most of the soreness was now behind him. Since he didn't know if he was a wanted man for what happened with the debacle at Lucidity and the ensuing chaos, he avoided going to the hospital. He found a payphone at an abandoned service station. He dialed 911, and told the operator that people were dying on Winfield Road. When the operator asked him what address she should call for the dispatch, he had hung up. For the moment, his conscience had been clear.

The glowing moon made visible the nighttime clouds. The rain, turning to razors of sleet, pelted the aluminum siding--static drowning out his reckless advance. He stopped at a front window, standing in ankle-deep mud. Peering inside the ground floor bedroom, he was soaked and couldn't help the shivers violently racking his spine. He also couldn't remember a happier time full of so much anticipation.

His breath condensed on the glass. He swiped his hand across it, not wanting to miss a second. A bare closet light bulb cast a wedge of dirty yellow light on the carpet in the otherwise darkened bedroom. Someone was in bed, the blankets pulled high to ward off the early winter chill. He looked nervously at his wrist, but was not wearing a watch.

The bedroom door opened a crack, a couple inches, a foot. His pulse seemed to double. The door opened wide, and Juliet entered. She took off her winter cap, stashing it in the pocket of her wool pea coat, her auburn curls falling in a rush to her shoulders. She looked at the window, seemingly right into Maury's eyes, but she would not be able to see him in his hiding place.

His arm was still in a sling when Juliet had found him. Having given up hope of finding her, he had moved on. He had lived off the cash Nolan Gage had paid him, renting a tiny sleeping room while slipping into a mild depression. He didn't make a concerted effort to hide from authorities, yet somehow he slipped through the cracks during the investigation of the tragedy at Lucidity.

Of all places for her to find him, he was at a bookstore, rifling through the newest tomes in the psychology section. She tapped him on his shoulder. When he turned to face her, and as realization sunk in, he nearly wept.

He figured she had been captured with most of the other dreams. But no. She had assimilated. She looked more comfortable in the urban setting than he felt. When he told her he loved her, she didn't laugh at him.

But now, Juliet walked over to the bed, a hesitance to her steps. She stood at the bedside and didn't move. As the seconds ticked away, Maury's anxiety increased. He looked to the driveway, down the street, as far as he could, but didn't see any sign of anyone approaching. But still, they had a limited amount of time.

Barbara, Juliet's dreamer, stirred, rolling over from her side to her back. Juliet's body tensed as she stood there. He wanted to beat on the glass.

Come on, get moving...

Barbara must have opened her eyes, must have seen her dream standing before her in embodied form. Her scream pierced the night. Even the rattle of the stinging sleet couldn't hide the sound. Barbara screamed as if screaming would wake her from this dream, but this was real--dreams were no longer just dreams, but snapshots stolen from the mind and given legs with which to walk, hands with which to grasp, a heart with which to pump blood and love.

Juliet struck with sudden and violent force. She leapt on top of Barbara, her knees on either side of her dreamer's torso. Her hands were at her throat, her slender fingers no longer graceful. Barbara's legs thrashed at the foot of the bed, her hands grasping at Juliet's forearms.

Barbara's struggle made it go faster, and for this, Maury was grateful. Her movements slowed, as if she were intoxicated, and soon one hand fell from Juliet's arms, fell flat on the blanket that had kept her safe and cozy until only a minute ago. She raked the blanket with her fingers as if in search of something, and then these movements also slowed to a twitch, slowed to nothing. Juliet had just murdered her dreamer.

Maury couldn't be more elated.

The sound of car tires grinding gravel jerked away his attention. He ducked--gaining as much cover as the dead flowerbed afforded him--as a Honda sedan pulled to a stop in the driveway. He hoped no one had seen him spying through their daughter's bedroom window. He could only hope that Juliet had seen the headlights flash across the bedroom walls.

Maury crawled around to the side of the house, and once clear of the driveway, he hurried to the back corner of the house. The sleetfall thickened, and his face felt raw and numb. Melt water dripped down his skin under his clothes, and he couldn't feel his toes. None of this mattered, not as long as Juliet was inside. He heard the front door open, and then slam shut. Then all was silent, the stinging sleet had disappeared, the rush of his pulse in his own ears ebbed. He had to do something. He couldn't let them find Juliet.

His mind raced, and all he could imagine was Juliet locked up by the government, locked up like all the other dreams that had found their immortality. Locked up in perpetuity, immortal yet trapped forever in a cell. Maury ran to the sliding glass door at the back of the house. If someone was going to be caught, it was going to be him. At least he could find release from imprisonment through death. Juliet did not have that luxury. Lights flicked on inside, one section of the house after another spurred to life. Maury picked up a metal patio chair, felt his wet hands freeze to the cold metal. When he had the weighty chair up over his shoulder and ready to swing, the sliding glass door opened. Juliet slipped outside, her eyes wide and luminous. Maury dropped the chair and could not help pulling her close in a nervous hug. She kissed him furiously, her warm lips like salvation. They ran away through the backyard before anyone became aware of their presence.

By the time they reached the rented car at the Laundromat parking lot four blocks away, Maury was frozen through. He hurried to the passenger side door and somehow was able to get the key in the lock to open it. Juliet gave him a peck on the cheek and climbed in.

Maury could feel every aching bone in his frozen feet, but pain was only a secondary thought now, pushed away by happiness. His life was starting fresh. Once inside, he turned the engine over, immediately blasting the heat on full.

"I didn't think I could to it." Juliet's cheeks were rosy and her eyes watered from the cold and sleet.

"I saw. I was afraid, too. I thought you were going to back out."

"She opened her eyes. When she saw me and was afraid, as if I was some kind of monster, a nightmare to escape from, I knew I could do it. I had to do it."

Maury leaned over, placed a hand on her stomach. Juliet wore layers of clothes under her coat, but Maury could still feel the beginnings of a swell to her belly. He might have also felt a kick from his unborn baby, but he knew it was too early for that. "You did what you had to do. Barbara could have…"

"I know. I'm still not happy about it. But the baby… I couldn't let anything happen."

Maury kissed her cheek, patted her belly with a gentle hand, and then put the car in reverse. He drove carefully, obeying all the rules of the road. He came to a full stop at all stop signs, and signaled when switching lanes. Maury Bennett was starting the life he didn't know he wanted until it fell into his lap, almost as if by accident. A life that seemed obvious now; a life of happiness and fulfillment. He wasn't going to do anything to ruin it.

Shortly after Kevin told his mom about Reid, and how his father abused him because he couldn't help going mad every once in a while, she started making phone calls. Her calls led to an investigation by the Department of Children and Family Services. A state mandated physical exam revealed that Reid had suffered two broken ribs that had never healed properly. He also had a chipped eyetooth, most likely caused by his father's balled fists. His torso and back were rife with bruises in various states of healing. Black, purple, brown--a riot of colors like a quickly advancing storm.

While Reid wasn't pleased one bit with the investigation, or the prodding of doctors or the questioning lawyers, his injuries healed. DCFS learned that his biological mom had moved to Europe the previous year, without letting her ex-husband or son know of her whereabouts. After weeks of chasing down dead end leads, they finally tracked her down. Her comment was short, and precise:

"Go ahead, take the little shit."

It took nearly a year of wrestling with the court system and DCFS, but by the time the leaves were falling the next year, Kevin had a brother. While not a blood brother, Reid seemed more of a big brother than he could ever imagine. Their brotherly connection was so strong, it seemed liked they had grown up their entire lives together. Once he got over wondering when the next punch would come, just because someone went a little mad, Reid accepted his new family, and eventually, he embraced them as his own. He left his juvenile delinquent trajectory and went to school regularly. Carin doted on him and treated him like her own flesh and blood.

The addition of Reid to their family came at a transitional time for all of them. It was a time of self-doubt and self-blame, of healing the wounds that would heal and learning to live with the ones that they would take to the grave.

Every once in a while Kevin would dream of Mr. Freakshow. Such an integral shaper of his life, it was not surprising for Kevin to wake every month or so knowing the Freak had been there, inside his head, a subject of his dreams. But since the night at their old house in Warren Cove, dreaming of Mr. Freakshow wasn't a nightmare. These dreams were of triumph, of overcoming loss and desperate odds. When Kevin would wake from these dreams, knowing he had encountered his one-time tormentor, he woke with a sense of calm.

NEWSLETTER

I have many projects that will come to fruition over the next year. To keep up to date on my release dates, and other exciting news, sign up for my newsletter.

Send me an email at glenkrisch@gmail.com. Use "newsletter" for a subject line, and indicate your preferred ebook format. I love to give away free books, including previews for unreleased works.

BOOKS BY GLEN KRISCH

NOVELS:

The Nightmare Within
Where Darkness Dwells
Nothing Lasting (forthcoming)
Arkadium Rising: Brother's Keeper, Book 1 (forthcoming)

2-IN-1 NOVELS:

Twice as Dark, Two Novels of Horror
(omnibus edition containing *Where Darkness Dwells* and *The Nightmare Within*)

NOVELLAS

Loss, a paranormal thriller
Brother's Keeper, a post-apocalyptic novella

COLLECTIONS

Commitment and Other Tales of Madness
Through the Eyes of Strays (from Dog Horn Publishing)

ABOUT THE AUTHOR

Glen Krisch has written three novels: *The Nightmare Within*, *Where Darkness Dwells*, and *Nothing Lasting*, as well as the novellas *Brother's Keeper* and *Loss*. His short fiction has appeared in publications across three continents for the last decade.

He is also an editor for Morrigan Books. As a freelance editor, he has worked on books by Tim Lebbon and Lawrence Block, among others.

Besides writing and reading, his interests include his family, simple living, and ultra running.

He enjoys talking to his readers. Feel free to stop by his website to see what he's up to: **www.glenkrisch.wordpress.com**

Made in the USA
Las Vegas, NV
05 August 2021